I0607508

CONJURE LAKE

REBECCA HENRY

Conjure Lake
ISBN # 978-1-80250-975-5
©Copyright Rebecca Henry 2022
Cover Art by Kelly Martin ©Copyright August 2022
Interior text design by Claire Siemaszkiewicz
Finch Books

Published in 2022 by Finch Books, United Kingdom.

Finch Books is an imprint of Totally Entwined Group Limited.

CONJURE LAKE

Dedication

For my mom and dad
and all our lake house memories…

Acknowledgements

I'd like to reference the author Rosemary Ellen Guiley and her books on witches, angels and Djinn, which I have found a world of information from, as well as mention the author Alice Hoffman and her book *Practical Magic* where the inspiration was born for the Ambrosia Hill series. I'd also like to reference the podcast *Superstitions* on Spotify as being another source of information and insight for the series. The TV show *Sabrina the Teenage Witch* on Netflix, which I am a huge fan of, also showed me there was a subculture for this genre and gave me motivation to write the series and *Conjure Lake*.

A big and heartfelt thank-you to my lovely and talented editor Angela Willingham for editing the first draft of *Conjure Lake*. Not only is she a true professional to work with as well as a wonderful human being but she is also a source of guidance and reliability for me.

Thank you to my social media assistant Fallak Tabassum for helping me promote and market *Ambrosia Hill* as well as being the first set of eyes on *Amethyst* in its infancy. Tabz is a source of stability and guidance and I am truly blessed to work with her.

A sincere and huge thank-you to the publishers and editors at Finch Books and the design team for all their talents, time and attention to *Ambrosia Hill* and allowing me the opportunity to tell my story through them.

I can't end my string of thanks without mentioning my beautiful daughter, Penelope Henry, and her talent modeling as Zinnia on my social media promotions and providing the series with a face.

And a big hug to my son, Jude, for always offering me his sincere opinions, support and enthusiasm as I sit at my keyboard for hours on end.

I would also like to acknowledge my dear friends Bailey and Elena and all the ARC readers for reading *Conjure Lake* and providing me with honest feedback, especially my husband Dave whose enthusiasm is priceless to me.

Prologue

The Cursed Tree of Conjure Lake
A nursery rhyme
(inspired by the rhyme *Who Killed Cock Robin?*)

Who killed the raven of Korwin Cottage?
I, said the tree. With a bow made from my trunk
and an arrow from my bark. I killed the raven
at the stroke of seven, for he is not permitted in heaven.
Who saw him die?
I, said the tree, with my nubby, twisted third eye,
I saw him die.
Who caught his blood?
I, said the tree. I caught his blood with luck.
And drank it up. Drop by drop in my silver cup.
Who'll dig his grave?
I, said the tree, with my long spindly pick and trusted
trowel.
I'll bury him wrapped up in a shroud,
six feet under the ground, never to be found.
Who will carry the coffin?
I, said the tree. I'll carry the coffin under my roots
and escort him to the devil's court.
Who'll toll the bell?
I, said the tree. With my scaly branches, I'll pull the bell.
And all the birds of the air will hear

the toll and know that their dead beloved raven fell. They will fly away in fear, for when the raven returns all of Conjure Lake shall burn.

Chapter One

The Sadness of Death

Serena closed the suitcase on her bed, zipping up what was left of her life in New York City, and slipped the tote bag carrying her sketchpad over her shoulder. Little remained to be done—everything had already been sealed in brown boxes and moved to a cold storage unit on the edge of the city. A lifetime of memories of baby books, photo albums, old Christmas decorations, her father's first guitar, her mother's easel—all packed and sleeping in the dark. Just like her parents, who now lay in the ground, side by side for eternity. The little things that had once made their house a home were now buried in their own coffins, never to be resurrected and soon to be forgotten.

After the funeral, Serena had vowed she'd never visit her parents' graves. There was no point. Rose and Edward Bancroft were now just two names written in stone atop a lonely hill at the back of a cold and isolated graveyard. Like her parents, she didn't believe in an afterlife. Neither her mom nor her dad had been religious—if anything, they were like scientists, putting faith in what science could prove. It seemed gruesome and unfair to leave their bodies rotting in the cold, hard ground. Serena never wanted to remember her parents as muted, decayed and sealed in a box six feet under the earth. Whatever made them human — whatever the soul was, if there ever was one — had departed the day they died. What was left in those graves was nothing but corpses.

Rose and Edward Bancroft had been killed in a car accident during a rainy afternoon drive to the library to pick up her little brother, Jack. The police officer who worked the scene assured Serena that they likely never saw the semi-truck that had smashed into their car, killing them both instantly. No, for them it began and ended with a glimpse into each other's eyes — a last look at this world in the face of their true love.

But for Serena and Jack, it was an end and a beginning. The end of a life as a happy family, and the beginning of something else — an eternity as orphans.

Suitcase in hand, Serena paused at the doorway, looking around her childhood bedroom for the last time. The walls echoed with memories, haunted by ghosts of sacred moments she'd never again share with her mother. Her first night home after the funeral had been unbearable. The absence of her parents had felt like a physical thing, a black void so large there was no room to breathe in their city apartment. It was as if their ghosts lingered in their belongings. Her father's reading glasses still lay abandoned on the coffee table next to the weekly paper. Her mother's apron hung forgotten by the oven.

A car honked outside, startling Serena from her reverie. A quick glance out of the window told her the cab had arrived to deliver them to their new life. Serena sighed as she dragged her heavy suitcase to the ground and rolled it down the empty hallway for the last time. "The taxi is here, Jack!" she called out to her brother. "We've got to get going if we are going to catch our train." He didn't answer, not that she expected him to.

Jack had always been quiet—more of an observer than a talker. Their dad had referred to him as "his little professor" because he always had his nose in a book. Most of his friends were the librarians who pulled aside books for him and brought him treats, usually delivered with a wink and a smile. Jack would glance up at them with a silent nod of appreciation, pressing all four of his fingers against the lenses of his glasses as he pushed them up his nose, leaving them eternally smudged with fingerprints. But after the accident Jack had stopped speaking completely. No one, not even his beloved wiener dog Tinker, could reach his island of grief.

From that terrible day and every day since, Serena had done all she could for her little brother. At age seven, Jack was far too young to be alone, so Serena had left her life behind at the University of California to be with her brother back in New York so he could finish the school year. Those first days had been hard. The thought of getting out of bed and making breakfast before their walk to Jack's school had seemed insurmountable, but they had managed. Now the school year was finally over and summer had come.

Serena stood in the foyer, eyes closed as she imagined her parents' laughter around the breakfast table, their kisses on their foreheads at bedtime. But nothing, certainly not wishes, could conjure them back.

Closing the front door, Serena sat beside her brother in the soft morning light on the sun-warmed front porch step, where Jack had his hand on Tinker's back, a book open in his lap. The cabbie laid on his horn, eying them with impatience. Ignoring him, Serena held out her hand and Jack wordlessly passed her his smudged glasses, which she cleaned on her shirt and handed back. He pressed them back up his face, smudging them again. Serena sighed and put an arm around her brother. Their mom had always been the one to clean Jack's lenses. Now there was only her.

"It's about that time, little buddy," she said softly. He nodded, his eyes still glued on his book, *A Guide to Surviving the Wilderness*. He closed the book with a sigh, then he and Tinker both looked up at Serena.

"I'm ready," he whispered. Serena threaded her fingers through his and gave them a squeeze. The cabbie honked again. Jack squeezed hers back. "If you ever cross a brown bear, make your body look bigger. Yell loudly and don't back down," Jack instructed.

Serena bit back a chuckle and nodded. "Sure thing, Professor Bancroft." She ruffled his hair and dropped a kiss on the top of his head. "Time to go," she said.

Days after the funeral, an official-looking envelope had arrived from a fancy estate attorney stating Serena and Jack had inherited a lake house on Conjure Lake in upstate New York. With everything else in chaos, it had seemed the answer to Serena's problems. She had vague recollections of her mother mentioning growing up in the mountains, but Rose never spoke about her parents, and the letter had been a surprise. Between the inheritance Rose and Edward left them and the money from their life insurance policies, Serena had enough funds to care for Jack and herself, but if they stayed in their city apartment, those funds would dwindle fast. Suddenly a new home—and a new life—had arrived, brimming with possibilities.

So Serena made the decision to move to the lake house with Jack once his school year was complete.

According to the estate attorney, their mother had inherited the house when her parents passed away. The lake house was fully furnished and had been winterized for year-round living, and Wi-Fi ready with internet. There was even an old pickup truck available for sale—for the dubious price of five hundred dollars—by the groundskeeper who had overseen the property for thirty years. If Serena so desired, she could keep the man on for a small monthly fee. Even though pickups were not her first choice in automobiles, she understood how valuable a truck would be living in the country. For five hundred dollars she figured she'd be lucky if it ran at all, and she was especially thankful there was a groundskeeper on hand to do the mowing and tackle plowing the road during the harsh winter months.

Jack had taken the news surprisingly well. He was fascinated to be moving "to the wilderness," which was what he called anything outside of New York City. Despite Corvin Grove having a population of nine hundred, compared to New York, that might as well be Timbuktu. Jack had read everything he could get his hands on about surviving the outdoors. Serena knew it was probably a coping mechanism, but figured the distraction was relatively harmless.

Jack was ready to be a boy again, ready to come out of his mourning. He didn't have many friends to say goodbye to other than his librarians. There were too many ghosts haunting their home in the city, too many shadows of memories so sweet they now ached like a sore tooth. Jack didn't want to be the tragic orphan who had lost his parents—he wanted to be like every other child his age. The change would be good for them, and Serena knew Jack needed normalcy in all its forms.

So they were headed to the Adirondack Mountains, an area neither Serena nor Jack had ever visited. All Serena really knew about her mother's past or her estranged grandparents was that Rose had hated growing up in an isolated back-country town. On her eighteenth birthday, Rose had traded in her barn boots for city shoes and never looked back.

But now there was only one way forward. Serena held Jack's hand and they walked down the front steps, suitcases bumping along behind them. At the curb Serena stared up at the picture window that once had been her mother's studio as the irate cabbie loaded their suitcases into the back of the taxi, muttering under his breath. The art studio overlooking the city park had been Serena's favorite place on earth. Her mother's studio had always smelled of wet paint and charcoal pencils, and Serena would sit across from her mom on the chaise lounge, sketching out drawings of the things inside her head while her mother painted at her easel.

Jack stood beside her with his arms crossed, his thoughts impossible to read in his dark eyes as he stared back at the apartment.

"Mom would've hated moving to our grandparents' lake house," Serena said to Jack as she wrapped an arm around his thin shoulder. "She spent our entire lives keeping the grandparents from us, and now we will live in her old childhood house. You'll probably even sleep in her old bed."

The cabbie slammed the trunk shut. Now that it was time to leave, Serena stared at her shoes, at the ground, anywhere other than the home they were about to leave forever.

"I wonder why Mom didn't like living on Conjure Lake. I guess it doesn't matter," Serena said as she kissed the top of Jack's head. "What's in the past will have to stay in the past. All that matters now is us and our future together." Serena pulled her brother in for a hug, and he smiled up at her.

"We will have fun kayaking every day," Jack said, his eyes bright. "You always wear your life jacket when you kayak. Lake water can suddenly become deep and before you know it you're a mile away from shore and struggling to get back to land." Jack rubbed his nose and pressed his smudged glasses up his face.

"And you will have an entire forest to explore." Serena smiled as she held out her hand for his glasses. She polished them again and passed them back. "There's over sixty acres on the property."

Serena wished she could share Jack's enthusiasm. He was excited to live on a private lake with no one around. Their nearest neighbor would be two miles away. Jack didn't mind that it would be a ten-minute drive to town. After all the attention from his parents' deaths, he welcomed the privacy, and really, so did Serena.

The past year had aged Serena, making her feel far older than her mere eighteen years. She had stopped going out on weekends, stopped using social media. She had grown annoyed by her vain friends who took endless selfies every hour and plastered them on the internet, and was turned off by her peers who made stupid videos of their classmates getting drunk at parties and making asses out of themselves. She no longer cared about staying involved in mindless activities or trying to get hot guys or girls to notice her.

It was as if the color had drained out of her world, and all the pointless things she'd cared about before no longer mattered. Even her sketchbook had been drained of color, and she now only drew in shades of black and gray. Serena had traded in a life of self-indulgence for a life of silent amity. Serena's world had narrowed until all she saw, all she cared about, was Jack. In the span of one night, Serena had been transformed from a modern college student to a grieving daughter and sister of a fragile little brother who needed a mom.

Though Serena had always been an artist like her mother, her sketchbook became a tool for how she viewed and processed the world around her. Now sketching meant more to her than just scribbles on a page—it was her sanctuary, the last link to her mother, a way to leave the sorrows of this world behind and enter a realm of serenity. Gone were the lip gloss and mascara and other silly items that used to line the bottom of her purse. In its place she only had her sketchbook and pencil, and they accompanied her wherever she went. It was her new makeup routine, but instead of painting her face, she was painting her soul.

Their mother had been a natural beauty with long, straight hair the color of starlight. When Serena was a child she would play with her mom's silken tresses, wrapping the shining locks around her tiny fingers as Rose read to her at night. Rose—even her mother's name was a beautiful thing. Serena and Jack had both inherited their mother's blonde hair, straight and soft like spun silk, though Serena kept hers perpetually in a bun, drawing pencils and pens stuffed in her hair for easy access. Their dark eyes, however, came from their father, deep and wide like dark pools full of secrets.

The train ride had been a long five hours and Serena was ready to exit the train and eagerly flagged down a taxi to take them to Korwin Cottage. She climbed in the backseat with her brother and wrapped an arm around Jack as she leaned her head against the window staring off into the beautiful scenery.

The cityscape was gone, replaced by picturesque hills and charming farmhouses. Serena poked her brother in the side and pointed out of the window. "Look, cows."

He glanced up from his book where he was reading about filtering your own urine for drinking water — gross. "Cows can detect odors from up to five miles away," he stated.

"Hmm. Good to know," Serena replied.

"Five miles, you say?" the cabbie called over his shoulder, a soft Jamaican accent curling his words.

"Yes," Jack answered, perking up to find he had an appreciative audience. "They have thirty-two teeth in their head, just like a human."

"Good for all that chewing." The driver nodded. He had been looking at the siblings with what Serena could only guess was curiosity. She knew it must look odd, seeing two kids traveling alone — permanently. He chatted with Jack about cows and trees, and what water was safe to drink in the wild, and what to do if they were bitten by a snake. Their chatter faded into the background as Serena stared out of the window, her sketchpad open in her lap, a pencil loose in her fingers. The drive upstate was beautiful, the landscape dotted with majestic rolling hills and the bright red barns of the country.

Before long, they saw a colorful highway sign welcoming them to the town of Corvin Grove, population nine hundred. Tinker squirmed with excitement in Jack's lap as they drove through the small town. It looked untouched, as if time had somehow slipped by this sleeping village, allowing it to remain undisturbed. Grand Victorian houses lined the one-way road leading to town, each one lovelier than the next, and Serena's fingers itched to sketch their imposing lines. Time enough for that later. Beautiful hanging baskets dripping with heavy blooms decorated their porches, and the silver waters of Conjure Lake glistened and sparkled in the waning sunlight as they drove down Main Street. Two humble restaurants sat alongside the village gift shop — an old-fashioned bakery and a rustic bar. There was a modest post office, a local hardware store and a Price Chopper for grocery shopping. The local school sat next to the village green.

"Look, Jack. That is where you will go to school next month." Serena pointed to the small elementary with tiny windows that lined the brick walls. A simple playground sat in the back with tall elm trees shading the swings.

Jack nodded his head, eyes serious as he studied the building. "Do you think they have a library?" he asked, his tone dubious. His elementary school in the city was more like a high school campus, grand and state-of-the-art. Thousands of students occupied the classrooms and only the top teachers worked there.

"You know they will." Serena smiled. She hoped the librarians here would love Jack as much as the ones back in New York. She put her arm around her little brother as the school disappeared into the distance.

Corvin Grove was perhaps the smallest town Serena had ever visited. With a population of nine hundred, the town was certainly small, but as she stared at the quaint buildings through the taxi window, she was comforted that it was large enough to feel like a community. Though she had never been there before, Serena felt a sense of familiarity as they exited the main street, passing the stone Catholic church that sat on the edge of town. A black gothic gate surrounded the church cemetery, protecting the dead that slept within its iron bars. Their new home on Conjure Lake was a ten-minute drive outside of town on a deserted country road. The cab turned onto Korwin Lane and rolled to a stop before the wrought-iron gate.

The cabbie turned around to Serena, his face apologetic. "Do you have the key for the gate, miss? If not, I'll have to drop you off here, and it looks like it's a hike to the house."

"Yes, I do," Serena said as she pulled an ornate skeleton key from her bag. "The estate attorney sent it, along with a key to the house." She got out of the cab and walked up to the imposing iron gate, the words *Korwin Cottage* scrolled across the twisting metal of the elaborate double doors. As she turned the metal key in the lock and swung the heavy gates open, the birds in the trees went silent, and Serena was struck by the peculiar thought that they were watching her. She shook her head. *Silly city girl.*

The cab passed through the open gate and slowly wound through the tree-lined dirt road. Though the sun was shining, little light permeated the dark woods around them. The trees grew thick and wild, and Serena was surprised to see a large home loom over them as they twisted through the tree-lined drive. Her eyes widened as she took in the sight.

Her mother's childhood home was nothing like the lake house she had imagined. The house sat back from the lake near the tree line of the forest, and a twisted, winding path of blood-red brick led up to the spiked iron fence that surrounded the cottage. Serena studied their new home. The house was ornate, more Victorian gothic in style, painted black with bargeboards that attached to the edge of the gabled maroon roof. The crooked chimney had the year 1666 carved in the center brick.

The cabbie whistled low as he slowed to a stop in the stone driveway alongside the cottage, making the sign of the cross as he whispered some quiet prayer under his breath. The moment he put the car in park, Jack jumped out of the back seat with Tinker following closely on his heels.

Jack spun a slow circle, and Serena's heart swelled at the sight of the silly grin he wore on his face. "Serena, look at this place! There's paths everywhere! And look at all the rocks along the shore!"

Serena was thankful that Jack wasn't put off by the creepy look of the house. She was certain their new home was the stuff nightmares were made of. Serena cautiously stepped out of the cab, wishing she could share in his excitement. She half expected the house to be made of candy with a sinister witch waiting inside to eat her and Jack. *It's so isolated, not another house in sight.* Serena scanned the dark tangle of woods behind them.

An old crab apple tree stood beside the cottage, blackened as if it had burned, but clearly alive. Serena placed a hand on its gnarled trunk. It looked rotten, as if it had died a hundred years ago, but still refused to fall. A cool breeze picked up from inside the woods. She shivered and wrapped her arms around herself, chilled to the bone from the sudden burst of cold air. And something else. Again, Serena had the sensation of being watched, and she looked up into the silent trees, wondering if leaving their home in the city was the right decision after all.

The cab driver handed Serena a suitcase, his eyes full of unease as he looked up at the house. "Looks like you two are in the sticks now," he said as he looked around the property. A frown creased his face. He pointed to a circular window facing them. "You've got some big spiders in these parts." A silky cone-shaped tunnel was anchored in the center of the window. The web looked more like armor than spider silk. Serena squinted her eyes. A black figure was trapped inside the tunnel.

"Sure hope you don't run into any black widows." The cabbie's words hung thick with perturbation and he wasn't doing a good job concealing his qualms about the cottage.

Jack ran over at the mention of spiders, adjusting the rim of his glasses. "Actually, black widows are not funnel weaving spiders. Funnel spiders are relatively harmless but they do venture inside houses looking for a mate."

The cabbie shivered and craned his neck to Serena as Jack spun on his heels and ran over to the cottage. "You'll be all right, though, won't you? I don't like the feel of this place." He gestured to the dark house, his concern genuine.

Serena took the suitcase from him and reached into the trunk for the other. "We'll be all right," she assured him. "This property has been in my family for many years. It's where my brother and I should be."

The driver looked unconvinced as he stared at the gothic home, but he nodded and wished Serena the best of luck before he drove down the dirt road, leaving the orphaned siblings behind.

Serena took a deep breath as she dragged her black and white paisley suitcase behind her. A shadow slid over Serena, and she turned around, puzzled. Nothing was there. Serena resumed her trek up the path and paused as she heard a swooshing sound. Serena had only just turned back toward the cottage when something large and black swooped down, nearly crashing into her. She covered her head as she ducked, crying out. The mass came again—a bird, she realized, and it grazed her shoulder, plucking out strands of her hair from her loose bun with its talons, and swooped into the woods, where it perched on a nearby branch. "What the hell!" Serena yelled. She stared at the giant black bird — a crow, she thought, or no, a raven. Too big to be a crow. Serena could see her own reflection in the oily black eyes of the bird. It cawed at her. Was that...blood on its beak? *Gross.*

It cawed furiously at her, as though she had disturbed its nest or something. Its beak was stained crimson red. Blood, she decided with a shudder. Serena watched as it rose into the air as if through levitation rather than flight. Another gust of cold wind ruffled Serena's hair as the raven stretched out its broad wings, and a chill stole over her body as its shadow passed over her once again. A small crab apple dropped from the raven's open mouth to land at Serena's feet.

Serena dropped the suitcases and picked up the apple and immediately hurled it at the raven, missing by inches. "Go away, you psychotic bird!" she shouted. "I'm not trying to hurt you. Just quit being weird and leave me alone! You are freaking me out! Go...fly up a tree or something."

The raven cawed again, as if annoyed, and opened its large beak to spit another tiny crab apple at Serena. She picked up the second apple and aimed. "I said go away!" she shouted as she weighed the apple in her hand, but the raven vanished amongst the shadows just as quickly as it had appeared. In a blink of an eye, it was gone, taking the dark shadow it had cast along with it.

Serena spun an uneasy circle as she looked for the menacing bird but saw no trace of it. *How's that for a welcoming committee?* Opening her hand, Serena inspected the tiny crab apple in her palm. *So weird. How can there be crab apples in summer?* She'd have to ask

Jack—or Professor Bancroft—about it. She turned the fruit over in her hand. It was weighted, too heavy for an apple. When she gave it a shake, there was a faint rattling noise from inside.

"What the heck? How can this be hollow?" Serena asked out loud as she examined the small apple. She had the sudden and ridiculous urge to take a bite, and she chuckled uneasily at the odd thought.

"Serena, come on!" Jack called from the brick path. He bounced excitedly on the cottage steps and pressed his glasses up his face, a fistful of onyx bird feathers in hand. "Look what I found!" Jack pointed to a spot on the ground below the spider's web. Serena's eyes traveled from the scattered feathers below the casement window up to the black mass inside the web and shuddered.

"A raven caught in a spider web, how is that even possible?" she muttered. "This place could make a sane person turn crazy." Serena threw the apple into the lake, dismissing the entire spectacle. Louder, she called out to her brother, "Be right there, Professor!" as she reached for the suitcases.

Chapter Two

The First Night

The old cottage sat above the ground with a deck that wrapped around the back overlooking the lake, a small island dotting the center. Down by the water's edge was a modest boathouse with a wooden dock connecting it to the shore. Serena's steps veered off the brick path as she made her way down to the boathouse, Jack and Tinker exploring close behind. Serena picked her way carefully over the rocky ground and onto the deck, thrilled to discover a two-seater kayak and a motorized fishing boat. The boathouse was lined with thick plank wooden shelving amply supplied with all the necessities for lake living. Along the shelves hung life jackets, fishing rods and tackle boxes.

"Jack! Come look at the boathouse." He thundered down the porch steps and flew past his sister, running to the water. Tinker barked happily at his side.

Serena watched them for a moment, smiling as the wind carried his conversation with Tinker back to her. "Hey, look at this! This is so cool!" Then he ran past her back up to the house.

Serena turned to the cottage and studied it again as she made her way to the house. It was certainly imposing, but maybe all country homes were a little isolated and strange at first. Her footsteps sounded hollow as she crept up the porch. She pressed a hand to the door and it swung open as though it had been waiting for her.

With a deep breath, Serena entered the cottage and cringed as the creaky door groaned as she shut it behind her. Serena's eyes traveled up the old warped stairs leading to the bedrooms on the second floor. A shiver shot down Serena's spine. The delicate hairs on her skin stood up straight and she rubbed at the raised goosebumps on her forearms. Serena craned her neck toward the landing and jumped as a shadow flickered like a flame out of the corner of her eye. "Jack?" Serena called up to the second story. She held her breath as she waited for Jack to respond. "Jack! You up there?"

"I'm in my new room! It's so great, Serena!"

Serena sighed as she let go of the railing. *Creepy old stairs.* She walked away from the staircase to investigate the downstairs. Serena was pleased to discover it was fully furnished and amply supplied with cooking utensils, silverware, plates, towels and bedding. The estate attorney had assured her the house was move-in ready with every amenity she and Jack would need to settle in. Serena had her doubts about how well-stocked the supplies might be, but it seemed fine. Great, even.

Serena stopped to admire the craftsmanship of the cottage. She itched to sketch the rooms, to see the lines of the building come alive with her pencil. Exposed wood beams lined the entire downstairs while dried herbs, garlic bulbs and lavender hung from the rafters above the solid farmhouse sink. It smelled earthy, like rain falling on soil. Serena noted the lack of a dishwasher, hence the reason for such a deep-seated sink to wash dishes. A grand stone fireplace separated the kitchen from the living room, large enough to warm the entire downstairs. Even though the house had been renovated to meet modern-day standards with full gas heating, Serena imagined how lovely the fire would be in the coming winter months.

Much to her surprise, off the kitchen was a simple but fully functioning greenhouse. The entire room was made of glass, except for the wooden plank flooring and frame. Serena recognized some of the herbs which still grew inside. Lavender, rosemary, lemon balm and peppermint. She leaned over to inhale their lovely fragrance. A wooden baker's table stood in the middle of the greenhouse. A mortar and petal rested on the table with dried herbs inside. Serena searched the bottom basket, pulling out mason jars, lids and labeling stickers.

"Gran must have been quite the herbalist," she muttered to herself while walking over to the potting shelves, not able to identify the other plants. Small silver spoons were used as herb markers sticking out of each pot—mugwort, patchouli, mandrake and wolfsbane. Serena delicately inhaled each herb, welcoming its unfamiliar fragrance. She had only smelled patchouli in oil form, packaged in tinted bottles sold from health food stores. The raw fragrance was overwhelming and exotic. She marveled at how well-preserved and clean everything was. It was as if her grandmother had just left for the store. But Serena knew that couldn't be the case. Her grandparents who had lived here were long dead.

"I'll have to buy some more herbs at a local farmers' market and keep up the supplies," Serena said aloud, a pang of longing in her chest. Serena missed her mom's homemade tea infusions from fresh herbs. Serena paused for a beat, clutching a hand to her heart, as she imagined her mother in the kitchen, brewing tea through a strainer. Serena pinched off a piece of lavender before closing the glass door behind her.

A small door at her feet caught her eye, and she opened it to reveal a pass-through that went outside the back door. Serena grinned. "How charming!" She'd learned about historic houses in school when her elementary class took a field trip to a historical town outside of the city. "This must be where the dairy farmers would put the daily milk through." She smiled, marveling that she had acquired such a rare old home. Despite her initial reservations about the cottage, Serena couldn't help but fall in love with its antiquated charm. Serena was thankful the house was more welcoming on the inside than on the outside.

Opposite the front door was a staircase leading to the two bedrooms. She padded up the creaky stairs and glanced into each room. Both bedrooms had low, slanted ceilings and diamond-paned windows. Serena was relieved to discover that the cottage had not only plumbing but also two full-sized master bathrooms off each bedroom. Jack must have already snuck in, she noticed. His bag lay on the blue-checkered bed in the smaller bedroom. His bathroom had a stand-alone shower.

Serena turned left into the room that would be hers and paused in the doorway, taking in the sight. A creepy antique rocking chair sat motionless by the window. A vanity with an oval black mirror rested in the far corner. She stepped across the room, opening the tiny drawers and feeling the velvet bottom of each one. Dainty perfume bottles sat inside in neat rows. She opened one of the blue-tinted bottles. The comforting scent of lavender escaped the bottle. She unscrewed the lid to the second bottle. Peppermint seeped out. More bottles of various liquids lined the drawers.

"I can use these to help me sleep at night." She inhaled the peppermint deeply, instantly calm. The door to the bathroom was open, and Serena gasped as she stepped through the doorway. A grand cast-iron bathtub sat in the middle of the bathroom. Its claw feet were ornate, intricate black wings etched along the sides. A bay window framed the wall behind the tub, exposing the dark woods behind the cottage. Serena ran her hand along the trim of the tub, stopping at a bar of untouched homemade black soap. She had always wanted a clawfoot bathtub, but never imagined she'd own one. She turned the handle of the Victorian faucet. Water freely flowed from the tap. Pleased, Serena turned off the faucet, squatting beside the tub and feeling immensely better about their new home. "Hopefully there are candles here," she said to herself. "I would love to take a nice hot bath later tonight."

Serena unpacked her suitcase, placing her clothes inside the antique dresser that rested against a window and her sketchpad on a simple wooden table in front of the window by the bed. Yes, she could rebuild herself here. She didn't know who she was anymore since she had lost her parents, but maybe this was where she would find herself, to become whoever she was meant to be. Serena craned her neck to stare down the path outside. Jack had returned to the boathouse, a long wooden stick acting as his sword as he chopped through the tall grass, blazing his own trail to the woods. Tinker barked excitedly at his feet. Serena's heart gave a squeeze. She glanced around for that psycho bird, but she didn't see it anywhere. Good.

She'd hate for it to scare Jack when he was so happy. Serena searched the trees, scanning the area for any sign of the raven. The image of the bird still burned in her mind, and she shuddered as she turned away from the glass.

Serena explored the bedroom for more treasures, opening and closing drawers, feeling a bit like an intruder. In the far corner sat an old trunk, and she scrutinized the rusty lock securing the latch. Serena was confident she could open it. Jack had accidentally trapped himself inside his bedroom a couple of years before, locking his door from the inside. Serena, being the only one home, had remained calm as she quickly googled how to pick old locks while she spoke to Jack through the bedroom door.

Serena had a talent for keeping her composure in dire situations, no matter how scared she truly was. She worked with steady hands, keeping her panic in check as she moved the pin inside the lock. Jack had been beside himself. That lock had opened easily enough, and this one seemed pretty straightforward. Serena examined the rusty lock and nodded as she got a hairpin from her toiletry bag and wiggled the pin inside the lock, feeling it twist.

Serena heard the magical click of the latch as her pin found its mark, and smiled as she lifted the heavy lid, releasing the trunk's secrets. Her eyes roamed over the items hidden away. A particular drawing caught her attention. She smoothed out the wrinkled page, noting how the ink was faded from the hands of time. The clipping showed the image of a beautiful woman with jet black hair, black eyes and pale skin. The name line read "Alice Lake, 1667." She marveled at how well-preserved the sketch was, considering it was nearly four hundred years old. This paper should be dust. The lady was solemn yet elegant. Serena traced the woman's face with her finger before setting it back in the trunk and lifting another clipping. This one was dated two years later. It showed the same woman, a baby in her arms. Serena concluded the images were from the local church. Must have been their newsletter, Serena thought.

Setting it aside, she looked deeper into the chest, pushing aside old candles, sacks of herbs, small glass jars, pieces of chalk, a black satin ribbon and black feathers. Raven, she guessed, like the beast outside. Serena paused at a tiny pair of antique baby shoes. They were small and delicate, and she fingered the torn laces, imagining what it had been like to have a baby hundreds of years ago.

Serena stretched and cracked her back, looking over the windowsill to where Jack played in the grass. He was still chopping down weeds with his faithful Tinker, who was barking happily. Serena rubbed her thumb across the laces of the tattered shoes and placed them side by side in her palm, mesmerized by their tiny size. They seemed so fragile to Serena, as if they would turn to dust at any moment.

"Why would my grandparents have old belongings of a woman from the 1600s? Maybe we are related to Alice Lake?" She stared at the image again, looking for any trace of resemblance. A squeaking sound emerged behind Serena. She slowly turned around, afraid of what she might discover in the room with her. Nothing was there. She scanned the room again before turning her attention back to the trunk and its belongings. Serena shrugged, placed everything back in the chest and shut the lid carefully. Someone had treasured these things, so she would, too.

As she began to stand up, she heard the squeaking sound again, this time louder and more aggressive. Serena whipped her head around and saw the rocking chair pause as if it had been moving. She walked over to the old chair and gave it a gentle push. It swayed back and forth at her touch and rested to a stop. "It's just a chair, Serena. Pull yourself together," she muttered. But she vowed to make firewood out of the creepy thing if it ever moved on its own.

Serena unzipped her suitcase and retrieved her laptop, placing it on the small desk that held her sketchpad. She reached for her phone and was grateful the estate attorney had given her the Wi-Fi login details. In a matter of minutes, she was up and connected. Serena quickly googled the name 'Alice Lake'. Nothing came up. She googled the lake house address, imagining Alice could be the original owner. Scouring the public records of the previous owners of the cottage, she was surprised to see the same name over and over. Korwin. That was her mom's maiden name.

Oddly enough, every name was Korwin, as if the old house had been passed down from daughter to daughter. *How progressive of the Korwins for the time period*, she marveled. Ownership usually passed from fathers to sons. The last person to own the cottage before her grandparents had been Ruth Korwin. Serena thought for a moment. That would be Rose's grandmother, and Serena's great-grandmother. How interesting that a lineage of Korwin women had birthed and died under one roof, a roof that was now her home. Something warmed in her chest. This was where she and Jack were supposed to be. This house was meant to be hers. She closed the laptop with a gentle snap. That was enough investigating for one day. The photo of

Alice Lake would still be waiting inside the chest tomorrow.

* * * *

"Serena! Serena! You won't believe what's back there!" Jack thundered up the stairs and his sweaty face appeared in the doorway. Serena sat on the bed with her sketchpad open in her lap, a cup of evening tea perched precariously on her nightstand. "We can take the kayak out tomorrow and go through the creek," Jack said, breathless. "It winds through the entire property!"

Serena looked up from where she was sketching the gnarled old crab apple tree and grinned. "Sure thing, Jack. Let's go after breakfast." Jack quivered with excitement, his dark eyes shining behind his smudged lenses. Serena held out her hand and he dutifully passed her his glasses. She gave them a quick polish, then reached out to ruffle his hair. "I mean, it's not like we got anything better to do, right?" She winked at Jack as she bent down to give Tinker a quick cuddle.

A glance out of the window told Serena night was falling. "It's getting dark," she said. "How would you like to make a campfire? You and Tinker can catch fireflies while I get wood from the woodpile."

"And a bucket of water." Jack nodded. "You should always have a bucket of water by a campfire."

Serena chuckled. "Yes, Jack. And a bucket of water."

Serena stretched and cracked her back before following her brother down the stairs and out through the door. The lake was still in the evening twilight. Not a single ripple danced on the surface, like it was made of glass. *A glass lake,* thought Serena. An entire lake made from a single piece of glass, trapping all life underneath. Serena shook her head, wondering where that macabre thought had come from. She was just as bad as that superstitious cabbie. This city girl was getting more than a little spooked by all this wilderness.

The sun was setting in the distance, streaks of orange and pink painted the sky. She knelt by a clear area near the water that looked perfect for a campfire and stargazing. Chairs ringed a firepit that looked to be recently dug out and cleaned.

"I can't remember the last time we had a fire. I'm actually looking forward to it," she called to her brother.

Jack appeared from around the side of the cottage, his arms weighed down with sticks of firewood, Tinker close at his heels. Serena rose to meet him. "I found an old flashlight in the boathouse, too." He huffed under his heavy load.

"Look at all this firewood. The groundskeeper must have continued to come here after our grandparents died. Everything is in good order, and it looks like the lawn has been freshly mowed." Serena glanced back at the cottage. "He must have a key too, because the house has been kept up and recently cleaned. Not what I expected from an abandoned lake house."

While Serena appreciated the gesture, she made a mental note to visit the town's hardware store the next day to have the locks changed. The house would feel more like theirs if they were the only ones who could enter. "I suppose I should inspect the pickup, make sure the keys are inside the truck and the old thing can start up."

Jack stacked the wood in a crisscross pattern, chattering to Tinker about how to properly build a fire, and Serena took Jack's flashlight over to the rusty red truck, peeking inside the window. It was unlocked, the keys in the ignition. Serena chuckled. Only in the country could people leave the keys in the ignition and not have their car stolen. She opened the squeaky door, running her hands along the dash. Some visible cracks stood out, but not a trace of dust. She sat on the worn leather interior, placing her hand on the steering wheel. Like magic, the key sparked life into the engine with a simple turn of the ignition. It hummed loudly, reassuring Serena it was reliable and in working condition.

"At least I have transportation for the morning when I head into town." Satisfied, she turned off the engine and locked the truck. Her old city habits wouldn't die just by being in the country. Not locking her car door was something she would never get used to.

Jack already had the campfire blazing—he must have picked up more from that survival guide than Serena had thought. The fire glowed brightly against the black sky and tiny white lights twinkled off in the distance. Serena sank into one of the chairs and counted the lights of the fishing boats, each one reflecting white rays into the water like starlight.

"It's so pretty here at night, isn't it, Jack?" Serena sighed. Night had truly fallen, and the stars appeared in the dark sky. When there was no answer, Serena sat bolt upright. "Jack? Jack? Where are you?" No reply. "Jack, this isn't funny, please answer me."

Serena stood and turned a full circle, surveying the property. Jack and Tinker were nowhere to be seen. Her breath squeezed in her chest. Something was wrong.

"Okay, I'm not going to panic yet. He's probably just off looking for sticks to burn. He's not far." Serena cursed the cabbie for infecting her with his unease and flicked on the flashlight. She tried to bury the seed of fear that had already begun to grow inside her mind.

A faint whimpering noise came from the rear end of the cottage. Serena shined the flashlight in the noise's direction. "Tinks, is that you?" she called into the darkness. "Tinks, come here, baby." Serena stood stock still, listening. Nothing. Serena placed the flashlight on the ground and clapped her hands together. "Tinker, come here, baby girl." Still nothing. Serena nervously looked around the cottage. She had no idea where her brother was, and full night was upon them, almost like an oppressive thing. No moon hung in the sky, and Serena's life in the city hadn't prepared her for such absolute darkness. Jack didn't like the dark.

Serena craned her neck, following the sound of another low whimper. *That must be Tinker.* She chewed on her bottom lip as another thought occurred to her. *What if it's not Tinker? What if it's something else, and Jack's out there in the night all alone?* She reached for the flashlight and tightened her grip.

"No," she said aloud to herself. "My imagination is getting carried away by this creepy house and the isolation." The house looked even more menacing in the night. Serena glanced up at the circular window and staggered backward as a willowy figure appeared in the glass. "Jack!" Serena called out and aimed the flashlight at the window. Nothing was there but the funnel web. Serena shook her head, trying to adjust her eyes to the dark. Her imagination was running away at full speed now and she needed to stay focused to find Jack. Serena took a step closer to the cottage, twigs snapping under her feet. She shined her dim light into the woods, but the beam hardly permeated the still night. Not even a breeze moved in the trees. Serena shuddered. "Where are you, Jack?" Serena called out into the night. "Please answer me!"

"Serena!" Jack appeared from behind the cottage, mud caked on his jeans. Sweat ran from his temples, and his face was tight with fear. He crashed into Serena, his small arms circling her waist.

Relief flooded into Serena. "Oh, Jack, thank God! You scared the life out of me! Where were you? I've been calling for you."

Jack leaned back, his expression panicked behind his smudged glasses. "It's Tinker. She's gone. I can't find her. We were over by that crab apple tree getting some twigs when she disappeared. I can't find her, Serena, and it's so dark."

Serena hugged her brother. "It's okay, Jack. She probably went off chasing a mouse. We'll find her."

Jack shook his head as he buried his face into her chest. "Tinker's never left me. Never. Something is wrong."

Serena bit her bottom lip. Her brother had a point. Hell would freeze over before that dog would walk off on Jack. Too late, she realized there must also be critters in the forest. Foxes and mountain lions, even a raccoon might think Tinker was a tasty treat. Dread rose in her throat, then a bark rang out in the night.

They both gasped. "You heard that?"

Jack whimpered. "She sounds scared."

The sense of dread grew stronger, and Serena shivered. The air grew colder by the minute. She surveyed the yard. There. The bark had come from under the deck of the cottage. Serena got to her knees and shone the flashlight under the deck. The light flickered, and she banged it once on the ground before it blazed again. The crawl space stretched out the full length of the house, leaving about two feet of clearance, maybe a little less. There were broken beams, pieces of old canoes, cinder blocks and a labyrinth of cobwebs blocking her view. Tinker whimpered again, but Serena couldn't see her.

"I think she's stuck under the house. Looks like there's a lot of junk under there. It's too dangerous for you to crawl through. There might be spiders." Serena handed Jack the flashlight as she zipped up her hoodie. "Aim the light where you think you hear Tinker, okay? That way I'll know where to go and I'll crawl in after her."

Jack's eyes widened with fear. "I'm scared, Sissy." He hadn't called Serena that in years. Serena wrapped a reassuring arm around his shoulders and made her voice stronger than she felt.

"She's okay, Jack. Her collar is probably caught on a piece of wood or a nail and she's scared because it's so dark," Serena soothed. "Once you flash the light on her, she'll start wagging her tail because she'll know you found her. Then I'll pull her out." Serena scanned Jack's face, trying to read his worry. "Once she sees you, she will be fine, I promise. But we have to be brave for Tinker."

Another yelp came from under the stairs and they both jumped. "Over there, Jack. It came from over there." Serena pointed to the far left of the cottage, the darkest part of the crawl space. Jack's light landed on the little dog, but Serena saw no movement. Tinker lay on her back, her glassy eyes staring into nothing.

"Serena! She's hurt! She's not moving, Serena!" Jack's voice cracked in terror. Serena dropped to her belly and army-crawled beneath the house. She didn't allow herself to think of the creepy-crawlies she was disturbing. She made a beeline for the little dachshund, talking softly to Tinker as she crawled.

"It's okay, Tinker. I'm coming, baby." The dog never moved, never blinked her eyes, and Serena feared the worst. Dust fell from the floorboards above her, and she coughed and sputtered, blinking grime from her eyes. She swiped at cobwebs, pulling the sticky film from where it clung to her cheeks and lashes, praying there weren't any spiders attached to them.

The smell of rot filled Serena's nose, strong enough to choke her, and she breathed through her open mouth. It couldn't be Tinker—it would be way too soon. The dog must have smelled something dead under here and come in to investigate. The smell of decay and rotting flesh grew stronger, and Serena coughed. The watery beam from Jack's flashlight dimmed, casting flickering shadows in the crawlspace. Shapes took form under the cottage—dark, hunched-over figures lurked in the corners. Her breath came in quick pants as fear trickled down her spine. *Wrong.* The flashlight wavered in Jack's hands as he sobbed.

Serena's hoodie caught on a nail, tearing from her shoulder, and her breath fogged before her. Cold. It was so cold. A scratching sound filled her ears, and Serena could just make out Tinker's still form ahead. She tensed, her eyes scanning the impermeable dark. The shadows closed around her, choking out the light, choking out her breath. Her teeth chattered, either with the fierce cold or fear, she didn't know. One and then another of the drawing pencils slid out of her bun, and her long hair spilled around her face. She squeezed her eyes shut. Something was down here—she could feel it. Her heart pounded.

"This isn't real," she told herself. "Nothing is happening to you. It's just your imagination. The dark is playing tricks on you, you big chicken. None of this is real."

Serena shook her hair from her face and tried to focus on where Tinker lay just ahead. It was so cold. "You have to do this," Serena said to herself under her breath. "Someone has to get Tinker, and there's no one else here, so it has to be you. Move," she commanded her frozen body. Something ice-cold slid down her cheek and she yelped, swiping at it with her bare shoulder as she startled into action and crawled closer to the dog. "Tinks, I'm here, baby," Serena said, a slight shake in her voice. She stretched out her fingers and grazed the little dog. Still warm. The flashlight blinked out, then there was only darkness.

"Jack, turn on the light!" Panic sharpened her voice, and again something cold grazed her cheek, almost like a caress. She jerked away, her hair tangling on a loose nail in the beams. "Jack!" she screamed. "Turn on the light!" She seized the little dog's collar, and dragged Tinker's limp body to her side. "I have her! Turn on the flashlight, Jack! Turn on the light!"

Jack whimpered behind her, banging the light against the wood. "It won't work!" he sobbed. "I can't make it come on!"

Serena cradled the dog against her as she tried to inch her way backward out of the crawl space. Her fingertips were numb with cold, but she could feel Tinker's racing heartbeat. *Alive. She's still alive.*

The scraping sound filled the crawlspace, and something warm passed over her face, like a hot, fetid breath. She gasped, panicking. *Something is definitely down here.* The ice-cold sensation slid down her face again, then her head jerked back, as if something—or someone—had a fist in her hair and was wrenching her head back, exposing her neck. Serena screamed as a sharp pain pierced the curve between her neck and shoulder. Her scream stopped abruptly, shocked out of her as ice poured into her veins from the bite. It was certainly a bite—there was no mistaking it. Serena sobbed as true panic flooded in. She was going to die here, with her helpless brother watching.

"Please, Jack," she begged. "Turn on the light."

The flashlight flickered back on and dimmed, and Jack's words were indecipherable as he sobbed. The grip in her hair loosened, and she was able to turn her head to Jack. The light shook in his hands, and when he shone it on Serena, he screamed, an unending wail piercing the icy night. "Serena's dead!" he sobbed. "Sissy's dead! It's eating her!"

Serena choked, squeezing her eyes shut as she clutched Tinker under her arm and slithered backward. An icy blast of wind buffeted her face, lifting her hair. Pain radiated from her shoulder, more than she could bear. She was frozen, like Tinker. Under her fingers she could feel the little dog's heart slowing. Ice slid through her veins, making everything slow. The bite. Somewhere through the fog of her mind she knew it was poison. Jack was right—she'd die down here. She knew it deep in her bones.

"J-J-J-Jack." Her teeth chattered in the cold. "Jack, I'm okay."

"No," he sobbed. "She's going to eat you."

Serena tried to move her head, but she was so tired, so cold. Her body felt as though it were filling with lead, her limbs were so heavy. Her eyes began to close...

Suddenly, something warm gripped her ankle, and she yelped as it gave a hard jerk. This was it. She tried to kick, but the grip was too strong. It gave another rough tug as the darkness closed over her.

Then she was free. The warm night air filled her lungs, and she looked up to see a tall figure silhouetted in the starlight. Tinker squirmed in her arms and broke loose, running for Jack. He huddled on the ground and wrapped his arms around Tinker in a death grip, hiccupping sobs into her fur.

"Are you okay?" A honeyed voice enveloped Serena, and someone placed a hand on her face. A warm hand — she leaned into it. She was alive. Hurt, but alive.

"There's someone down there," Serena whispered, her eyes blinking open. "Someone bit me."

A soft chuckle warmed Serena, and she felt arms go around her. "You're okay," a velvety female voice assured her. "Nobody's under your house. You must be our new neighbors from the city." A warm hand smoothed over her back, calming her. "You're fine. You're safe," the voice soothed. "But why the hell are you crawling under your house? There could be snakes."

Serena felt groggy, as if she were coming out of a fog. "It bit me..." she mumbled. *So tired.*

Warm fingers grazed her injured shoulder, and she jerked. "Yep," the stranger murmured. "Something got you good. Let's get you in the house and look at it. Can you stand?"

Serena shivered as the adrenaline dwindled in her system, leaving her drained of any strength. "I think so," she whispered. Gentle hands gripped her arms and helped her to her feet, arms going around her to steady her. Serena looked up into the face of her rescuer.

The stranger was tall and lean, dressed in jeans with a black T-shirt. She wore a baseball cap, shielding her face from view. Dark hair spilled from under her cap. Serena blinked as her vision blurred and her head felt too heavy for her small shoulders. The stranger gave

Serena a little shake before Serena passed out, collapsing onto the hard ground.

Serena awoke. Her eyes were blurry, and she squinted to focus in the blinding light. Her shoulder hurt, and she winced when she tried to touch it.

A hand stopped her. "You're awake," the voice said brightly. "You sure gave your brother a scare. He was convinced someone was eating you under the porch. It took four cookies to get him to calm down. Hope you don't mind."

Serena sat up, blinking. She was indoors, on a strange couch. *My cottage, that's right.* Tinker got under the house, and when Serena went after her... "Something bit me, I think," Serena groaned.

"You said that already," the stranger — no, a girl — grinned. Serena could find no words as she stared up at the girl kneeling beside her. Her face was squared, with a narrow brow and a sharp jaw. Serena was taken back by how pretty the girl was — athletic-looking with strong slender arms. She grazed her calloused fingers softly over Serena's bare shoulder, and she shuddered, not from the cold. Serena gazed from the girl's long fingers to her strong forearms, thin but attractive veins traveling up her arms, suggesting she worked with her hands often. Her shaggy dark hair stuck out from under her baseball cap, falling around her ears. Serena focused on the girl's gray eyes as the girl frowned, concern creasing her lovely face. Serena realized too late she was staring, and she blushed furiously.

"My name is Ashton," the girl said. "I live on the other side of the island over there." She waved in the general direction of the dark water outside. "I was on my boat and saw your campfire and house lights on. There hasn't been anyone on this property for years. I wanted to make sure you weren't squatters."

Ashton looked over at Jack. He held Tinker in his lap, wrapped up in a blanket like a baby. He pet her gently as he watched Serena. He seemed calm. "I heard your brother screaming," she continued, "so I docked my boat and ran over. That is your brother, right?" Serena shook her head yes.

Ashton bent down next to Jack, giving Tinker a gentle pet. "Keep her wrapped up in that blanket. It'll make her feel more secure. You've all had a scare. Maybe you could get some of those cookies for your sister?"

Jack nodded, and lifted the bundle with Tinker in his arms and carried her off in the direction of the kitchen.

Ashton turned to Serena. "Think you can sit up? I need to look at that bite." Ashton helped Serena rise to a sitting position, then lifted a crocheted blanket from the back of a chair and wrapped it around her, leaving one shoulder exposed. She sat in the ottoman facing Serena. "Well, you know my name and why I'm here, but I don't know your name." She smiled.

"Serena," she whispered. "This used to be our grandparents' house, but now it's ours."

Ashton nodded. "I'm going to look in the bathroom's medicine cabinet. I should clean that bite before I leave."

Serena watched this unknown person moving around her unfamiliar house. Ashton's cropped hoodie fell above her belly button, a silver bar pierced her tan skin, and she wore a pair of skinny jeans with white sneakers. At that moment Ashton towered in the tiny cottage, though she appeared to be around Serena's height. Ashton returned with a cloth, a bottle of peroxide and some ointment.

Though her shoulder burned with an icy fire, Serena felt herself calming. It was nice to be fussed over, to be taken care of. She didn't realize how much she had missed it since her mother had passed, and all the emotions from the past year filled her throat. She swallowed, unable to speak.

Ashton's gray eyes moved from Serena's to examine the bite. "Mind if I touch it? This might hurt a bit." Serena nodded. Ashton trailed her fingers over the tender skin, and Serena hissed a breath through her teeth. Ashton nodded. "Stings, huh? It looks pretty nasty," she said, her voice low. "I'm not sure what bit you. An animal of some kind? A raccoon? Hmmm. Whatever it was, it only had two front canines. Maybe a snake. Or a spider, probably, though honestly it looks pretty bad for that. Your brother said it was a vampire." She chuckled, and goosebumps rose on Serena's arms.

"He was really shook up." Ashton opened the peroxide and dabbed some on Serena's shoulder. The peroxide fizzed, turning the bite white. Serena inhaled deeply through her nose. "Does that hurt?" Ashton asked, concerned. "Usually there's not a lot of discomfort when using hydrogen peroxide to clean bites."

Serena bit her lip as the icy pain traveled deeper into her neck. "It's fine," she said in a whisper.

"I know you're shaken up over what just happened, but try not to worry about being here," Ashton said as she patted the wound, her fingers gentle. "The lake has a way of playing tricks on you. The stillness, the quietness, being away from neighbors and streetlights. It can be a lot, especially if you are used to city life. Sometimes the silence can be deafening. It's a lot to get used to, but you will. And before you know it, you will grow to like the privacy and quiet that comes from living on the lake."

Serena could hear the girl's affection for the lake in her voice, her words surrounding Serena like a blanket of sincerity. Serena wanted to believe her, but it wasn't the dark or night creatures she feared on the lake. It wasn't the isolation or lack of city noise that scared her. It was the unknown that Serena feared. The things she could not see but feel. She knew something—or someone—had been in there with her, something that couldn't be found under a microscope or explained in a science textbook.

Ashton removed her baseball cap and ran a hand through her dark hair as she waited for Serena to speak, but she was silent. "The wound is festering," fretted Ashton as she smoothed some ointment over it.

For a long moment Ashton worked in silence, her eyes darting up to meet Serena's, then back down to the wound. "Kind of weird, right?" she said, stealing another peek at Serena from under her baseball cap as she carefully placed gauze over the bite. "Some girl just shows up at your new house late at night and offers to help you dress a colossal spider bite." Serena kept her eyes locked on Ashton. "Definitely not your ordinary welcome to the neighborhood greeting." Ashton smiled, trying to settle Serena's nerves. She rubbed her palms on the front of her jeans and stood up. "All done."

Serena pressed her fingers on the bandage. The bite stung with the same familiar icy pain that penetrated deep into her body. "I saw a funnel web on one of the windows, but Jack said funnel weavers are harmless." She shuddered as the pain branched out into her arm as well. Serena rubbed her shoulder, suddenly feeling too exhausted for company. "Thank you for helping me tonight and for coming over to inspect the fire."

Ashton smiled, giving her a gentle nod. "Would you like me to check on the dog before I leave?"

Serena frowned, thinking about Tinker and what condition she might be in. She'd been so focused on Jack that she hadn't even thought about Tinker until now.

"I'm good with animals, dogs especially," Ashton continued. "I don't mind checking on her before I head back."

She nodded, giving Ashton a small but genuine smile. Ashton smiled back. Serena was not accustomed to accepting help from people in general, let alone strangers, but Ashton seemed sincere, and she had a quiet but reliable kindness to her. Still, Serena was no starry-eyed fool, despite how undeniably attractive this Ashton girl was. If Ashton truly was a nice person to have as a neighbor on the lake, time would tell and Serena wasn't going to let her physical desires cloud her judgment. Even though Ashton looked hot as hell with her belly-button piercing and baseball cap. "Yes, I would appreciate that, thank you."

Ashton called out to Jack, not wanting to startle him in the kitchen. "Hey, buddy, mind if I come in? I can look at your little dog. I just want to make sure she is okay," Ashton added.

Jack sat motionless at the kitchen table with Tinker wrapped tightly in a blanket like a butterfly inside a cocoon. Jack's entire focus was on the dog in his lap. "How is she doing?" Ashton asked as she made her way over to Jack. She knelt beside the chair, keeping her attention on Tinker. Carefully, Ashton rubbed the bridge of Tinker's nose. The dog closed her eyes in response to her gentle touch.

"She likes that," Jack whispered.

"I had a dog a few years ago," Ashton said quietly. "She always loved it when I would rub the bridge of her nose. She was afraid of thunder."

Jack looked at Ashton. "Did a monster try to eat your dog, too?" he whispered.

"Nope." Ashton chuckled. "She just went the way of good old dogs." Serena leaned against the doorframe, watching Ashton lean over Jack and Tinker. Ashton was even prettier in the light, Serena noticed, and looked to be around her age.

"What type of dog was she?" Jack asked.

"She was a great dane." She laughed. "The most beautiful, majestic great dane the world has ever known. She was regal and strong, but kind and soft-spirited. A true gentle giant. Such a beautiful girl." Ashton tilted her head back as she laughed again, and Serena smiled, too. It was a nice laugh. "She would bring a grown man to his knees with one growl." Ashton lightly elbowed Jack in the arm. "She was about as big as you, and probably just as tough. When she stood on her hind legs, she was as tall as me!"

Jack laughed, eyes wide with wonder. "Scooby-Doo was a great dane. That's because people thought they'd ward off ghosts and evil spirits."

"Is that right? Well, she was a beauty, that's for sure, but one roar of thunder and that dog was as scared as a church mouse being hunted by a field cat." Ashton's face lit up as she spoke of her beloved friend. "Genevieve would try to hide under my bed during storms, but she would forget how massive she was and only her head would fit under the bed frame, leaving the rest of her exposed."

Jack laughed again, and the tension melted out of the room. "I would try to coax her out with carrots." Ashton's head tilted up toward the ceiling. "She loved carrots! Her absolute favorite snack. But nothing worked during a thunderstorm. She was just too scared."

Jack leaned closer to Ashton. "What did you do to help her?"

Ashton once again placed her slender finger on the bridge of Tinker's nose. "I crawled under the bed with her and did this." Ashton's finger stroked Tinker's long nose, putting the little dog to sleep. Jack looked down at Tinker, then up at Ashton, his eyes warm with affection.

"Hey, buddy, your glasses are dirty. Want me to clean them?"

"No," he answered, his tone serious as he glanced up at Serena in the doorway. "Serena likes to do it. It makes her feel useful."

Ashton turned to look at Serena, and they both laughed. Ashton rose, moving to Serena's side. "Will you be okay when I go?" She pulled her phone out of her pocket. "I live close by. Well, close enough to where I can get to you in a few minutes by boat." Serena stared at the floor, suddenly shy. The thought of having someone nearby was a comfort.

"Just a few minutes by boat?" she asked.

"Yes, give me your number and I'll text you now so you will have mine and you can call me or message me if you feel...unsettled about anything." She chose the word carefully.

Serena smiled. She was so accustomed to being alone and taking care of Jack she had forgotten what it felt like to have someone to rely on, a friend. After her parents' death, Serena didn't have time for friends. Maybe Ashton was right, maybe her imagination had run away from her. Maybe the sudden change of life was too much too soon, and all she needed was to go to bed and wake up in the daylight to see things clearly. In any case, she was thankful Ashton had come by. Now she knew someone in the area, and they weren't as isolated as she had thought. It didn't hurt either how good-looking Ashton was. Serena bit her bottom lip thinking about Ashton's silver belly-button ring.

* * * *

Later, Serena sat in the overstuffed chair in Jack's room next to his bed. She was beyond tired from all the commotion, but she couldn't bring herself to sleep away from Jack. Her sketchpad lay open in her lap, and Ashton's lovely face stared back at her from the page. Jack slept fitfully, and Serena would smooth a hand over his hair to calm his dark dreams. Tinker curled tightly in his arms. Serena remained half awake, watching her brother battling nightmares as he slept. Wishing she could ease his distress, she sang to him their mother's lullaby, hoping it would calm his troubled dreams.

"The night has come to take you to sleep. The stars have come to wish you sweet dreams. The moon watches over you, the Luna moth sings to you and I am here beside you. Sleep sweetly my love, fall to sleep, my little love."

Jack's body went still and his breathing became steady until finally, it was a calm, and tranquil breath of someone in a deep peaceful sleep. Once satisfied Jack was safe and sound in his own dreams, Serena gave in to her exhaustion and closed her eyes, her sketchpad falling to the floor.

Chapter Three

Small Town

Serena woke up the next morning worried about her little brother. She had stayed by his side through the night, brushing Jack's flaxen hair away from his forehead as the morning light streaked through the pane glass window, etching diamond sunbeams across his face. He looked so peaceful when he was sleeping, just like he did as a small baby when their parents would let Serena hold him, rocking him in their mother's special rocking chair.

Now that the sun was peeking over Lake Conjure, Serena felt she might have overreacted the night before. Maybe Ashton had a point—maybe her imagination had gotten the best of her. Maybe she was bitten by a giant blood-sucking spider with enormous fangs. It was certainly possible. More plausible than the alternative—that there was a creepy monster out to eat her.

Jack twitched in his sleep, his dark eyelashes fanning over his soft cheeks as he stirred. Serena knew she had to get Jack's mind off the night before. They needed to do something fun, something to help him get back into the spirit of being on a beautiful mountain lake. Perhaps a tour of their new town and a visit to the library. Surely that would make Jack feel more at home here.

Serena rubbed a hand over her tired eyes, then gave Jack a soft shake. "Time to wake up, Professor. We have a big day ahead."

Jack rolled over and pulled his pillow over his head. "Children need sleep, Serena," he mumbled into his pillow. "Disturbing my circadian rhythm can interrupt restorative sleep."

Serena smirked as she pulled the pillow off Jack's head and swatted him with it. "Well, excuse me, Professor! But I thought we'd visit the library today."

That got Jack's attention, and he immediately sat up, wide awake. "Do you think we will need to verify our new address in order to get a new library card?"

Serena shook her head and chuckled. "I'll take care of all that. You just worry about whatever you need to research for your next dissertation. Get dressed and meet me outside, okay?"

Jack nodded as he reached for the glasses that sat on his nightstand. "I'd like to learn more about the local flora and fauna native to this area. And the area's history!" he called out to Serena's retreating back.

"Sounds good to me, Professor!" Serena called over her shoulder as she descended the stairs. "Don't forget your shoes!"

Serena wanted to get an early start and head into town. She settled into the rusty old pickup and fired it to life. The truck rumbled, idling, while Serena made a mental note of everything they needed to get today. Groceries were a necessity, so they'd stop at the Price Chopper Serena had noticed on their way into town.

The library, of course. And maybe the hardware store. Motion caught Serena's eye, and she looked up to see Jack descending the porch steps, a book clutched to his chest and Tinker following behind.

"Look what I found!" he called out to Serena. "A book—*A History of Witches*! I think some of them were from around here, but most were from this place called Salem. Where's Salem?" He pulled the passenger door open and it groaned loudly in protest. Tinker leapt up beside him, wagging her tail as Jack buckled his seat belt.

"Salem actually isn't too far south from here. I think I saw a sign for its exit when we drove up here. Salem, Massachusetts, is where the infamous witch trials took place. I didn't even realize New York had a town named Salem until recently. What are you reading again, exactly?" Serena leaned over to examine the cover. "Witches? Won't that be creepy?" After the previous night Serena had all the creepiness she could take.

Jack rolled his eyes. "Only bad witches are creepy, Serena," he said in his know-it-all voice as he cracked open the book in his lap.

"Well, let's hope we don't run into one of those," Serena teased as she put the old truck into gear and puttered down their tree-lined driveway.

She drove the old hooptie of a truck to Price Chopper to purchase some ingredients to bake Jack his favorite breakfast—blueberry pancakes.

The library had not yet opened, so Jack waited in the truck with Tinker huddled beside him while Serena shopped. Tinker looked down at the book, seemingly reading along with him as he flipped through the pages. As he turned the pages, he stumbled upon the history of witchcraft in Salem, New York. The only useful information the book offered was that a witch trial was held in Salem during 1777, eighty years after the infamous witch trials of Salem, Massachusetts.

Motion caught Jack's eye, and he looked up in time to spy a woman wearing a long floral dress with squared-toe shoes unlock the library's front door. Jack quivered with excitement at the prospect of all those books he'd never seen before, just waiting to reveal their secrets to him. He popped his head out of the window and scanned the streets of the small town. The town was quiet at this early hour, and Serena was still inside the grocery store.

"What do you think, Tinker?" he asked his dog. She looked up at him and wagged her tail. "Do you think I can go inside, or should I wait for Serena?" Taking Tinker's silence as a yes, he pushed open the creaky pickup door. "You hold down the fort here, Tinker, and tell Serena where I went." Tinker put her front paws on the truck door window. He turned back and gave Tinker a thumbs-up before he entered the building.

Libraries had always been Jack's most favorite place in the world. The smell of dusty book bindings and old paper always soothed him, and he took several deep breaths, taking in as much of the comforting library smell as possible.

The woman in the floral dress leaned over the library counter to make eye contact with Jack. She had gunmetal gray hair curled close to her head, popular with grannies all over. She squinted at him from behind her horn-rimmed glasses, and her mouth formed a firm line. She brought her finger to her mouth as she hissed, "Shhhhhh." Jack looked around. They were the only ones in the building.

Jack had never met a librarian he couldn't charm. He walked up to her and pressed his glasses up his nose, offering her a wide smile. The corners of her mouth turned down into a frown as she stared down her nose at Jack. "What may I help you with, boy?" Her words were cold, like frost before a harsh winter, and immediately Jack missed the old library back in the city.

Undaunted, Jack continued to beam at the grouchy woman. "I am looking for a book on Salem, New York."

The librarian pulled her glasses down the bridge of her nose and with her pointer finger beckoned Jack closer. "Come here, boy."

Jack shuffled forward a step, but came no closer. She was definitely not like the librarians back home.

The old librarian's lip curled as she stared down at Jack. "What is your name, boy? I know everyone in this town, and I know I've never seen you before."

Jack shuffled from one foot to the other as he stared down at the ground, fighting tears along with a wave of homesickness. He wondered if this woman was even a librarian at all. She had a cruel face, and looked like she had never baked cookies a day in her entire life. Or even smiled. Not like the librarians back in the city. His lower lip wobbled.

"Well, boy?" The woman crossed her arms as she stared down at Jack. "I asked you a question. What is your name?"

"His name is Jack." Serena's voice swept over her brother like a blanket and Jack instantly relaxed as his sister's hand rested upon his shoulder. "And I'm Serena. We just moved to Korwin Cottage."

The old librarian gasped as she took a step back. She eyed them warily as she fingered a small gold cross around her neck. Her eyes moved over the two of them, resting on the large bandage on Serena's neck before she looked away. "I assume you know how to use a computer, boy. You can access the online catalog." The librarian busied herself by straightening a stack of paper, then lined up the pens on the counter, her eyes down.

"Jack," Serena snapped, irritation sharpening her words. "His name is Jack, not boy."

The woman's eyes darted to Serena before looking away. She mumbled something under her breath. It sounded like a prayer. Serena glared at the woman before she knelt down to Jack's height. "Come on, Jack," she said as she rubbed a soothing hand in circles on his back. "Let's find your book and get out of here."

Serena took her brother's hand and guided him toward the back of the library, passing through aisles of books. Jack peeked over his shoulder and caught the librarian watching them through a small hand mirror. She narrowed her cold stare at him, and Jack swallowed as he turned around. "She's watching us, Serena," he whispered, his shoulders tense. Serena looked over her shoulder at the librarian, who startled and dropped her mirror. It shattered on the ground, and the old woman's face was pale as she turned around to appear busy. She looked afraid.

Well, that was...unsettling. "Don't pay her any attention, Jack," Serena murmured to her brother. "She's seriously whacked. What a mean old witch. Just find your book so we can get the heck out of here."

Twenty minutes later Jack took a stack of books to the front desk. Serena stood by the library's exit, watching as the librarian's hands shook as she printed Jack a library card and checked out his books, never once looking up.

Serena tapped her foot, annoyed. What was wrong with this woman? How could she treat Jack that way? She made a mental note to ask Ashton about the kooky librarian.

Serena held the door open for Jack, and he hugged his stack of books to his chest as he crossed the parking lot to their junky pickup, his face drawn. Serena was furious with the librarian. How on earth was a crazy woman like that working with the public? It was baffling. The entire point of the trip was to make Jack excited about his new home, and now he wouldn't even meet Serena's eyes. She looked up and caught the old librarian staring through the window at them. When Serena met her gaze the woman dropped below the windowsill, then crept back up to peek through the glass at them. *So strange.* Serena shook her head. *I guess they don't get many newcomers here.*

On their way out of town, they stopped by the hardware store to arrange for a locksmith to come out later that day and change the locks on all the doors. "Do you want to stay in the truck with Tinker, Jack?" He looked over at his big sister and nodded yes, one of his new library books opened in his lap. Serena looked down to see what he was reading. There was a drawing of a woman in pilgrim clothes being hanged. *Good grief.* Shaking her head, Serena let out a long breath and stepped out of the rusting truck. They'd talk about his choice of reading materials later. Serena only hoped he didn't give himself nightmares.

The hardware store was small, with a limited selection of items. It had enough to appeal to the daily needs of country life—inflatable rafts, pails, shovels, gardening tools, seeds, pots, hinges, nails, a few power tools and items that might come in handy for the odd job around the house. However, the options available were scant, and if one were looking to paint their room cobalt blue, they would have to settle for baby blue. Serena opened the store door. A bell ran above her head informing the owner and his wife of her presence.

The woman behind the counter was middle-aged with a crop of wiry red hair with streaks of white sticking out amongst the red like frozen branches in winter. The lady glanced down at Serena as she stacked cans of paint. Her cold blue eyes pierced Serena like daggers from behind her wide-rimmed glasses. Serena focused her attention on the woman's husband, keeping her shoulders straight and her head held high. Serena wouldn't be intimidated by small-town folks with small-minded opinions and Serena knew this one was busy forming a hasty judgment.

Serena eyed the husband's uniform, spotting the name Bob stitched in red thread above the left shirt pocket. She was relieved to see Bob was more welcoming than his wife.

"Well, hello, little lady! You must be new here!" he boomed. "I never forget a pretty face," he said, winking as he eagerly set to placing her work order. "What's the name, and where's this headed?"

"My name is Serena. And yes, I'm new here." She smiled. "My brother and I recently moved into Korwin Cottage. Do you know the place?"

Bob dropped his pen, and Serena jumped when she heard the crashing of a dozen pints of paint clattering to the floor. She turned to see the man's wife staring at her, her mouth open, aghast. Clearing his throat, Bob picked up his pen and continued to fill out the work order. "Korwin Cottage, you say? No one has lived there in a long time." Serena watched as his wife haphazardly stacked paint cans, unable to take her eyes off Serena.

She scrunched her nose, confused. She knew that newcomers in small towns always set locals on edge, but this was getting ridiculous. "Yes, it was my grandparents' home. It was left to me."

"You live in Korwin Cottage?" the wife asked, interrupting their conversation. Serena wasn't accustomed to small-town living, but she knew enough about people to keep answers short and to the point.

"I do." That was all the reply she was going to give. The woman seemed miffed and darted her husband a cantankerous glance.

"Nobody has lived there for quite some time," the woman replied, echoing her husband's words. She tilted her head, staring at Serena through her thick-rimmed glasses.

Serena just nodded, knowing she was irritating the woman by not volunteering her private life. "This is a small town," the woman went on. "I know just about everybody who's ever come through here. I didn't hear anything about a new resident occupying the old cottage." The woman's eyes narrowed on Serena.

Serena kept her shoulders straight and avoided eye contact with the woman as she signed the work order, offering Bob a quick smile. "I'm Serena. I'll be staying here permanently, so I'm sure we will see more of each other."

Serena wondered how much this woman knew about her grandparents, considering they must have frequented the local store for household goods. She was tempted to ask but decided against it. Better to let things unfold naturally than force them. So far everyone seemed a little insane, but perhaps that was what happened when people lived too long in the boondocks.

Serena was careful not to catch the eye of the woman, who was staring at her avidly. She could tell this woman liked to gossip and Serena didn't want to find herself caught up in small-town chatter. Between the crazy librarian and the rude hardware store woman, she had no doubt that she'd be the topic of conversation at the next bingo night held at the local church. Serena eyed flyers for the event at both the grocery store and the library. It seemed to be the hip thing to do on a Saturday night in Corvin Grove.

At the door, Serena opened her tote bag to drop in her work order receipt. Behind her she could hear the husband and wife speaking in low voices. "That girl is too young to be out on that lake all alone in that old Korwin Cottage," the woman said to her husband.

Bob sighed, his voice low. "She seems like a good girl. I feel guilty watching her drive off like this knowing she's going back to that cottage, after everything that's happened there. Come the first winter, she'll pack up that pickup and head back to the city."

The woman snorted. "That girl should pack up and head out now if she knows what's good for her," she muttered under her breath.

The door chimed as Serena opened it to leave, and she felt their eyes on her back as she crossed the parking lot. She schooled her face into something calm and kind, and climbed into the old pickup. Jack didn't bother looking up from his book. "How was the hardware store?" he asked, his eyes still on his book.

"Just peachy." Serena sighed as she put the old truck into gear and pointed it toward their new home.

* * * *

"Who's hungry?" Serena asked as she put away groceries. Serena wasted no time in the kitchen. "I'm making your favorite, blueberry pancakes." She smiled. Jack was relieved to be back at the cottage and dropped his haul of books on the kitchen table.

"In the future we can get fresh blueberries from the farmers' market in town," she called out to him. "The people at Price Chopper said they have one every Friday. So, we can have locally grown blueberries every week for our pancakes. It can be a new tradition we start."

"Maybe we could gather our own," Jack yelled back. "I read that blueberries are native to this area."

"That sounds like fun. Maybe we will put you in charge of blueberry gathering. You can be Captain Blueberry." She winked at her brother. "And I even got fresh peaches and strawberries. Maybe we can bake muffins for tomorrow's breakfast."

Jack scrubbed at his nose. "It's Professor Blueberry, actually."

She swatted Jack as he walked past. "Take your books upstairs, Professor Blueberry." She laughed, and he dodged her as he skipped up the stairs with Tinker, arms full of books.

Serena pulled on an apron she had found hanging in the pantry. She was surprised to discover the pantry was a few degrees cooler than the rest of the house. *This must have been a cold pantry where they kept perishable food before refrigerators*, Serena thought as she touched the cool stone shelves.

Tires rolling on gravel echoed in the driveway, and Serena looked out of the kitchen window to see a blue truck parked next to her own.

"Who would come here?" she wondered aloud as she removed her apron and placed it on the counter before walking out of the back door. A man both round and tall waited by the side of the house. His arms were crossed, and he wore denim overalls, heavy work boots and a permanent scowl. Traces of motor oil stained his nails and knuckles.

Serena extended her hand. "Hi, I'm Serena. Can I help you?"

The man turned his head and spat tobacco in the driveway near her feet, his eyes on the house rather than Serena. "Are you here alone, or did your brother move with you?"

Serena dropped her hand as she raised her guard. "And how would you know about me or my brother?" she asked, her tone sharp. She placed her hands on her hips. "Who are you?"

The man glanced at Serena, then turned back to the house.

"Deaken Ward. I was your granddaddy's groundskeeper, but I suppose now I'm your groundskeeper." He moved the chewing tobacco around in his mouth. "At least that what's the estate attorney informed me."

Serena nodded. Somehow when the estate attorney mentioned a groundskeeper, she had imagined a sweet and gentle old man. This man was old, but not old enough to be a grandparent who wore dentures and used a cane. Deaken's salt-and-pepper hair and defined wrinkles showed his age, but he looked strong and healthy. The man before her didn't appear to be sweet or gentle, but if he was truly the caretaker of the property, he had done an impeccable job.

"Yes, I live here now." She gestured to her red truck parked beside his. "Thank you for selling me your pickup. It came in handy."

Deaken waved his hand in the air. "It was nothing. I wasn't using it and figured you could use a truck if you're gonna be living out here permanently. It was your granddad's truck. He left it to me when he died." He spat again into the driveway. "You'll be residing here full-time, I presume?"

"Yes, my brother and I will," Serena replied in a matter-of-fact tone.

He nodded. "Well, I hope you find the condition of the house to be satisfactory. I worked hard keeping it up and making sure everything was in order. I've been looking after that house my whole life." He pointed to the boathouse with his thumb. "You got a small fishing boat, gassed up and ready for use. It ain't much, it's just an old rudder your granddaddy used to get to and from the neighbors. He didn't believe in spending a fortune on those fancy big engine speed boats." Deaken spat again, and Serena curled her lip in disgust. "Can't say I blame him on that."

Serena turned over his words and nodded, connecting the similarities she had with her grandfather's practical way of thinking. She knew so little about her grandparents, and could only guess at their personalities by the things they left behind.

"There's also an extra can of gasoline on a shelf," Deaken continued. "I come by once a week to maintain the lawn, stock up on gas, chop wood for the woodshed and other supplies you might need. In the winter I plow the main road so you can get into town. I'll also make sure you ain't snowed in." He nodded to the truck. "If your truck is up to its roof in snow, I'll shovel it out." He pointed over his shoulder to the winding gravel road. "School bus won't come out here, so your brother will have to walk to the end of the road every day to catch it. Can be a difficult walk in the winter if the snow is too high. I'll keep a solid path for him."

Serena nodded. This Deaken sounded surly, but she could deal with that. He was a hard worker, and he seemed to take pride in keeping the Korwin property in top shape. Serena thanked him for his diligence and appreciated the extra help. She wasn't a mountain girl and wasn't accustomed to chopping wood and plowing roads.

Deaken stomped dirt off his boot from the gravel driveway. "You know my fee. Your lawyer said you agreed to keep me on as your hired help. I expect my pay on the first of the month. I only take cash, but I assume you are comfortable with those terms."

"Of course, that's not a problem," Serena said.

He nodded. "I live off Korwin Lane by the main road. My house is not on your property. It's the town's land. I keep to myself, but I'm your nearest neighbor by foot. I've lived here my entire life, and I value my privacy and space. You don't bother me, and I won't bother you."

"That shouldn't be a problem," she said, trying to catch his eye, but Deaken stared at the ground. *Hmmm. Not a talker. That's probably for the best.*

"Good," he grumbled. They both turned at the sound of the front door opening. Jack and Tinker spilled down the front steps. Jack came outside to stand by his sister, and Serena placed her arm around his shoulder.

"Jack, this is our groundskeeper, Mr. Ward."

"Deaken is fine," he grunted. He looked down at Jack, scanning him carefully with his right eye. Serena noticed his other eye was unmoving and dull. Glass then. *Maybe that's why he doesn't make eye contact.*

"Nice to meet you, Deaken," Jack said, extending his hand.

To Serena's surprise, Deaken reached out and shook it, a smile creasing his stern face. "You like to go fishing?" Deaken asked.

"I've never fished before," Jack replied as he shoved his glasses further up his nose. "But I read about it in my book. Fish like to eat worms, leeches, minnows, crayfish, crickets and grasshoppers."

Deaken nodded. "Books will only get you so far. The only way to learn is to do it. Now that you live on a lake, that's gonna have to change. There's fishing rods and a tackle box in the boathouse. I can show you how to line a reel and add bait to the rod next time I come to mow the yard."

Jack beamed up at Deaken and Serena smiled to see it. She could see he liked the idea of learning how to fish, and Deaken seemed to like Jack. *Maybe women make him uncomfortable.*

Deaken cleared his throat. "You will like it here, son. It's a good place for a small boy. I spent my whole life here, working with your granddad. Just don't go out on the lake without your sister. It gets deep quick all right."

"All right," replied Jack. "You should always wear a life jacket on the water, even if you are a strong swimmer."

A shadow passed over Deaken's stern face, and he glanced at Serena, his expression dark. "I reckon life jackets are a good idea. Make sure you wear one, boy. Don't want to end up like your grandpappy." He turned on his heels, heading back to his truck.

"What do you mean by that?" Serena asked.

Deaken paused, not turning around. "They say your granddaddy died in a fishing accident."

Serena was astonished, and she looked uneasily at the water's edge. "I never thought to ask how my grandparents died. I never met them. Are drownings common on this lake?"

Deaken still had his back to Serena, his hand on the handle of his truck door. He was silent for a long moment. "No, not common," he finally answered.

"What about my grandmother? Do you know how she died?"

Deaken's shoulders rose in a shrug. "She followed your grandpa not long after," he answered.

Serena nodded. That she understood. Her parents had loved each other like that. It was better that they went together—that way they never suffered being apart.

"One more thing before I go." He turned to face Serena, his one eye meeting Serena's gaze. "I was informed by Bob down at the hardware store you've arranged to have the locks changed today."

Serena straightened her shoulders. "Yes, I have. Glad to know there is a sense of privacy and discretion in this town."

Deaken snorted. "Small town, people talk."

"Is that a problem that I'm having the locks changed?"

"No, ma'am, it's your call. Just keep in mind I am the only person who has spare keys to the house, so once the locks are changed you might want to find a good hiding place to stash your spare or search for another soul that's not ten miles away to give a key to. Last thing you want is to be locked out of the house during a winter storm." Deaken paused, breaking eye contact with Serena before adding under his breath, "Or worse."

"Well, do you blame me for changing the locks? I mean no offense, but you are a total stranger."

His lip curled. "I may be a stranger, but I am also your hired hand, and it's in my best interest to maintain a healthy working relationship with you. Jobs are scarce out here. Besides, I've worked in this house my entire life. Before I was the groundskeeper, my father had the job. Our families have been connected through the generations, you might say." He opened his truck's door, sliding inside.

Serena walked up to the truck, "I'm a city girl. I don't trust people simply because they work for me or my deceased grandparents. I just don't feel entirely comfortable with you having full access to my house."

Deaken spat once more near Serena's feet. "I understand that concern and respect your decision. I'm just informing you, this isn't the city, and me not having a key may be a poorer decision than your fear of me having one." He paused for a moment to point at Serena's neck. "Spider get cha? The funnel ones like to enter inside houses and have been known to crawl into beds."

Jack piped up. "They are attracted to our body heat because they think it could be a mate."

Deaken smirked. "Smart boy you got there. Did one bite ya while you were sleeping?"

Serena covered her bandage with her hand and stared coldly at Deaken, not knowing how to answer his question and not wanting to. He looked over at Jack. "Bye, son. See you soon and be safe on the lake."

Serena kicked a pebble into the grass as she and Jack watched his truck rumble down the curving driveway. "What an odd, pompous old man. This is my house, and I should decide who has a spare key and who doesn't. And it's none of his business what bit me."

She looked out into the lake. Her nearest neighbors were spread out wide around the shore. Nothing but water and woods surrounded her, and now she was all alone to care for her little brother. She sighed, unsure what to do. After all, Deaken had been trusted by her grandparents for over thirty years, and from what she could tell, he didn't steal, ransack the place or murder them in their sleep. The townspeople knew Deaken, so it wasn't like a psychotic maniac had a spare key to her house. She thought about how clean the house had been, how there wasn't a speck of dust to be found, the stack of firewood around back and the spotless greenhouse. She glanced up at the old cottage. Maybe she was being hasty. If Deaken really wanted to break in, all he would need was a big rock to smash through one of the greenhouse windows. "Maybe I am overreacting." She pulled the pencils out of her bun and rewound her long blonde hair, sorting her thoughts. He seemed grouchy but harmless. Just an old hermit that liked to keep to himself.

Serena looked around for her brother. Jack was kneeling in the grass collecting duck feathers that were scattered about.

"I like Deaken. We are going to fish together. I feel better knowing Deaken has a key, Serena. What if you're not here one day after school?" He looked up at his sister's face. "I'm okay with living out here, I really am, but I'm not used to being alone. Deaken seems nice and I feel better knowing he's close by and could get to me if you can't."

Serena sighed, bending down to pick up a feather. "Then it's settled. Deaken can keep a key if it makes you feel more comfortable." Jack nodded, reaching for the feather in Serena's hand. *Oh, what the hell, I'll let him keep a key for now. If he poses a threat, I can always change the locks later.*

"Come on, silly. I'll call the hardware store and then I'll make us breakfast." Jack and Tinker scampered up the cottage steps behind her.

* * * *

"Jack, I have a great idea." Serena flipped the third pancake into the air, catching it in the middle of the iron skillet. "Let's go on an adventure." She looked over at Jack as he sat impatiently at the planked wooden table, his eyes glued to the pancake. "It will be fun! We can take out the two-seater kayak. I'll do all the paddling and we can even bring Tinker."

Serena scanned her brother's tired face, hoping to see a spark of excitement in his eyes. Yesterday he had been so excited about kayaking. After that scare, she hoped he'd still be excited about exploring their new home. "We can go across the way to the other side of the lake by the island. See who our neighbors are."

Jack gave his sister a knowing look. "New neighbors like Ashton?" he asked. Serena laughed as she blushed. That kid was always too smart for his own good.

Serena placed a plate full of pancakes in front of him and dropped into the chair across from him. Tinker sat at Jack's feet, her adoring eyes expectant as she stared up at him. "If you don't hurry and eat those pancakes, Jack, Tinker sure will." Serena giggled as she swiped a pancake from Jack's plate, breaking it into tiny pieces. Jack smiled as Serena dropped a piece into Tinker's eager mouth.

"Look, the sun's out!" Serena implored him. "It'll be fun. We can wear our life jackets," she teased.

Jack shoved a mouthful of pancakes into his mouth, humming as the warm blueberries trickled down his throat. "You mean when we go see where Ashton lives?" he teased back.

Serena's face warmed as she turned away. "No, I mean if we do see where her house is, that will be good information to have, in case we ever need anything, like help with the boat or gas furnace."

"Or maybe just to come over and cuddle up with you in a blanket," Jack said, smiling broadly.

Serena hit him lightly on the arm. "Stop that, Jack!" Her face was red as a tomato, and Jack laughed with his mouth full of pancakes. Serena was happy to see Jack laughing, even if it was at her expense.

"Sure, let's go. I'd like to see Ashton again anyways." Jack shoved the last pancake in his mouth, licking the blueberry juice off his lips.

Serena wondered what it would be like speaking to Ashton the next time she saw her. Would things be awkward? Did she think Serena was crazy? Serena touched her shoulder where Ashton had bandaged it. Serena had sketched her last night—her strong hands, her warm gray eyes.

Serena wasn't sure if Jack's statement was accurate or not. Ashton had popped into her mind once or twice that day. Okay, maybe a little more than that. A follow-up visit was definitely in order. She owed her a massive thank you for rescuing her from being eaten, or at least saving her from her own panic. Now that the sun was shining, she felt a little silly about her freakout under the porch. Maybe it was just a spider, like Ashton said. But she had been so sure someone—or something—had been there with her. She couldn't shake the feeling that she was missing something.

But seeing Ashton again was not the main reason she wanted to go on the lake. Serena was curious about exploring the area and seeing the other neighbors. She was agitated being so disconnected from everyone. People in town and on the lake knew one another, but she had no idea who anyone was. In the city, Serena was acquainted with everyone in their building. Serena enjoyed having neighbors to bump into as she came and went from their New York City apartment. Here she felt isolated, adrift. It was time to meet some neighbors and build a new community of friends. And maybe see Ashton again, too.

Chapter Four

Lake Cauldron

Serena stood in the boathouse with her hands on her hips as she examined the map of Conjure Lake someone had tacked up on the wall. Probably her grandfather, or Deaken, she supposed. The lake was a modest eight miles long, with scattered islands popping up throughout its span. Each island was large enough for a single home, a boat dock and a shed. Island property came with a sister boat dock accompanied by a small patch of land across the lake to keep their vehicles.

Serena pondered over the extra hassle island life possessed. One would have to load all their groceries and shopping from their vehicle into their boat then lug it all to their house. Serena had spotted a sign hanging up by the cash register inside Price Chopper offering deliveries to residents of Conjure Lake and its islands, a service she considered using herself during the harsh winter months. Serena could only spot a handful of houses on either side of her cottage. She wondered if the majority of Conjure Lake residents resided past the main island, the one where Ashton lived.

Serena and Jack kayaked to Ashton's house first. Her island covered by thick evergreens, creating a personal northern oasis. The lake shimmered in the sunlight, and golden sparkles glittered on the gentle ripples. Serena loved kayaking and hoped her passion for being on the water would help calm her.

Jack sat in the front with Tinker on his lap, an orange life vest securely hugging his chest. The little dog wagged her tail happily as they made their way down the lake. The water was translucent and clear by the island, with smooth crystal currents running through. Jack leaned over the kayak, pointing to a school of trout swimming by. Serena tilted her head back as the sun kissed her freckled face, filling her body with penetrating warmth. Jack leaned over the side to count the fish, rocking the boat.

"I bet there are over twelve fish here, Serena! Trout can live up to twenty years. How old do you think these guys are?"

Tinker barked as a fish jumped in the air, landing back in the water with a grand splash. "I think Tinker wants to jump in and chase the fish," she said. Jack laughed.

Serena took her time as they approached the neighboring island, pausing often so Jack could count more fish. She allowed the boat to coast, and pulled out her sketchpad to draw a few lines of the fish cutting through the water. She was in no hurry to rush the beauty of the day. Her brother was happy, laughing and playing with his dog. All the darkness he had experienced the night before was gone for the moment. Serena pressed her hand to the bandage on her neck that concealed the bite that festered and pulsed with the beat of her heart. She shook her head, brushing off the icy sting that coursed through her body like an electrical current.

A house sat along the shoreline, quite close to the water. A barrier of stones kept the water from lapping the thick carpet of grass covering the island, and a long wooden dock adjoined the shoreline, extending over the water some fifty feet out.

"Look, Jack." Serena pointed to the shore. "That must be Ashton's house." Serena paused, examining the home as she steered the kayak up to the dock. It was a modest but sophisticated log cabin with a very high, flat sloping roof that ran along the entire length of its angular log walls. Serena stared at the cabin's impressive structure, admiring the grand, multicolored stone chimney that shot straight into the sky like a beacon. Two large walls made of glass lined the front of the cabin, blurring the lines of its exterior and the interior space until she couldn't tell exactly where the outside met the inside.

The island was abundant with thick white spruce trees surrounding the back and sides of the cabin, leaving a small but generous clearing in the front, allowing a glorious view of the lake and, ultimately, the front of Korwin Cottage, Serena's new property. She turned her head back toward her cottage, narrowing her eyes to get a better view. Serena could see how a campfire would attract attention from where she was.

Serena stepped gingerly onto the dock then extended a hand to assist Jack and Tinker. Ashton and an older man—her father, Serena could see the similarities in them even from a distance—were outside sanding an unfinished fishing boat, which was mounted upside down on a ladder frame in the middle of the front yard.

"Do I just call out and say hi?" she asked Jack, not sure if she had the nerve to go through with her brilliant plan anymore.

Jack wrinkled his nose at her. "Sure, why not? That's the whole point, right?" Jack, being only seven, didn't understand the complications of being eighteen. Thankfully, Serena didn't have to decide. Ashton spotted them and waved, pulling off her cap to swipe at the sweat on her face.

"Hey there! You found the place." Her smile was broad and welcoming, revealing dimples in her cheeks that Serena had somehow not noticed the night before. Serena blushed. *Don't pay attention to the dimples*, she scolded herself. *Be sensible. So what if Ashton's extremely pretty? You just met her and you have enough going on. You don't have time for crushes, Serena.* Dimples were her undoing, and she was irritated to see Ashton had the cutest pair she had ever seen.

Serena took a deep breath and smiled, still a little flustered. "I wanted to take Jack out on the lake and see where our neighbors live." Serena turned behind her, looking over the lake. "So far, I only see you." She smiled shyly.

Ashton shrugged and winked, and Serena's heart skipped a beat. "You'll have to take the fishing boat out if you want to meet the other lake folks. There's a few of us out here, but we are spread out."

Ashton grabbed the rope attached to the front of the kayak, securing it to the dock. Her shorts revealed a set of tan legs with a tattoo of an anchor below her knee. Jack set Tinker down on the dock before throwing his arms around Ashton in a tight hug. She looked surprised but delighted, and returned his embrace.

"You are the nicest person in all of Corvin Grove," Jack said into her shirt, his voice muffled. Ashton looked over at Serena, her eyebrows high.

"We went into town this morning and the librarian was...less than welcoming," Serena explained, her nose scrunched up in distaste.

Ashton laughed. "That's Mrs. McElroy. She's been an old grouch my entire life. She'd always threaten to spank us and accuse us of stealing books. Who steals books from a library? They give them away for free!"

Jack leaned back in his hug to look up at Ashton. "She watched us with her little mirror."

"It was weird," Serena agreed.

Ashton's lips thinned, as if she didn't think it was funny at all. "Ever sanded a boat before, Jack?" Ashton asked.

"No, but I've read about it. It looks pretty interesting."

Ashton chuckled, then stopped when she saw Jack was being serious. "Go have a look," she said with an encouraging wave. "My dad is a nice guy. He'll show you how."

Jack plodded his way over to where the man stood. He had a kind face, and leaned over to pet Tinker. Ashton watched as her father began to show Jack how to sand along the grain, then turned back to Serena.

"And how about you?" Ashton teased. "Did you read about sanding boats in a book, too?" Her playful smile danced upon her chiseled face, revealing those irresistible dimples again.

Serena's face grew hot again, and she cursed herself for betraying her intimate thoughts. She shook her head, hoping Ashton would just think she was winded from the kayaking. "Nope. Jack is the researcher of the family." The word family caught in her throat, and she coughed. "Well, of the two of us," she amended. "But I'm a quick learner."

Ashton raised her eyebrows. If she noticed Serena's stumble, she made no sign of it. "Well, that's good then. I could always use an extra set of hands." She pointed her thumb in the direction of her father and Jack, who was studiously explaining the correct way to sand a boat while Ashton's father fought a smile. "My dad likes kids." Ashton grinned. "He's already having a good time teaching Jack how to sand the boat."

"It looks like Jack is teaching him." Serena chuckled. "Is this a hobby of yours? Something you two do together?"

Ashton's gray eyes were warm as she observed her dad. "It started that way years ago. My dad is a carpenter. He built our house. It was my mom's dream to live in a log cabin. This was her vision. Every detail, every design came from her. My dad just executed it."

Serena raised her eyebrows. "Wow, your mom is talented. To come up with a design like this is impressive."

Ashton adjusted the rim of her cap, looking away. "She was an artist. She loved to draw. She had been sketching this cabin her entire life." Ashton turned back to face Serena. "When I was five, Dad wanted to build a father and daughter fishing boat. Something we could work on together." Ashton bent down to pick a blade of grass, fiddling with it. "The first one came out perfect, a real beauty. In fact, we still have her."

"Her?" asked Serena.

Ashton blushed. "Yeah, we name our boats."

Serena chuckled. "I know sailors used to do that as a superstition. It was to bring the boat good luck — or

Rebecca Henry

was it to keep bad luck away?" Serena shrugged her shoulders. "Depends on how you look at it, I suppose."

"Did Jack read that in a book, too?" Ashton teased, and when Serena blushed and grinned, she knew that he had. Ashton twirled the blade of grass between her fingers, looking out into the lake. "That's true. They also believed that it was bad luck to change your boat's name. You would have to do a de-naming ceremony."

Serena raised her eyebrows. "Jack didn't tell me about that. What's a de-naming ceremony?"

"It's really simple. You write the current name on a piece of paper, then fold the paper and place it in a wooden box. The magic bit is when you burn the box and scoop up the ashes and throw them into the sea. Then and only then can you rename your boat." Ashton turned to Serena, a grin on her face. "You can use a de-naming ceremony for anything, even people. My mom's midwife performed a ring gender test on her when she was pregnant with me."

Serena cocked her head, unable to tell if Ashton was being serious. It seemed like she rarely was, if those charming dimples were any indication. "What's that?"

Ashton took off her cap, shaking out her long hair. "It's an old wives' tale that can determine the sex of a pregnant woman's baby. Mom was beyond eager to know what she was having. My dad was convinced I would be a boy, but my mom wasn't so sure. She said throughout her pregnancy she was craving honey. She told Dad that was a sign I would be a sweet but strong and capable female."

Serena scrunched her face, and Ashton's gray eyes went wide as she fought a grin. "It's true! So the local midwife performed the ring gender test by attaching an amethyst crystal to a piece of string and dangled it over her belly. If it moves to the left, you're having a boy, and if it moves to the right, it's a girl. Well, according to Mom, that crystal didn't just move, it swung all the way to the right like metal being pulled by a magnet. My dad had his heart set on naming me Ashton after his brother who died young, and Mom agreed that even though I would be a girl, they would name me Ashton, and if I grew up to not like my name, they would simply hold a de-naming ceremony for me to change it." Ashton looked at Serena, her eyes playful and mischievous. "But I love my name and couldn't imagine being anyone else other than an Ashton."

"Magic, crystals and de-naming ceremonies. Sounds like witchcraft," Serena teased.

"My mom was something else," Ashton agreed. "I think she just liked a good story. Like Jack over there." They both looked over to where Jack chattered cheerfully to Ashton's father, a small but genuine smile on his face as he nodded along to whatever the little professor was telling him, then looked back at each other, laughing again. Serena couldn't stop the flush from creeping up her neck every time Ashton smiled at her. *Was she this cute last night?*

Flustered, Serena glanced over at Jack. "Has your mom designed other houses on the lake?"

Ashton rubbed the back of her neck as her gaze grew long over the sparkling waters. "Mom's not here anymore."

Serena recognized Ashton's discomfort. It mirrored her own when talking about her parents, a familiar feeling she was accustomed to lately herself. "So, what happened after you and your dad built your first boat together?" Serena asked, changing the subject.

"My dad received countless offers to sell the boat, but of course, *Iris* was special. He would not sell her. So, he made another and when that one sold, he made one more. Before he knew it, he had orders coming in regularly. Now this is what we do." Ashton held out her arms with a flourish. "We make boats and sell them all over the state and up the coast to New England."

Serena smiled inwardly at the thought of having such a simple but rewarding profession. Being a shipwright was artistic, though rather than creating a painting or a drawing, Ashton created beautiful boats. "How nice to have a career where you can work from home and use your hands," Serena said with sincerity.

Ashton rubbed her forearm. "It's not glamorous, but I like it, and it's what I want to do with my life."

"To stay here on the lake and build boats every day with your father." Serena's words were soft. How she would give anything to be as fortunate as Ashton. To work side by side with her parents, doing something they both loved. Grief threatened to overwhelm her, and she forced herself not to think about the days she spent in her mother's studio, creating art side by side. Someday those memories wouldn't be a dagger to the heart. Someday they'd be warm and soft and comforting. But not today. Not yet.

Ashton's eyes were soft, watching her. If she noticed a change in Serena's demeanor, she didn't mention it. Serena didn't know her well, but in the little time she had, she knew Ashton to be perceptive and kind.

"Yep, right here with Dad. Or at least until I build my own house someday on the other side of the property. But basically, yes, you are looking at my life career at the ripe age of nineteen."

Nineteen, Serena mentally noted. *One year older than me.* Serena looked around the property. "Will you give me a tour? I'd love to see *Iris* and any projects you're working on."

Ashton and Serena walked over to where Ashton's father was bent over a boat, Jack beside him. They both stood up as the girls approached. Like Ashton, her father wore a baseball cap, and had the same gray eyes and dark hair tucked away underneath.

"Dad, this is Serena. Serena, my dad, Kevin Bates. She moved into the Korwin Cottage."

Mr. Bates shot his daughter a concerned look before quickly wiping it away to remove his work gloves and shake Serena's hand.

"It's nice to meet you, Mr. Bates," she said.

"Call me Kev. It's a pleasure, Serena. How nice to see some young life in the Korwin Cottage." Mr. Bates nodded to Jack, who pushed his smudged glasses up his face with all four fingers and grinned before returning to his eager sanding. "Looks like I got a recruit." His smile was warm and paternal. Serena turned away, forcing the lump in her throat to recede. It had been so long since she'd heard a father's voice, it was almost her undoing.

Kevin's brows creased together as he glanced over the lake at Korwin Cottage. "Settling in all right? Not having any issues with the property, are you?" His words were an invitation for Serena to talk about the night before, but she wasn't ready to relive the fear she had experienced. Serena forced a smile and shook her head no.

Kevin nodded. "Korwin Cottage is a rare beauty, a true historical property. It was the first house built on Conjure Lake. It has the potential to be a charming home. But old homes have a way of playing tricks on you. Don't let any bumps in the night scare you off."

The bite on Serena's neck pulse at the mention of Korwin Cottage. "Historical or haunted?" she muttered under her breath.

"So, it's just the two of you living in the cottage, is it?"

Serena's heart dropped into her stomach. She knew this question would come up eventually with the town's folk. She was just hoping it wouldn't come up today.

"Yes, just us." She looked at the ground, unable to meet anyone's eyes.

Mr. Bates nodded with understanding. "Well, you and Jack are welcome to visit us anytime. It's nice to have neighbors close by again. Have you made it into town yet?"

"Yes," Jack answered as he rubbed his nose. "We went to the library. The old lady there watched us with her little mirror."

Like Ashton, he didn't laugh. "Yes, I think Mrs. McElroy might have dementia, though she's always been a bit strange. It must be the new faces making her nervous. She thinks everyone is a witch or demon out to hex her, hence the mirror."

"What do you mean?" Serena asked, confused.

"She's just a grouchy old kook," Ashton explained. "She's what I'd call a 'superstitious Catholic,' which means she goes to church, but she also charges her crystals in the moonlight. I'm serious!" She laughed when she saw Serena's expression.

"It's just an old wives' tale, or maybe it's a regional thing, I don't know." Mr. Bates looked uncomfortable. "She says a Catholic can't look a witch in the eye, so a mirror protects her from a witch's stare. I've known her most of my life and she's always been that way."

"Are there witches here preying on sweet little old librarians?" Serena asked incredulously.

"Nope." Ashton answered, a playful smirk on her face. "No witches. And no sweet old librarians, either. Just old sourpuss Mrs. McElroy." Ashton reached over, curling her hand around Serena's bicep.

"I'm going to show Serena the workshop and *Iris* before they head back home."

Mr. Bates tipped his hat, resuming his place next to Jack. He glanced back, peering at the two from under the brim of his hat "Do you think they'll be okay, little buddy?" he asked Jack.

Jack looked up, watching as the girls trekked to a wooden structure at the end of the property. He pushed up his glasses, then resumed his sanding. "I think they're going to kiss in your boat."

A surprised laugh escaped Mr. Bates' lips before he ruffled Jack's hair and got back to work.

* * * *

Ashton's fingers were light on her back as she led Serena to the other side of the shore, guiding her through a copse of trees and pointing out holes in the ground so Serena wouldn't trip. They stopped at a large shed made from redwood cedar resembling their log cabin.

"This is where we keep our tools and supplies, but mostly, we work here during the winter months, or when the weather isn't conducive to being outside."

Serena whistled as she took in the clean workshop. It had two massive skylights and one large window facing the lake. A finished boat sat in the middle of the room. Serena ran her hand along the boat. The name *Alice* was painted on the side. *Like the woman in the sketch*, Serena thought.

"This boat is for a local customer. It's almost finished. It just needs sealant. Then we will deliver it to Miss Yolanda. She lives on one of the streams out in the woods that flows into the lake."

Just like in the Korwin Cottage boat house, this workshop had a large map of the lake framed on the wall opposite Ashton.

"This looks so similar to Conjure Lake, but it's called Lake Cauldron." Serena leaned in, examining the blue lines extending from the lake. "Did they change the name, what, hundreds of years ago?"

"It's a long story actually, and I mean story literally." Ashton chuckled.

"Well, how many streams are on Conjure Lake?"

Ashton shrugged. "There's a few of them around Conjure Lake. They flow down from the mountain and run through the woods before opening into the lake. You and Jack should explore one on your kayak. It's peaceful back there."

Ashton leaned over Serena's shoulder and traced a long finger along a blue line on the map. She stood so close Serena could feel the heat of her against her back, her body prickling with awareness. "This map is old. An antique, like a lot of the people around this lake."

Serena caught a glimpse of one of Ashton's dimples. A joke, then. Serena smiled as she turned to face Ashton. Ashton's eyes were still on the map, though they had a teasing glint that made Serena's stomach do a flip-flop.

"Townsfolk believe Conjure Lake was once a larger lake that spanned over thirty miles, feeding countless streams throughout the mountains." Ashton raised her eyebrows at Serena. "Legend says that the new settlers came from Europe with black witchcraft and a curse fell upon the land. Lightning fell from the sky and struck a tree whose roots ran deep under Conjure Lake, causing the lake to split into two."

Serena studied Ashton, no longer sure she was joking. "Do you believe that?" she asked.

Ashton shrugged. "I don't, but there's a lot of superstitious people around here who do. Legend has it that the Native Americans abandoned this land and resettled to Lake Cauldron. They left their village and everything they owned, but what they did take with them were two orphaned twin girls whose surname was Fern. The natives stole the sisters from the new colony and hid them under a pile of furs as they fled this area. The twins were rumored to have the mark of a white witch on the backs of their necks, and the tribe knew the girls were in danger. If the sisters stayed here on Conjure Lake, the dark witch would find them." Ashton shook her head with a sigh. "It's just an old legend. I've never seen Lake Cauldron. I believe what I can see."

Ashton leaned forward to trace the map again. "There are a couple of old-timers that reside in the woods that run along the creeks, like Miss Yolanda. This lake is a decent size, spanning eight miles around. That gives you a lot of area and most of it is protected land and can't be built on. Then you have the mountain range all behind the lake. There aren't many residents on this lake, but the ones that live here have spread out, taking acres of land for their own property. Most of it is family land, like your house, passed down for generations. It's nice though. It keeps our lake private, preventing the lake from becoming another summer spot for tourists. Lake Cauldron is supposed to be somewhere over these mountains" — Ashton snorted — "but of course you need to be a witch to find it." She shrugged, pausing for a beat. "Only witches can travel between Conjure Lake and Lake Cauldron. Makes sense, I guess, if you believe in that sort of thing."

Serena ran her hand over the smooth edge of the boat. "This boat is for an old woman? Does she live alone?" The thought bothered her. A woman living alone in the woods seemed incomprehensible to her. "Isn't it terrifying? Is it even safe?"

Ashton laughed. "Miss Yolanda isn't your ordinary woman. Local folks say she's a witch."

Serena crossed her arms. Now she knew Ashton was teasing. Her dimple didn't dare to make an appearance, but her eyes were bright with mirth.

"A witch? As in the occult?" Serena asked, concerned.

Ashton giggled. "No, nothing that dark. She's known in town for her herbal concoctions and eccentric ways. She's a recluse. She rarely leaves her house. She only goes into town when it's absolutely necessary. She has a small following, country folk who believe in her craft. Mostly young girls seek her out, the ones that want a love potion or some nonsense like that. Miss Yolanda is odd, there's no mistaking that, but she's harmless."

Serena's face pulled into a tight frown, and Ashton eyed her unease. "She's nothing to worry about—I'm sorry I brought her up. Everyone around here is superstitious. I think it comes from being so isolated. You'll see. Actually, we're lucky to have her here. The nearest hospital is quite a drive away, so people go see her for minor complaints. She can make herbal remedies that can help you. She brews a mean cup of tea and she has the most incredible herb garden. Miss Yolanda has devoted her life to becoming an expert herbalist."

"There's a greenhouse at Korwin Cottage. I wonder if my grandmother was an herbalist, too," Serena pondered aloud.

"Maybe." Ashton shrugged. "I don't think I ever talked to your grandparents. They kept to themselves, but I'd run into Deaken sometimes." Ashton stood up tall and glared at Serena with her arms crossed in an uncanny impression of Mr. Ward. Serena laughed, and Ashton beamed at her. "What a grump. Anyways, when I was younger, I broke my leg. The road to town was blocked because of bad weather, so my dad called Miss Yolanda. She paddled over to our house with her witch bag. That's what everyone calls it, but really, it was more like a medical bag. She set my leg, rubbed St Johns' wort on it and made tea from catnip, skullcap and valerian." She made a face. "The concoction tasted like death, but it worked for the pain."

Serena nodded, understanding that a woman with such intense knowledge of herbs could be useful in the country. Still, the mention of a witch set her on edge. This place was too different and strange to her, and this occult talk made her stomach flutter after her freakout under the porch.

Serena crossed the workshop to run a hand over the smooth wood of a finished boat. The name *Iris* curled in lovely script on the side, and she traced the carved name, admiring the craftsmanship.

"I think your boat is lovely," she said. "You have real talent, it's no wonder you can make a living off your work."

Ashton grinned, making those irresistible dimples pop. "What about you? Do you have any hobbies?" Ashton leaned against the counter. Her arms flexed without effort, and Serena pretended not to notice how well-defined Ashton's triceps were, or the annoying heat that once again flushed her cheeks. Ashton had a slender, athletic build, womanly but strong. Serena couldn't help but admire her. She'd never officially dated a girl, but she'd had crushes before. Her first and only kiss with a boy had been when she was fourteen at summer camp, and she knew immediately that she didn't want to repeat it. But she was drawn to Ashton and her easy smiles.

Serena willed her pink cheeks to cool before answering, "I draw. Well, I sketch."

Ashton raised her eyebrows. "I could use your talent. Part of being a shipwright is sketching out the plans." She smirked. "Want a job?"

Serena laughed, waving her hand in dismissal. "Maybe one day, but for now, sketching is something I do for pleasure."

"Could I see your work?" Ashton asked, and Serena's grip tightened on the tote bag she shouldered that held her sketchpad.

She hesitated a long moment. "Sure, I guess." She opened her bag and handed Ashton her sketchbook, suddenly nervous. She felt the strong urge to rip it back.

But instead of flipping it open, Ashton stepped up into *Iris* and settled on one of the seats. She set the sketchpad in her lap and looked up at Serena expectantly. Serena took a deep breath then stepped into the boat and settled beside Ashton, their shoulders brushing.

Serena kept her gaze locked on the sketchpad in Ashton's lap, but she could feel Ashton's eyes studying her profile. After a quiet moment, Ashton opened the book and began flipping through the pages.

Heat crept up Serena's neck, leaving her feeling embarrassed and even a little exposed and vulnerable to have Ashton look at her work. She had only shared her sketches with her mother Rose during those long, quiet afternoons in her studio. She let out a long breath she hadn't realized she was holding when Ashton stopped on a page.

"Wow, this is that creepy old tree in your yard," Ashton whispered, her voice reverent. "This is incredible. You really captured the feel of it. It's alive. I mean, I know it's alive — it's a tree. But it *feels* alive. Like it's breathing." Her fingers traced the twisted, curving lines of the bark. "It's unsettling, actually."

She continued to flip through the book, making soft sounds in her throat when she stopped on a sketch of her mother. "This is your mom," she said quietly. Serena's throat filled with emotion, and she nodded. "She looks like you — beautiful like you." She smiled, then flipped the page with a sharp inhale. Serena realized her mistake a moment too late, and they both stared down at the sketch Serena had drawn of Ashton the night before, of her gray eyes sparkling under her hat, of her strong wrists and long, tapering fingers. "This is me," she said with awe. "But prettier."

Serena looked up at Ashton's face. "No, it's just right," she said with a shy smile. "It's not finished yet."

Ashton's gaze dragged up to meet Serena's eyes. Serena bit her bottom lip nervously, and Ashton's eyes dropped to her mouth. The boat suddenly felt too small, and Serena was aware of every place her body pressed against Ashton's, her honey and cedar scent filling Serena's nose. Her stare dropped to Ashton's hands.

"I really should be going," Serena said. "I need to make lunch for Jack."

The air between them felt charged, as if a lightning storm buzzed between them. Neither of them made a move to get up. "Serena, can I ask you something?" Ashton said, her voice soft as she closed the sketchpad in her lap. Serena tucked a strand of her blonde hair behind her ear, unable to meet Ashton's intense gray eyes. "Have you ever kissed a girl before?" When Serena shook her head, Ashton smiled, her dimples popping. "Would you like to?"

Serena held her breath, her eyes wide as she met Ashton's gaze and nodded.

Ashton watched Serena as she leaned in, waiting for any sign of her changing her mind. Instead, Serena leaned forward and met Ashton's full lips with her own. Every atom of her body blazed alive, and when Ashton reached up to cup Serena's face, she leaned in to the touch. Ashton tasted warm and sweet and soft, and a low hum buzzed in her throat as Serena deepened the kiss, her arms coming up to skate down Ashton's strong, bare arms. Their embrace grew heated, their kiss deepening as their breathing grew frenzied. Suddenly there wasn't enough room in the boat—enough places they were touching, and for a long moment they lost themselves to the heat between them, their soft moans and fumbling the only sound in the workshop. Too soon they broke apart, both panting, and looked at each other with something like surprise before they both laughed.

Whatever awkwardness, whatever spell was between them had broken, and they spent the morning sitting beside each other, fingers interlaced and shoulders brushing as they talked easily about everything and nothing. Conversation flowed easily, and Serena was able to forget all about eerie houses, spider bites and monsters under the porch. Serena told Ashton about her mother's studio, her brother's library and the day her parents died, about how she had left college to take care of Jack.

Ashton squeezed her hand as tears traced down Serena's cheeks, and she leaned in to kiss them away as she told Serena about growing up on Conjure Lake, and the girls she'd have summer flings with only to say goodbye in the autumn. Most of their customers were family men with young, pretty daughters who took to Ashton like heat scorching the desert. Nothing serious ever came from the summer girls she met, and they'd moved in and out of her life like the tide, and Ashton was just fine with that arrangement. She might spend a couple of weeks or a month at most with one, but they belonged to one world, and Ashton to another.

Serena knew instinctively that whatever was between them was no summer fling, and she liked hearing about their home from Ashton's lips. Ashton loved her life, as isolated as it was, and didn't need the bustle of people to keep her company. She was a mountain girl through and through. Mr. Bates had tried to encourage Ashton to attend university, to go to school, meet other girls, date, but Ashton already knew her profession. She had her life mapped out and couldn't justify the cost or time lost in university when all she wanted to do was right in front of her.

The bright morning sun rose in the sky and passed into early afternoon, the day timeless as the girls lost themselves in their idle conversation and slow kisses. Serena shivered, a chill passing through her body as she finally noticed the dimming sunshine. She leaned her head on Ashton's shoulder and sighed. "I need to get back to Jack. I'm sure he's worried. Or hungry. Or driving your dad crazy."

Ashton huffed a laugh as her long finger traced the small blue veins on Serena's wrist. "Let's go find them," she agreed. As they climbed out of the boat, Ashton placed her hand on Serena's hip. Her touch was as light as a feather as she guided Serena through the open door of the workshop, but Serena could feel Ashton's hand like a scorching hot rod. She stepped into the fresh air, certain her touch would linger on her body for the remainder of the day, and expected to discover a burning red mark on her skin.

Jack was sitting on a bench with Mr. Bates, a glass of lemonade in one hand and half a cookie in the other. Tinker sat at his feet, happily chewing on the other half of Jack's cookie. Jack looked up at them and pressed his glasses up his face, a bright smile on his face.

"Hi, Serena! Mr. Bates was just telling me about all the species of fish in the lake. He even pointed to the best fishing spots by our house. I'm gonna ask Deaken if we can go out there when he teaches me how to fish."

"That's great, Jack! I'm sure you will be a master fisherman in no time." She winked at her brother, then met Mr. Bates' eyes and smiled with gratitude.

He patted Jack on the shoulder. "Jack and I just about have this boat ready for sealant. He's a great helper."

"Thank you for teaching him. Jack, are you ready to go home for lunch?"

His dark eyes were teasing behind his smudged glasses. "Are you finished kissing Ashton in the workshop?"

Ashton barked a laugh, and Serena flushed as she chuckled with embarrassment. "That's enough out of you," she scolded. She grinned at Ashton's dimples peeking out. Mr. Bates just shook his head, a small smile on his face.

"Come on, stinker. It's time to go." She looked down at her feet shyly, and thanked Mr. Bates again for entertaining Jack.

"It was my pleasure. It's good to see young life here on the lake. Last time I've seen a youngster enjoy Conjure Lake was when Ashton was a small fry." Mr. Bates looked off into the water. "It's been far too long. This lake could use some young life back in its waters."

Serena and Jack buckled their life jackets before stepping into the rocking boat. Ashton handed Serena her tote bag and sketchbook, then squatted beside them. Her gaze searched Serena's face. "I could come by this evening if you'd like some company later."

It sounded more like a question, and Serena nodded with a soft smile. "I'd like that," Serena admitted, desperately willing her face not to go crimson. Ashton grinned, her dimples popping as she pulled her baseball cap back on her head.

Ashton nodded and gave the kayak a push-off as she called out, "See you tonight!"

Jack waited until they coasted out of earshot, the only sound the chirping of the birds and the paddle sluicing through the water. "Your face is red again, Serena," Jack quipped.

Serena placed her hand over her mouth, her eyes wide. "I know! Ugh. I'm working on it, Jack."

Jack snickered. "I think Ashton likes you."

She laughed. "I think I like her, too." She turned around, looking back at the log cabin. "She's just a friend, I think." Her face grew solemn, filled with seriousness. She turned back to Jack, her expression delicate, almost vulnerable. "And to be honest, Jack...I think I could use one."

Chapter Five

Tainted Flesh

Serena paddled in the direction of their cottage as Jack leaned back in his seat and closed his eyes. A few hours of sanding in the mountain air had tired him out. Serena gazed at the sky, watching the clouds change forms as they moved through each other like a dance. She took her time getting back to the cottage, and allowed the kayak to drift as she opened her drawing pad in her lap and sketched out a few lines. The shape of Ashton's cabin, the curve of *Iris* the boat. The column of Ashton's graceful neck under her baseball cap.

Jack surrendered to the heaviness of sleep, drifting off into a secure dream. His little arm twitched now and then, exhausted from all the work he had done with Mr. Bates. He looked so young, so fragile, and Serena sketched the sunlight filtering through the trees that danced on his sleep-slackened face.

Serena rested the paddle across the kayak, feeling the waves of the lake move back and forth, rocking her in a delicate lullaby. She loved being on the water. It invigorated her, awakening all her senses. Rose and

Edward had sent Serena to summer camp every July when she was in middle school to get her out of the city. It was during those three summers Serena had learned to kayak, giving birth to a lifelong passion.

Serena leaned over the kayak, looking into the depth of the water. An orange-spotted sunfish darted next to the boat, its tiny speckles of blue scales reflected brightly in the sun. It stopped, hovering by the kayak. Serena gently placed her hand in the water, wondering if she could get close enough to touch it. The sunfish remained still, not shying away from Serena's presence. Slowly Serena moved a little closer to the fish, willing it to come near. The fish remained perfectly still, its eye fixed on Serena's hand. A tall reed of seaweed waved beside it in the water, its stem long and thin. Serena leaned a little further, inching closer to the sunfish, the seaweed brushing against her hand. Serena watched as the little fish swam like hell in the other direction, and she trailed her fingers in the cool water, the wet leaves of seaweed tickling her fingertips. But when she lifted her hand to grip the paddle, her fingers became entangled in the seaweed. No, not entangled — trapped. She yanked her hand, but the seaweed only tightened impossibly, cutting into her wrist. She yelped as she jerked her arm. The reed had wrapped itself around her finger, and seemed to grow tighter with every pull of Serena's arm.

Serena tried to pull her hand loose, but it latched on even tighter, slithering and twisting up her fingers and digging into her wrist. Serena choked back a shriek, not wanting to scare Jack, and she stared in horror as the reed burrowed into her flesh as if it were alive. As if it were trying to devour her. A pattern of deep green vines burned into her hand, and her breath came in pants as she scraped her hand against the side of the boat, desperate to remove the green image of the weed deep underneath her flesh but it wouldn't come off. It had inked her skin like a tattoo.

Frantic, Serena quickly made her way back to the cottage, paddling with a feverish speed, careful not to disturb Jack. The banks of Conjure Lake had never felt so far away, and her hand burned against the oar as she paddled as hard as she dared. She cursed the lake for being so broad. Jack slept on as they glided into the boathouse. Serena stepped from the boat and tied it to the dock, thankful Jack had slept through the whole eerie ordeal. She didn't want to give him any more reason to be fearful about their new environment. She carried his still form up to the house, careful to keep from touching him with her green, vine-twisted tattooed hand. It burned with cold — like shards of ice. She laid her brother gently on his bed and kept her hand tucked in her jean pocket until she was able to reach the solitude of her bedroom.

Serena ran to the bathroom, locking herself inside and turning the faucet to full blast, as hot as it would go. She scrubbed at her skin with a bar of black soap she found under the sink until it turned scarlet. If anything, the green twisting reeds looked starker against her raw skin, the green blooming deeper. She squeezed her fist, frightened as she thought back to all of her brother's lessons on survival. But while he'd warned her about poison ivy, poison oak and poisonous berries, he had never mentioned anything like this. She stared at her hand. She was certain she'd never heard of something like this happening. Serena looked inside the medicine cabinet, grabbing a bottle of rubbing alcohol, but the macabre marking still would not vanish.

Serena groaned in frustration as she hurled open the door and pounded down the stairs to the kitchen. Shuffling through the cabinets, she found what she was looking for and mixed together a salt scrub with sea salt, lemon juice and olive oil. She gritted her teeth as she scrubbed at her raw skin over the kitchen sink, focusing on each leaf as she desperately tried to erase the marking. Tears welled in Serena's eyes as she scrubbed her skin until it bled. But it was no use. All her ministrations only made the curling leaves a lurid green against her flesh, its vibrant image as deep as before.

She slumped at the kitchen table and stared at her aching hand. No amount of scrubbing could take it off. Maybe a soak in the tub would do her good, or at least calm her down enough to figure out what to do next. How quickly this afternoon had deteriorated. Was it only an hour ago that she was kissing Ashton in her work room? It seemed a lifetime ago compared to the misery she felt now.

Serena slumped back up the stairs to her bathroom and ran the tub faucet as hot as it would go. She gathered lavender and peppermint oil from the bedroom vanity and placed a few drops in the hot water as she sat on the edge of the tub, watching the oils swirl and blend. Her neck still hurt from the night before, and she carefully peeled back the bandage Ashton had placed on her bite. She grimaced at her reflection in the mirror. The bite hadn't gotten any better. If anything, it looked worse—the puncture marks were still raw, refusing to heal. She sighed as she tossed the bandage into the trash bin. "Spider bites, seaweed poisoning. What's next, Serena?" she asked her reflection.

Shaking her head, Serena undressed and delicately slipped into the porcelain tub, submerging her body into the warm water, which welcomed her like a flower closing its petals for the night. Instantly she calmed, relaxing as the aroma of the herbs seeped into her pores. She closed her eyes and for a moment allowed herself to forget about the strange marks that stained her fair skin. She sank deeper into the clawfoot tub, the warm water lapping at her belly like a giant tongue. She ran her hand along her stomach, welcoming the sensation.

She held her wrist before her — still marked in the twisting green vines. She brought her left wrist to her nose and inhaled the sweet scent of lavender which lingered on her delicate skin, allowing her senses to be lost in tranquility. Her mind wandered to the image of Ashton's smoky blue-gray eyes and strong hands. She sighed, remembering the soft touch of Ashton's lips upon her own. Another sigh answered hers, sending a soft, warm breath over her skin. With a gasp, Serena sat up, the water sluicing from her body. But no one was there. She was alone.

Unnerved, Serena ran her hands through her hair and sank further into the tub. This place was giving her the creeps, and she couldn't shake the feeling that she was missing something — something key, something fundamental, something just beyond her grasp. She reached for the bar of black soap and once more scrubbed her wrist, but the more she scrubbed, the deeper the markings became, as if they were mocking her.

Frustrated, Serena tossed the soap on the ledge of the tub and closed her eyes once more as she sank under the warm water. She held her breath a long time, allowing her thoughts to roam back to Ashton's face as she listened to her own heartbeat echo through the warm bathwater. She released a long breath in a slow line of bubbles, then sat up. Or tried to. Two ice-cold hands gripped her upper arms tight, pushing her down against the bottom of the tub. She had no breath left to scream, and she thrashed and jerked against her assailant. Water churned and splashed as she struggled, but whoever was pushing her down refused to release their grip. True panic gripped Serena. She knew if she didn't get out now she'd drown. Her chest screamed for air as she bucked against the strong arms that gripped her. Her lungs spasmed, and she sucked in a deep breath of bathwater.

And Serena was free. The phantom grip on her arms vanished, and Serena surged from the tub and tumbled wet and soaking to the rug, choking and coughing up water. She gasped for breath as she tensed, ready for another attack. But no one was there. She was completely alone. Her coughs turned to sobs as she curled on her side on the bathmat, cold and wet. "Why am I experiencing this? Why am I hearing, seeing and feeling things that aren't real? I feel like I'm losing my mind."

Serena's wrist began to burn, and she sat up to examine it. If anything, it seemed to flare and pulse with a deeper shade of green. With shaking hands, she drew a towel around herself. Her heart was thumping in her chest, and she wanted the marking gone. It didn't belong on her skin—it felt intrusive, like a violation. It was green and wild like the seaweed that had touched her, and she was certain that this was abnormal. She knew she'd never heard of man-eating, tattooing seaweed. But the mark was clear as day. There was no point in arguing the impossibility of it when the evidence burned right there on her flesh.

She needed to get up and check on Jack. Instead, she stared out of the paned window deep into the woods behind the cottage. She needed reasonable, logical explanations for the strange events happening to her. Everything had felt upside down since she'd lost her parents, and now she was apparently losing her mind.

She looked intently at the dark trees surrounding her home, watching as they began to move in the breeze, first a gentle sway, then wilder, as if a storm was approaching inside the woods. Serena looked deeper into the trees, watching as their branches moved savagely, synchronizing in a ritual dance. A black figure, small and obscure, sat at the top of a high branch. Serena crawled closer to the window as she drew the towel tight around her, narrowing her eyes on the tiny image. It thrust into the air like a bullet shooting out of a gun, aiming for the cottage.

Serena squinted her eyes as the black plumage came into view. *Omigod, it's that crazy bird from yesterday*, she realized with a start. Between the spider bite, Ashton and almost drowning in her own bathtub, she'd forgotten all about the damn thing. The giant raven flew toward her, crashing against the paned glass. Serena leapt back, stunned by the ferocity of the black beast's attacks as it hurled itself over and over against the glass.

Serena was no ornithologist, but she didn't need her brother to tell her this was abnormal behavior. She watched in horror as it attacked the glass with a force that would break the neck of any normal bird. Serena knew instinctively this was no ordinary bird. It oozed a sense of dread, of despair, of hate, and fury. The paned glass cracked under the bird's relentless onslaught, and Serena cowered beside the tub, watching in horror as the glass cracked, then shattered. Serena held her breath, looking around for some kind of weapon to bash the bastard with as soon as it breached the windowsill.

But just as quickly as the attack came, it stopped. The room rang with silence. When nothing happened, Serena crawled to the window and slowly, carefully raised her head to peek over the sill. Was that crazy bird still there? Shaking, Serena looked around, but she didn't see anything. Wait. There it was, silhouetted against the dark shadows of that monstrous tree. Its deep red eyes glittered with malice as it watched her back. *Red eyes?*

Serena stumbled to her feet, her fear giving way to anger. "What do you want?" she screamed at the giant bird. It squawked as it took to the air, its enormous wings flapping, the force of its wind shaking the house. The hideous crab apple tree seemed to move and undulate in response, and hundreds of crab apples, a dizzying, impossible amount, rained down from its twisted branches and rolled and piled on the lawn.

Serena pulled down a bathrobe that hung on the door and shrugged it on as she ran out of the bathroom, fleeing down the stairs, through the kitchen and out through the back door. She grabbed the long stick Jack had used as his sword and brandished it at the beast, daring the bird to come closer. It squawked again, its shrill scream sending ice coursing through Serena's veins. It shot down, racing toward Serena, its violent wingbeats filling the space with an echoing croak.

Serena stood amongst the rotten crab apples that littered the lawn and gripped Jack's stick like a baseball bat, taking aim and swinging as the bird swooped down to attack her. She cracked the stick through the air. It passed through the raven like a shadow, and the monstrous bird swooped down, its talons tangling in Serena's hair. It took off in flight, jerking a wad of Serena's wet, blonde hair from her head. Her eyes swam with tears from the shocking pain, and she blinked them away as she followed the bird's flight. It looped through the hideous crab apple tree, circling the trunk before it vanished from sight. Serena collapsed in the grass, rotten crab apples squishing beneath her knees.

Jack appeared in the doorway, his hair disheveled and glasses askew. Serena looked up at him from where she sat slumped in the grass in her bathrobe, her hand pressed to her tender scalp. Jack ran over to her. She was staring into the ominous tree. Tinker stood on the porch, pacing back and forth frantically, not coming any closer.

"Serena are you, all right!?" Jack was frightened and confused. Serena understood the feeling. "What are you doing?"

Not wanting to frighten her brother, Serena tenderly touched his arm, offering comfort. Whatever was happening to Serena, she couldn't tell her brother. She was all he had. What would he think if she told him she was losing her mind?

"I'm fine, Jack, it was only an irritating bird. It flew at me while I was in the bathroom. The glass is broken. It must have been blind and lost its way."

Jack nodded, looking up into the dark tree, and Serena had the sudden urge to shield her brother from the tree, to prevent the tree from looking at him. Which was insane. Trees didn't have eyes. But Serena felt as if it were alive. Watching her. Mocking her. Its tall branches were twisted and deformed, and Jack shuddered when he spied the black bark that appeared scaly like a serpent. Jack adjusted the frames on his glasses as he examined the black scales.

"I learned in school that birds fly into windows to defend their breeding territories. They think it's another bird and not their own reflection."

Serena snapped her head toward Jack. "Why would your teacher tell you something like that?"

Jack shrugged his shoulders as he pushed his smudged lenses up his face. "There was a cardinal that would always fly into our classroom window, pecking at the glass. Sometimes he would hurt himself and fall over." Jack wrinkled his nose. He didn't seem to like the crab tree any more than Serena did. "It is a creepy tree," Jack whispered. "I don't like it. It doesn't like us, either."

Serena watched her brother for a long moment, unnerved by his words. But she knew what he meant. The tree felt alive, malevolent, and the crab apples around them reeked of overripe rot. Serena agreed, wishing the damn thing was off their property. Maybe if Deaken were to cut it down, that ungodly raven would fly off and find another ghastly tree to haunt.

"Don't worry, Jack. I'm all right." She paused, seeing the worry in Jack's eyes, and he continued to rub a comforting hand up and down her shoulder. "Really, I'm fine." Serena rose to her feet, almost slipping in the rotten crab apples. "Why don't you go inside and do some of your assigned reading for summer. I'll be right in after I scrape this gunk off my feet." Sure enough, her feet were coated in the overripe mush of crab apples. "Step carefully, Jack. We don't want to get any of this gross goo in the house."

"Wash it off soon, Sissy," Jack said, his tone quiet. "I don't like that tree." His eyes were uneasy behind his smudged glasses, and Serena found a clean spot on her mush-covered robe to clean them off. She put them back on his face with a kiss, and he beamed at her. She pressed a kiss to the tip of his nose the way their mother used to, and swatted him as he giggled and dashed up the steps, Tinker's tail wagging as she followed behind.

Serena watched them vanish through the front door, then turned to survey the yard. She walked to the back of the house, her sticky bare feet clinging to pine needles that crunched loudly underneath her gait. She spun around, noticing that all the trees had resumed to their normal, placid state.

Serena bent down to examine one of the strange crab apples, the flesh smearing her fingers and clogging inside her long fingernails. The rotted apple was crimson with a thick liquid oozing out of the side. Serena felt drawn to the apple, as if bewitched, and her tattooed fingers brought the ghoulish fruit to her lips. She bit into the apple, overcome by a metallic taste violating her tongue. She spat the bite onto the ground, then swiped at her mouth. It came away red. Blood. She was wiping blood from her lips. Horrified at her actions, she looked inside the apple to discover a small bird embryo, pale and translucent. She gasped in revulsion. She picked up another apple, smashing it against a rock. Like the first, there was an unborn embryo curled up, lifeless inside its womb of death.

Serena gagged and spat as she dashed around the yard, gathering up the hundreds of monstrous crab apples and their bloody carcasses and dumping them into the fire pit. Her robe was a smear of fruit and gore, and she breathed through her mouth to stop herself from puking. Desperate and defeated, she stumbled to the boathouse, grabbing the gasoline tank and a pack of matches. She poured the gasoline on top of the apples, drenching them in amber liquid before she lit the unholy things on fire. A vile black smoke spiraled from the apples, circling the sky in a dark cloud. She tried to calm her breathing, racking her brain for any reasonable explanation for everything that had transpired over the last hour, but there was no logic in which science could explain the disturbing discovery. She turned to the crab apple tree, cursing it for bearing fruit. She looked at the gasoline tank in her hand, tempted to torch the damn thing right here and now.

"I should burn you down!" She cursed the tree as it stood before her, tall, dark and ancient. She wanted it gone, but she knew better than to set it on fire. Her brother the professor had lectured her enough about fire safety, so she was well aware of the risks of forest fires. As Serena climbed the steps for her second bath of the day, she decided she would call Deaken in the morning and insist he cut the tree down as soon as possible. Tomorrow, even. She wanted it gone.

* * * *

The lights from Ashton's fishing boat twinkled on the lake as her boat silently slid through the dark and tranquil waters of Conjure Lake. Jack was waiting on the steps, the fire from earlier still burning black smoke in the night sky. Serena came outside to meet Ashton, her freshly washed hair twisted in a bun and speared with a pencil, a long-sleeved sweatshirt hiding the tattoo on her hand and wrist. Ashton hopped off her boat and secured it to the dock. "Ahoy!" she called out. "I come bearing gifts!"

Serena smiled to see the dimple-popping grin on Ashton's face as she held up a tiny tin box.

"What did you bring me?" Serena asked. "I hope it's expensive!" she teased. She was relieved to see Ashton, the bright light in this otherwise bizarre and frightening place.

"I wasn't talking to you, Material Girl," Ashton teased back. "I brought something for you, Jack," Ashton said, sitting down next to Jack on the steps. "It's a compass. Every good explorer needs a reliable compass so you don't lose your way on your adventures."

Jack's eyes were wide with wonder. "The compass was invented in China. It uses the Earth's magnetic field."

"Um, that's right, Dr. Jack." Ashton chuckled. "Any other interesting facts about compasses?"

Jack stared off into the distance, his dark eyes thinking. After a long moment, he finally answered, "Some people use them for divination. Fortune-telling."

Ashton looked up at Serena, her face scrunched from trying not to laugh. "What people are those, Professor?"

Jack turned to face Serena, his tone serious. "Witches," he answered.

A chill went down Serena's spine, and she laughed awkwardly, not wanting him to know he'd spooked her. Again. "Let's see your new compass," she said as she thumped down on Jack's other side. He took the round object out of the box. It was lovely with a bronze body and a green needle. Jack pointed the compass straight and the needle responded by moving north.

"Now you know where north is." Ashton pointed. "You are exactly right. The ancient Chinese invented the compass, forever changing the world. Explorers could travel freely, not having to rely on the sun or stars for direction."

Jack moved the compass about, pointing in different directions, amazed by the movement of the needle. "This is great. Thank you, Ashton."

"You're welcome. I thought you could use one now that you are on your way to becoming a great explorer." Ashton leaned forward to meet Serena's gaze. "You and your sister have an entire lake to explore. I want a full report on everything you discover."

Jack promised to catalog his adventures and went inside to check out the direction of his room. "I read that your bed should face east for a proper night's sleep," Jack informed Ashton before making his way inside.

"My mom used to practice feng shui. Our parents' bed always faced east," Serena explained, staring up at his bedroom window for a long moment before turning back to Ashton, their knees brushing on the steps. "That was awfully sweet of you, Ashton," she said.

"You're welcome. I like Jack. He's a sweet kid. My dad actually got the compass for him. I guess they had a really good time today."

Serena scooted closer to Ashton, wrapping her arms around her legs. The night was quiet, the only sound was the water lapping at the docks, and the song of summer cicadas and frogs. Lightning bugs dotted the dark trees, twinkling like fairy lights.

"My dad gave me a compass when I was Jack's age. I thought it was the greatest thing and used it all the time." Ashton's eyes turned soft, and she smiled at the memory.

Serena stared into the fire, remembering her own father. Edward would never be able to teach Jack about such things. It made her heart hurt, a pain she desperately tried to hide.

"My mom's name was Iris." Ashton's voice was gentle, like petals on a flower.

Serena glanced at Ashton, awaking from her daze. "Was?" she asked.

"She died when I was nine. My dad never fully recovered from it. We don't talk about her much."

Serena closed her eyes, not understanding how one world could be so cruel. "Ashton, that is a pain no one should endure. I'm terribly sorry for your loss."

Her words were a whisper sent out into the universe as a prayer for all children suffering from an empty heart. The loss of a parent was a void that time itself could not cure—the pain was permanent. It never healed, but people just learned to adapt.

Ashton placed her hand on Serena's knee. Her touch was comforting and warm. She gave her a gentle squeeze. Serena covered Ashton's hand with her own. "I don't even know how we ended up here, Ashton. I was just an ordinary college student, focusing on my future, and then suddenly I'm a single mom moving to a lake in the middle of nowhere." She laughed, turning her face up to the night sky. "I didn't even know my grandparents," she confessed to the stars. "I never met them in my life, and now I'm living in their house with all their belongings. It's so strange because, at the same time, I feel as if I belong here, but I have no idea why."

Ashton squeezed Serena's knee, then turned her palm up to interlock fingers with her. "That's because you do belong here. This house is your family's history."

Serena shook her head. "My mom left this place when she was eighteen. She never spoke of my grandparents or this house. I don't even know how my grandparents died."

Ashton paused, as if choosing her next words carefully.

"There was an accident. Your grandpa was on the lake miles out. The lake can be extremely deep at parts. A storm hit and his boat capsized." Ashton bit her bottom lip before continuing. "It fell on top of him and he drowned."

Serena cupped her hands over her face. "Another tragic accident." She removed her hands, running them over her damp hair, taking a deep breath. "Then what happened to my grandmother? Deaken said she died not long after."

Ashton shook her head. "All I know is she drowned a week later, near the same place he went down. They said it was an accident, but…"

Serena closed her eyes. "That's so sad. Maybe she didn't want to live without him. My parents were like that—totally devoted to each other. My parents were killed in a car crash, but they went together. I hope that's what they would have wanted, though I know they wouldn't have wanted to leave Jack and me alone." Serena sighed. "How cursed can one family be?"

Ashton stroked her thumb over the back of Serena's hand, then lifted it to see it closer. "What are these markings on your wrist?" she asked quizzically. "Did you get a tattoo in the last five hours?"

Serena cursed as she slid her hand into the sleeve of her sweatshirt.

"No, it's some kind of seaweed poisoning, I think. I must be allergic to the algae in the lake."

Ashton pulled back on Serena's arm and pushed up her sleeve to get a hard look at the image on her skin. "Algae never leaves marks on the skin, that's for sure," she remarked as she turned Serena's wrist one way and another. "This looks like stonewort, but it's harmless and there's no way it could cause a reaction like this. This looks as if it went under your skin, like it's still there."

Serena pulled back her hand, making a fist. "Maybe it's some weird allergic reaction. I know it looks insane, totally out of the norm, but I'm sure in a couple of days it will fade and go away. If not, I'll see a doctor. I'm sure some hydrocortisone cream or a strong steroid ointment will cure it."

But Ashton's face was worried, her gray eyes stormy as she bit her lip and studied Serena. "First a spider bite, and now this." Her fingers grazed Serena's shoulder, sending a pulse of cold down Serena's arm. "May I?" she asked softly, her fingers stalling over the bandage. Serena gave a quick nod, and Ashton lifted the corners of the adhesive, pulling it free from the wound. "Geez, Serena. Your bite hasn't healed at all. It's still oozing and doesn't look any better." She frowned, a small crease between her eyebrows belying her concern.

Serena exhaled, enjoying the soft touch of Ashton's gentle fingers. "I know." She sighed. "I tried everything in the medical cabinet, but it isn't getting better. And it still hurts, as if it just happened, as I've just been bit."

"It must be the venom. Well, that helps narrow down what bit you—something that has venom in its fangs."

Serena's jaw dropped, and she smacked Ashton on the shoulder. "Oh, that's a comforting thought," she teased. "Something with poisoned fangs."

Ashton smirked, taking Serena's hand. "That's what I'm here for." She grinned. "To offer you comfort whenever you need it."

Serena smiled. She knew Ashton meant it. Her large eyes twinkled like stars that fell through the night sky from heaven. Serena turned away from her stare. She hadn't relied on anyone to take care of her for the past year. Her friends had been too self-centered to be concerned about a friend who was grieving the loss of her parents. She didn't know one person her age who had any idea what it was like to be a single mother at eighteen. Ashton was a stranger, someone she'd just met, yet she was able to reach inside her thoughts and pull out her deepest emotions. A mirror to reflect them back to her. It frightened Serena. She was used to being alone, taking care of herself. Serena wasn't sure if she was more afraid to let Ashton in, or to be rejected when she left. If she had learned anything this past year, it was that people left, either by choice or through death—in the end, everyone left.

Ashton rubbed her free hand over Serena's knee, and Serena's heart quickened in response. She didn't want to feel this way. It was too soon to be falling for someone she'd just met, yet she couldn't deny the way Ashton's touch affected her. There was too much craziness to deal with here, and she was too much of a mess to think about getting in a relationship. Still, she shivered as Ashton ran her fingers along Serena's leg, tickling her skin. Her eyes were burning bright, and she could feel Ashton's intense gaze on her face.

"Tell me what you are thinking," Ashton whispered. "Where did you go just now?" Her face was close, her breath soft against Serena's cheek, and if she turned her head just right, she could graze Ashton's lips with her own. Ashton rubbed Serena's blonde hair between her fingers

Serena bent her head, avoiding her face. She knew Ashton wanted to kiss her. She could feel her desire for her. It was what she wanted too, but she turned away. It wasn't fair to Ashton to get involved when Serena's entire life was in such chaos. What could she give Ashton other than pain and insanity?

"What's wrong, Serena?" Ashton breathed. "It feels like you have the weight of the world on your shoulders."

Serena shook her head. "Ashton, I wish things were different. I like you. A lot." She swiped at her eyes. "I just am too much of a mess right now to get involved with you. Maybe once things settle down. But right now I'm hardly able to take care of myself, let alone Jack. I can't kiss you under the stars like everything is okay. It's not."

Ashton stared at Serena a long time, as if putting together what she wanted to say, then discarding it. Finally, she said, "I know you are feeling a lot of things right now — fear, confusion, uncertainty. I don't want to add to your problems." She lifted Serena's chin to gaze into her eyes. "But I do want to be here with you, to sit here with you and your problems, and be a friend in any way you need. And maybe that will become something more later on, when you are ready." She smiled. "That's what I want, at least. I woke up this morning desperate to see you. And then you appeared in the water and glided up to my house. It felt like a sign, like I had summoned you there. I thought maybe you might have felt the same way."

Serena swallowed. "I do," she said quietly. "I feel that way, too."

Ashton's customary grin lit her face, making her dimples pop. "Well, then I guess we'll just have to be friends for now. Can you show your friend your sketches?" she asked.

Serena smiled, feeling lighter. Maybe she couldn't do a relationship right now — she was too much of a mess for that, but a friend…a friend would be nice. "Sure, I have just the sketch to show you."

Serena stood to get her sketchpad from where she'd left it on the kitchen and padded back to the porch to drop down beside Ashton. She'd shown Ashton some of her more recent sketches that morning, but this time she flipped to the front, her fingers lovingly running down the page as she flipped through them, showing Ashton her sketches of her parents, her mother's studio, their old view of the park. Glimpses of a life lost. Serena's voice turned hoarse as she flipped through the pages. It felt like laying her broken soul bare and letting Ashton sift through the pieces.

At last Ashton got to the page that held her finished portrait. "You finished your drawing of me," she breathed, her eyes soft. They both looked down at the drawing in her hands of Ashton's intense eyes, the dark hair and chiseled features. The face was kind but strong, with a compassionate expression.

Serena was surprised to see Ashton blush. She hadn't seen her flustered yet, and she knew her next sketch of Ashton would be her face right now, shy and proud and tender. "No one has ever drawn me before," she said sheepishly. "This is how you see me?" she asked in a gentle voice.

"It's how you present yourself to me," Serena responded.

Ashton understood what the drawing meant. To give Serena time. She closed the sketchpad, vowing to be there for Serena, in whatever way she could. She leaned back on her elbows and watched the night sky. It was quiet, and easy to feel they were the only two people on earth, as if the stars were putting on a show just for them.

They talked easily in the dark. Ashton had never been in love, she told Serena. When her mother died, Ashton had vowed to never fall victim to love's spell. Growing up, she saw what love could do to a person. Her parents had been made for each other. Her dad used to spin her mother around, planting kisses on her neck in the garden. Iris would always laugh, rubbing her hands through Kevin's hair as she accepted his kisses. They had been inseparable ever since they were children. Iris would wait for Kevin every morning outside of school. In spring Kevin would show up with an iris bloom he'd picked from his own garden. They grew up best of friends, side by side, doing everything together. Until one day they discovered they had grown up and what they felt for each other was more than childhood friendship. Ashton told Serena how everyone in town knew they would get married. Their mothers used to sit at the playground and plan out their children's future as the two friends climbed trees and swung on the swing set. It was undeniable to everyone who saw them together — they were soul mates and destined to fall in love.

Ashton told Serena about how she used to feel like she was the luckiest kid in all of Corvin Grove. Her parents were in love, and because of their love they were a happy family. Most of Ashton's friends had parents who fought all the time, cursing at each other for their annoying habits. It had left a bitter taste in Ashton's mouth. She didn't understand why people would marry someone they didn't love or even like for that matter. Ashton would spy on her parents from a tree branch as they held hands, walking barefoot through the garden together. Iris loved flowers and planted the most beautiful wildflowers in all of Conjure Lake. Ashton laughed as she told Serena about how some townsfolk would say that if they walked barefoot through Iris' garden, they would find true love. Ashton used to walk barefoot through her mother's garden and hoped one day she would have the kind of intense love her parents found in each other.

Ashton's voice turned rough as she told Serena about how everything changed the day her mother took her last breath. After Iris' garden died, nothing seemed to grow, as if spring itself refused to visit their garden after the loss of such a lovely woman. Ashton stopped walking barefoot. She never removed her shoes, even sleeping in them in her bed. Kevin was so devastated over the loss of his wife that Ashton believed her father's heart broke in two. The only reason her dad survived was because of her. Ashton was the other half of Kevin's heart and she alone kept him going. Iris was one half of Kevin's heart and Ashton was the other.

During the last days of Iris' life, Ashton would listen behind the bedroom door as her dad would sit with Iris, weeping about what was to come. Iris made Kevin promise that he would continue after she was gone and not stay in grief's darkness. She told Kevin that her dying wish was for him to live the rest of his life in joy because Ashton deserved a happy childhood. *"She will feel my absence more than you will, my love,"* Iris had whispered to him. *"A little girl needs her mother, and I am leaving our precious daughter. You must promise me to always be a source of strength and happiness for that child. If you don't, then I will never find peace in death."*

Kevin had wept on Iris' chest. He didn't want her to go where he could not follow, yet he knew she was right. Kevin would never remarry, never find another love or kiss the lips of another woman. That life died with Iris. But he would be a father to their daughter. He would uphold his promise to his dying wife and spend the rest of his life waiting to be reunited with her. His focus on Ashton and her happiness.

The dark felt like a confessional as Ashton poured out her heart to Serena, knowing Serena would hold its broken pieces like precious glass, then maybe reshape them in her sketchpad into something beautiful, like the rest of her drawings. Ashton knew her pain was safe with Serena, who felt so deeply and suffered so much. Ashton had never wanted to feel that unspeakable anguish of losing her soulmate. The pain of her mother's death was almost unbearable. She was too frightened to fall in love after that.

Yet here she was, here *they* were, under the stars on the porch with the waters of Conjure Lake lapping against the shore. The air was full of jasmine, and all her fears of love seemed petty and sad, now that she had someone who looked at her the way her father used to look at her mother. In her last conversation with her mother, Iris made Ashton promise that she would surrender her heart and let go of her fears and fall in love when it came to her front door. To cherish and protect and nurture it, wherever it was found.

But it didn't come to her front door. She had to drag it out from under a dirty porch in the dark of night. And now that she had found it, she wasn't going to let it go.

Chapter Six

The Root of Evil

Serena was already waiting underneath the shade of the crab apple tree with her hands on her hips as Deaken pulled into the drive early the next morning.

"You're up early," he growled as he slammed his truck door and walked over to her.

"I couldn't sleep," Serena said, pointedly ignoring his sour tone. "I keep thinking about this damn tree. I want it gone."

Deaken crossed his arms over his chest, his one eye meeting Serena's gaze in a challenge. "You want it gone."

Serena's eyebrows rose at his derisive tone. "Yes. Now. Right now, like this very second," she retorted, matching his mocking annoyance. "I want it cut down and chopped into a hundred pieces so I can burn each log in the fire and watch every bit turn into ash."

Deaken shook his head as he stared at the ground. For a long moment he was silent. "Tree comes with the house," he finally said.

Serena's jaw dropped. "The hell it does," she sputtered. "This is my house, my property and my tree. And I want you to cut that tree down. Immediately."

He sucked his teeth before responding to Serena's demand. "Well, I hate to disappoint you, little lady, but I can't cut it down. That's *your* tree."

Serena turned on him, her eyes narrowed and her fists clenched. She hated being patronized by men. "Why the hell not? You're a big strong man. You could cut through this tree with a chainsaw in minutes."

Deaken snorted. "It's not that simple."

Irritated, Serena threw her hands in the air. "Yes, it is! This is my property, and you are its groundskeeper. You just don't want to do it because you don't like me." Serena glared at him. "And you think I'm young and foolish." She took a step closer to Deaken, closing the distance between them and lifting her chin in defiance. "You don't have to admit it. I read it all over your face the second we met. You resent me for being your new employer, a young, spoiled girl from the city. Well, excuse me for losing my family and having nowhere else to go. My only option was to come here to this ancient house with this wicked tree!" Serena turned to stomp off toward the boathouse. "Forget it! I'll do it myself."

Deaken tracked her as she returned to the tree, his hands still on his hips as he glowered at her. Serena hoisted an axe in her hands like a baseball bat. Throwing a glare over her shoulder at Deaken, she braced herself for an enormous swing at the trunk.

But just before she swung, Deaken snagged the wooden handle, stopping the blade. "You can't cut it down with that," he growled.

Serena struggled with the axe, but Deaken's grip was unrelenting. "Yes, I can! I may be small, I may be a female, but I will cut this tree down with this axe and I'll stay out here all day and night until this bloody thing comes crashing down."

Deaken tightened his grip around the axe, his jaw clenched. "I'm not saying it's because you can't do it. It's because your tree cannot be cut down. Period."

"Let go of my axe, Mr. Ward. I'm not in the mood for your riddles." Her tone was low and dangerous, and whatever Deaken saw in her eyes made him let go of the axe and take a step back. "Fine. Then by all means, have at it," he said.

Serena threw one last glare in Deaken's direction as she swung the axe with every fiber of her being, the force of impact sending painful reverberations up her arms. But when the blade hit the tree, nothing happened. Not a single cut slashed into the bark. Frustrated, Serena swung again, smashing the blade into the tree, but not a dent was made. She tried over and over, plowing the axe into the tree until she fell on the ground in exhaustion, her arms shaking from fatigue. Hardly a single mark marred the twisted bark of the tree, as if she had merely scratched it. Serena turned to the blade, running her fingers over the warm and sticky black sap on the edge. No, not sap exactly. Thinner. Like blood—sticky, coagulated blood. The same dark matter oozed out from the scales, dripping onto the ground. Serena didn't need to consult her brother to know this was abnormal. "I don't understand," Serena huffed, exhausted. "Why is this tree so unnatural?"

Deaken sighed as he held out his hand to Serena and helped her to her feet. She was surprised by the gesture.

"It's blood," he affirmed. "Don't touch it," he said as she swiped her fingers across her jeans. "It is a cursed tree. You won't be able to cut it down, burn it or dig it up. It's an ancient tree. Its roots are thick and strong.

"Listen, girl. There are things in this land that are evil, things that cannot be explained through science or reason. That tree of yours is one of them. I don't know how much you believe, or are willing to believe when it comes to the occult, but this tree is the very center of all things wicked in this land."

Chills ran down Serena's spine, and she shivered despite the morning heat. The axe slid from her grip to land at her feet in the grass. Serena had never been one to believe in that nonsense before...but she had also never experienced such strange phenomena.

"I... I'm listening," she stuttered.

Deaken watched her face carefully. "In every religion," he continued, "there is a cursed tree. The Christians have the fig tree Jesus cursed for not bearing fruit, and in the Egyptian Book of the Dead, the Egyptians have the sycamore tree, where the soul of the deceased finds blissful repose. But in these parts, this is the cursed tree of the occult. Do you understand?"

Serena shook her head as she stared at the tree. The diminutive marks she'd made with her axe had already healed over. "I don't understand, but I do know something is wrong with that tree—something evil."

Deaken nodded. "You can feel its curse. So could your mother. Yes, I knew Rose. I knew your mama when she was little. Your mother sensed it—believed that tree was evil. Rose was a sweet girl, but she was scared. She said she saw the darkness lurking here, waiting to consume her. She said it haunted her dreams. She tried to convince her parents to move, to get out while they still could, but they were old-fashioned. They didn't listen."

He paused to swallow, as if it hurt to speak of the memory. Serena remembered Deaken had been close to her granddad, and her heart gave a squeeze of sympathy for the grouchy old man. "They loved this place," he continued, "and believed they needed to stay as keepers of the tree. To watch over it and prevent its evil from reaching others. Your mom disagreed."

Serena fought the sudden tears that pricked behind her eyes. Deaken watched her, one eye on her, the glass eye looking at the forest beyond. His voice was low as he continued, "Her ultimate mistake was thinking she could flee from Conjure Lake and the curse would forget about her. But it never forgets about a Korwin. Your tree knows your blood, and it will find you no matter where you go."

Serena held up her hands as she stumbled backward. "Curse? Are you telling me that my family is cursed because we inherited a family cottage on a lake with a blasted tree that bleeds? That's preposterous," she said shakily. "So now I'm going to die like my grandparents did?"

Deaken watched her, his eyes landing on the bandage at her neck. "And your parents. I don't think their accident was an accident." He touched his neck, gesturing to hers. "Something got you, didn't it? I know this seems impossible, but you know what bit you. Deep down, you know what it was." Deaken pointed at Serena's wrist where the deep green leaves twisted in an intricate tattoo. "And now you've been touched by the mark."

Serena defiantly pulled her sleeve down over her wrist.

"Your parents' death, this house, your recent injuries…none of it is a coincidence, Serena. And your tree is the center of it all."

"My tree. *My* tree. Why do you keep calling it *my* tree?" Serena lifted her arms in offering, as if someone would appear out of thin air, claim the tree as theirs and release her from this bleak nightmare.

Quick as a rattlesnake, his hand shot out to grip her wrist. He twisted it up so the garish green of her leaf tattoo was visible in the morning light. "This tree knows you. It got its mark on you. It's watching you. This tree is cursed, and so is your family line. This is your tree." He dropped her hand just as quickly. "You and your brother are in danger. You can run from here, but not from the curse. Your parents are proof of that."

They both turned to gaze at the wicked tree. Its branches waved in the still air as if it were mocking them. Serena closed her eyes. "So Jack is in danger," she said.

"So are you, if you got any sense," he said. Deaken took a step closer to Serena, his brown eye looking down on her. "I'm sorry you are the one who inherited it." Deaken crossed his arms. "And for the record, I don't dislike you because you're young and my employer. I choose to have this job, and I choose to stay on because I want to help you." Deaken rubbed the stubble on his chin, sighing heavily. "I stayed on because I care about this place. I couldn't leave you and that small boy here all by yourself with no one to look after ya. Not after what happened to your grandpa."

Serena closed her eyes, fighting back the tears that were threatening to be released. "And my grandmother?"

"And your parents," Deaken said softly.

"So everyone knows about my past and the family curse?" Serena crossed her arms, turning her head away from Deaken. "All the townsfolk... Ashton?"

Deaken shrugged his shoulders. "All the old-timers do, yes. That Ashton girl has lived here a long time. I'm sure she heard the nursery rhythm of the cursed tree of Conjure Lake."

Serena snapped her head back. "There's a nursery rhyme?" she sputtered.

Deaken bent his head, leaning in as if he didn't want the tree to overhear him. His eye met hers, and she shivered again as he began his rhyme, his gaze locked on hers.

"Who killed the raven of Korwin Cottage?
I, said the tree. With a bow made from my trunk
and an arrow from my bark. I killed the raven
at the stroke of seven, for he is not permitted in heaven.
Who saw him die?
I, said the tree, with my nubby twisted third eye,
I saw him die.
Who caught his blood?
I, said the tree. I caught his blood with luck.
And drank it up. Drop by drop in my silver cup.
Who'll dig his grave?
I, said the tree, with my long spindly pick and trusted trowel.
I'll bury him wrapped up in a shroud,
six feet under the ground, never to be found.
Who will carry the coffin?
I, said the tree. I'll carry the coffin under my roots
and escort him to the devil's court.
Who'll toll the bell?
I, said the tree. With my scaly branches, I'll pull the bell.
And all the birds of the air will hear

the toll and know that their dead beloved raven fell.
They will fly away in fear, for when the raven returns
all of Conjure Lake shall burn."

Serena's breath came in short gasps as she tried to calm herself. "What a horrible, gruesome poem." She shuddered. "Kids say that? If Ashton knows that rhyme, then why didn't she tell me?"

Serena burned with fear and betrayal. Did Ashton know about the curse and not warn her? She'd made it sound like Serena was crazy for thinking something scary was under the porch. But she *knew.* Ashton had welcomed her to the cottage, made her believe like there was nothing wrong with Conjure Lake, that everything happening to Serena was explainable. Yet, she knew. Ashton knew of the nursery rhyme. She must have known Serena and Jack were not safe at Korwin Cottage.

"I don't know about all that." Deaken shrugged. "Girl seems nice enough. Young people don't want to believe, Serena, just like your mother didn't want to believe. They try to reason the supernatural away with logic and science, until ultimately it's too late and there's nothing left to reason, because you've been marked by the tree. And once you've been marked, there's no escaping your fate."

"My fate!" Serena paced back and forth in the shadow of the wretched tree. "My fate, Deaken, is taking care of a young, heartbroken boy who lost his parents. That's my fate. Not this, Deaken. Not this!"

Serena pointed at the tree, and as she did, a searing pain stabbed her neck at the bite wound. Serena yelped as she touched her hand to the bite and saw blackened blood smeared on her fingers. The wound pulsed with ice, more black blood soaking the bandage. She craned her neck toward Deaken.

He stared at the blood-soaked bandage. "It's the curse. It's getting stronger. Tree's got its claws into you now. But there's a woman who can help you. She's been battling this evil her entire life. She can't make it go away, but she can teach you how to protect yourself. That is, if you wish to stay."

Serena shook her head. She didn't know what she wanted or what path to take. Run away, put the house on the market, find a two-bedroom apartment somewhere in suburbia and start over with Jack? Was all this even real, would she even be able to start over?

"Is leaving an option?" she wondered aloud. "If I'm marked, like you say, can we escape the curse?"

Deaken shook his head. "You already know the answer to that. Your mother tried to escape. I think you should see the Wise Woman. She lives deep in the woods where this evil can't find her. I can tell you how to get there, if you like."

"You could show me where it is?" she asked hopefully.

He hesitated. "I could show you how to get there, but if you want her help, you must go alone and bring her a gift. Otherwise she will not accept you."

Serena huffed out a breath as she stretched open her arms. "A gift for a Wise Woman? And what gift could I possibly have that's of value?"

"It's not money she's after," he said, shaking his head. "Bring her a token from the earth. Something pure plucked from nature itself."

Serena bit her lip. "And why can't you take me if you know so much about it?"

"It doesn't work that way." He shrugged. "I can draw you a map. I'll stay here with Jack. Watch over him while you go. Best take your kayak, as she lives on a stream of the lake and the water is too shallow to go by the fishing boat."

Serena's shoulders dropped in defeat. "That's kind of you. And what do I say when I get there? That Deaken Ward sent me, that I live in Korwin Cottage and I'm the one who inherited the cursed tree of Conjure Lake?"

Deaken snorted. "Sounds about right. She'll believe you. In fact, she probably already knows you're coming. I'm sure she's expecting you."

"How could she possibly?" Serena asked. "I only just arrived here."

"She knows things." He nodded. "You'll see."

Serena went into the house to check on Jack as Deaken went into the boathouse to sketch a map for her. Jack still slept snug in his bed, his arm around Tinker. She shook him gently.

"Hey, Professor," she cooed as he reached over to pull on his glasses. "Deaken is here to show you how to fish."

Jack sat up in bed, instantly awake as he reached for the compass he had strung on a string. "There are over one hundred and sixty-five species of fish in New York's lakes," he said as he pulled his compass over his head and settled it on his chest.

Serena chuckled as she kissed his sleep-mussed hair. "That's a lot. You better get started then."

A pajama-clad Jack rolled out of bed and flew down the stairs, Tinker on his heels. Serena's chest squeezed. For him, for Jack, she'd go see this Wise Woman. If Deaken was telling the truth, if this place was really cursed — and Serena felt a certainty in her bones that it was true — then she'd do anything she could to protect her brother. Resolved, she touched her aching shoulder, where the pulsing pain of the phantom hands still gripped her, and she trudged back down the stairs.

Deaken's map was accurate and easy to read, and she was surprised and grateful at his turn of attitude. He acted like such a grouch, but much to Serena's surprise, he was helping her. She gathered supplies for her trip as Jack dug for worms in the yard, chattering endlessly to Deaken. He stood with his arms crossed, grunting in acknowledgment at Jack's words, his stern face cracking into a rare smile. Serena smiled to see it. Jack had a way with people, and it seemed even grim Deaken wasn't immune to his sunny charms.

Serena looked over her supplies as she hitched her tote bag and sketchbook higher on her shoulder. She felt confident she could find the Wise Woman and be back in a few hours. Jack appeared to be in safe hands, and he was excited to spend the morning fishing with Deaken. Serena went into the greenhouse, gathering the biggest leaves off the herb plants, selecting lavender, chamomile and peppermint. She placed them in one of the mason jars and tied a piece of twine around the lid and dropped the jar into her tote bag, having no idea what an appropriate gift was for a river-residing medicine woman. "I hope this will suffice as a suitable gift for the Wise Woman," she muttered aloud to herself. "If anything, she can make a nice infusion from the leaves."

Serena made her way to the boathouse, stopping to give Jack a hug before she left. "You have my number," she told him as she kissed his hair. "The phone line inside is hooked up. Call me if you need anything, okay?"

"Don't worry, Serena. I'll be fine! Maybe I'll catch us a fish for dinner!"

Serena laughed. "That would be incredible."

Deaken followed Serena into the boathouse. "He'll be fine," he rumbled. "I'll watch over him while you're gone."

"I haven't left him since our parents died." Serena cupped her mouth, surprised she'd shared such vulnerability with the gruff man.

"Then this will do both of you some good." He nodded. "Follow the map, stay on the route and you should reach the Wise Woman within an hour. You'll know you've found it when you see a gray house with a purple door. We will be here waiting for you when you get back."

Serena didn't know if she should thank him or be irritated for sending her on this ridiculous quest for a Wise Woman. She got inside the kayak, placing the tote bag of jars and herbs in the back pocket of the seat.

"Just take care of Jack while I'm gone," she said as she pushed off from the dock. "I'll see you soon."

Deaken squinted his eye as his gaze followed Serena. She paddled away, drifting out of sight.

Chapter Seven

The Wise Woman of Conjure Lake

Serena was uneasy being back in the kayak. She wished she could have taken the fishing boat. After learning of her grandparents' deaths and the incident with the seaweed, the last place Serena wanted to be was on Conjure Lake, let alone in a kayak that now seemed vulnerable to the deep waters.

Thankfully, she would not be on the lake for very long. She found the entrance to the stream leading into the woods. Deaken's directions were accurate and easy to follow, and she was making excellent time. It was peaceful in the woods away from the lake and, for a fleeting moment, Serena forgot about the malevolent tree in her garden.

The stream had a whimsical quality to it. Lush trees formed a canopy as she made her way through the narrow stream. The shore was lined with beautiful wildflowers that were tall and white, stretching high toward the treetops. She paddled to the edge, plucking one from the ground. Serena placed the flower to her nose, inhaling its delicate fragrance. A water lily. Those were her mom's favorites. She couldn't have missed her mother any more than she did at that very moment. Serena turned the flower in her hand, thinking of what her mother would say, knowing Serena was on her way to see the Wise Woman. Would her mother laugh at such a ridiculous thought, or would she be disappointed to learn that her daughter had allowed a small back-country town to taint her view of reality? Or, even worse, would Rose be afraid for her daughter? *Have I become simple-minded like some of the locals here?*

But something spoke to Serena as she stared into the white lily. Its petals were wild and pure, innocent and untouched by the outside world. "Mom would be sad to see me in such pain," Serena said aloud. "She wouldn't want me to keep running, to uproot Jack and move again because of fear. She would want me to stay and make this work, not only for me, but also for Jack." Serena placed the lily inside the kayak's pocket along with the tote bag. "All right," Serena said in a reassuring voice into the woods. "I'm committed. I'm going to see the Wise Woman and I'm going to resolve this."

The stream curved in a serpent pattern, a long S that snaked along a narrow path. Serena knew she was close to the Wise Woman's cottage by the legion of wind chimes hanging in the trees by the water's edge. Some were made of shells, others from sticks and branches. Some had strange markings, like symbols from another time. Serena noticed an upside-down triangle in one chime and another was in the shape of a square with an X running through the corners that had a line going down the middle. There was also a symbol of a large square with a triangle inside with an even smaller triangle. Oddly, she wasn't afraid of these bizarre markings. Instead, she felt protected as she continued down the stream. They were comforting to her, familiar, even though she had never seen anything like them in her life.

Serena stopped the kayak as she came to an ash-colored wooden cottage with a violet door. The house was small — very small, in fact. The grand chimney took up the entire roof of the two-story house. By the look of it, the house only had one large room downstairs and possibly a bedroom upstairs. Serena noticed a dilapidated boat docked on shore, the name *Alice* written on the side. Ashton had been working on a boat called *Alice*, she remembered.

Serena pulled her kayak onto the bank, laying it next to the old boat. She lifted her tote bag carrying her sketchbook, mason jar and lily out of the back seat pocket before making her way to the cottage. The sun shone down through the trees, landing on a path of cobblestones. Six large stones shaped a circle by the front of the house. Two logs lay inside, forming a cross. Serena bent down to touch a stone when a deep voice spoke, startling her.

"It's the symbol of earth, everything I live, breathe and stand for. If you've come here looking for love, fortune or fame, I suggest you paddle your pretty ass back to the city."

Serena dropped the lily and stood upright. A gnarled old woman stared back at her, a wild halo of gray hair surrounding her deeply lined face like a corona. Her dark eyes were cloudy with cataracts, and she wore a tattered floral housedress and men's boating shoes. Serena knew instinctively this was the Wise Woman she'd come to see, though she was shocked that this woman knew where she came from. She glanced down at her Converse, her ordinary jean shorts and her plain black T-shirt. She wasn't wearing any jewelry or makeup. How did this woman know where she was from?

"You're just assuming I'm from the city because I've never visited you before, or you would know who I am because of the townspeople talking," Serena said.

The woman came closer, her boat shoes thumping on the hard ground as she looked down at Serena. "I know you're a city girl because you reek of it."

She turned around, heading back to her house, her long dress tailed behind her, dragging dirt as she moved. "Only a city girl would have such poor manners, coming all the way out here without bringing me a gift." She spat on the ground. "You probably heard about me from a friend at one of the prestigious northern colleges downstate. The Wise Woman of Conjure Lake, the one who can make your heart's desire come true. The one who can make any boy fall in love with you. Well, why don't you take your hollow heart and go back to your empty life where you belong amongst the pollution of this world. Leave me be. I have no use for city girls." She stood on her front porch with her arms crossed.

Serena marched up to the house, placing the jar and lily at the old woman's feet. "I am not an empty city girl. I am just a girl, just me. And I'm here because I was told you are the only person in this cursed place that can help me protect myself and my little brother from something dark that's been attacking me since the day I left my polluted life and came here to this land of hell."

The woman spun around, grabbing Serena by the arm. She looked hard into Serena's eyes, past her pupils, past her soul and into the very beginning. "You're a Korwin."

She said this as a fact, not a question, but Serena answered anyway. "Yes, on my mother's side."

The old woman sniffed hard with her long nose, her wide nostrils flaring as she did. "But your mother is dead. Your father, too."

Goosebumps rose on Serena's arms, and she found she couldn't look away from the old woman's cloudy gaze, like a fly trapped in a spider's web. The woman's grip on her arm tightened almost painfully. "Yes," she answered again.

"Your brother, he has your eyes as well. Same color, same deepness. He sees."

"Yes," Serena rasped. "We look very similar."

Without warning the old woman leaned forward and caught a bead of sweat from Serena's forehead with her pointer finger. Serena's eyes were wide as she watched the woman lift her finger to her mouth and run it along her tongue. Serena gasped, shocked and a little revolted by the woman's movements.

"Your flavor is sweet, like young love. You're a stupid girl. I taste it on you like nectar from a flower." The old woman spat on the ground, as if disgusted by the sweetness as she dropped Serena's hand. "First love never dies — it stays with you for all time. The only cure for that is blood," remarked the woman drily.

"I'm not a stupid girl, and I'm not here for some dopey love spell." Serena straightened her shoulders, trying to keep her footing in this bizarre situation. This wasn't working out the way she planned at all. "And I'm certainly not the first person to fall in love. But anyway, I'm not here about that. I have real problems." A warning note escaped her voice.

"Ha! You and everyone else. But you've never loved one like yourself before! You want this, you've always wanted this and now it is staring at you dead in your pretty brown eyes."

The woman shook her head knowingly, as if certain of a fate Serena was not privy to. "You will suffer the consequences. Love only brings heartache and, my dear, you have suffered enough heartache to last one lifetime. Trust me, girl, I've been visited by too many young fools wanting love and once they receive it, the love turns to obsession and ruins them forever."

Serena lifted her head, looking up at the woman. "Like I said, I don't want love. I want protection," she said soberly.

"I'm offering you protection, girl, protection from yourself. You are too vulnerable. You still see your parents in your life, walking among you, but they aren't here, girl, they're dead, buried in that cold cemetery you refuse to visit. Back in life, the one you ran from."

Serena's hand trembled from the woman's insults, and she was unnerved that the woman knew she hadn't visited her parents' grave. Serena wanted to spit in her face and head back to Korwin Cottage, away from her prying eyes. "You know nothing about me," Serena said defiantly, her hands now formed into fists.

"Ha! But don't I? I know you don't sleep at night. I know you stay awake, peering out your bedroom window, waiting for the darkness to come for you. For love to find you, for help to save you. But you know it's out there. It wants you." The woman gripped her arm again, holding up her wrist where the tattooed leaves twisted around it. "It's seen you. It's even visited you."

The woman squinted her eyes, taking a step closer to Serena. "You shouldn't be here. You should go. Head back to your house, collect your brother and leave. You don't belong in Conjure Lake." The woman spun on her heels, turning her back to Serena as she moved to the purple front door.

"I don't belong anywhere!" Serena shouted. Her hands shook with rage. She was done with riddles, done with half-truths and games. She had a brother to protect, and she would not be dismissed anymore by anyone.

The woman craned her neck back to Serena, and this time placed her thumb upon Serena's forehead. "I can see you, girl. I see many things. You've been touched." The woman removed her thumb, taking a step back from Serena.

Serena threw her hands up in the air. "I've been touched, bitten and haunted by a black raven. My bathtub tried to drown me, and the tree in my yard is cursed, producing dead embryos inside its fruit. I have no idea what I'm up against, and no clue how to protect myself or my brother. My groundskeeper thinks I'm not safe, not just here but anywhere, because of the cursed tree on my land. He said I can't outrun the curse. He sent me here to see you. He said you can help me."

The old woman reached out to snatch a hair from Serena's head. She yelped as the old woman turned and opened her door. "Groundskeeper, huh? That old fool. I know him well. Don't just stand there like an idiot. You might as well come in. Leave your jar of herbs by my door, and the lily, too. Whatever you brought with you stays outside. Only your spirit and truth can enter my home."

Serena rubbed her scalp where the old woman had pulled out her hair. With a hesitant sigh, she opened her tote bag and placed the jar and flower by the purple door. She stepped over a line of salt before entering the woman's house.

The room was dark, cluttered with furniture. A narrow set of winding stairs hid in the corner leading to the upstairs. Dried herbs and homemade amulets of snail shells tied on ropes and onion braids hung on exposed beams. Serena had to duck as she made her way through the clutter to stand by the old woman at the fireplace. The woman took the strands of Serena's hair and threw it into the fire. Black flames rose, taking the form of a raven. The woman spoke to Serena, not taking her eyes off the fire.

"This is my home. It is not a house like yours. Everything in here is here for a purpose. Each amulet, each besom broom, each shell and every herb has a purpose. Even the color of my front door serves a purpose.

"I am not a doctor, a mother, a priest or a therapist. I am a witch, known amongst my kind as a kitchen witch, a Wise Woman. I do not convene with the devil. I commune with nature. I am a healer. I use the elements of the earth for my craft. Plants, stones, flowers and trees. I use them all to make potions and herbal remedies for protecting the hearth and home. I have the gift of sight. I can see through your clothes to your nakedness. I know what is inside you that makes you ill. I can see into your very organs, pinpointing the source of your disease. There are many species of witches. This is mine. This is what I am and why you have sought me out."

The woman removed her eyes from the fire, glowering into Serena's face. "And what manner of witch are you?" she asked.

Serena startled, surprised. "Um, I'm not. You are? That's why I'm here."

The old woman grimaced. "We'll see. The flames tell me you're being pursued by a wicked entity, the spirit of a powerful witch who is centuries old. She is not like me. She is dark and black as the night without a moon. She is deadly, collecting souls. This witch takes the form of a raven and lives deep inside your tree. The tainted fruit you speak of, those are the dead she has gathered. The souls she has taken with her to hell."

Serena felt faint. Her legs trembled, threatening to give out on her. Ravens, curses, souls in hell. How had this madness become her life? She reached for the back of a stuffed chair, willing her body to stay strong.

"Do you need me to stop? If this is too much for you, girl, go. Like I said, pack up your things, collect your brother and leave. The door is there." The witch pointed her gnarled bony finger to the side.

Serena shook her head. She would not give in to fear, not anymore. "No, I'm staying," she demanded, her voice strong. "And you are going to help me defeat this witch."

"Ha! I admire your spirit, girl, I truly do!" The witch laughed raucously. "But you have no training, and you would need a lifetime of my knowledge just to make you worthy of one battle against this entity. And even then…" The old woman shrugged.

"Then why do this?" Serena said angrily. "Why bring me inside your home to tell me these things if you didn't believe I have it in me to fight? That I have what it takes?"

The woman's eyes, though cloudy, missed nothing, and they speared through Serena to her soul. "Because you are a Korwin. Though you don't even know what that means."

"Then tell me." Serena swayed back and forth. Nausea was rising in her belly.

The woman watched her for a long moment, then sighed. "Sit down, girl, you look faint. I'll brew you some tea." The woman walked to the kettle, placing herbs into a strainer. Serena dropped into a wooden chair at the table, feeling drained. "Don't get sick on my chair, girl!" the woman barked from the stove. "Place your head between your legs. The tea will settle you soon."

Serena did as she was told, rocking back and forth, impatient for the tea. The woman walked back to Serena carrying a mug, her long gray dress flowing on the floor as she moved. "Drink this. You will feel better in a moment."

Serena sipped the bitter fluid, its raw matter traveling to her stomach. She felt it advance with each gulp down to her stomach, where it sat warm and calming. "Thank you," Serena breathed.

"I use ginger. That's what gives it bite." The woman nodded, proud of her tonic.

Serena chewed on a chunk of the shredded root, her queasiness diminishing. A curtain of silence fell between them and Serena used the moment to gather her thoughts. "You said I can do this because I'm a Korwin. What does that mean?"

The old woman poured herself a cup of tea and settled into the seat across from Serena. "It means you come from a historical line of witches. Your grandmother was a witch, Edith Korwin. Your house, your land and your abilities all came from Edith. She married your grandfather because she became pregnant from her lover, but he died, and Edith was alone to raise a little one by herself. Even though Edith was a witch, she did not believe in abortion.

"Witches have ancient ways of losing a pregnancy. We believe in a woman's right to choose. That belief is sacred to us. No matter what the decision is, we honor it. Edith was very maternal and wanted her baby. She came to me, eager to learn the sex of the unborn babe. I could see into her womb. I saw what was lacking between the unborn baby's legs. She was carrying a girl, your mother Rose. Edith wanted Rose to learn the craft, like all Korwin women in your family, but Rose left, never to return to Korwin Cottage or to her mother."

The old woman paused and looked up at Serena, her cloudy eyes keenly moving across Serena's face. "You look like her. Your mother, I mean. It broke Edith and at times I thought it would destroy her. She stayed alive, hoping one day she would meet her grandchildren. Edith eventually married, but kept her maiden name. She learned to love her husband. He was, after all, deeply in love with Edith. And to be fair, he was a good and honest man, though I can't say much about the company he kept. Your grandmother, now she was everything to him." The old woman was silent for a long time, and Serena wondered why the woman was telling her this, and if she were waiting for Serena to speak.

But just as she opened her mouth, the old woman drained her tea and stood, turning back to her kitchen. "Girl, run outside and get some water from the stream. Flowing water. I want it moving. Fill up this pitcher and come back." The woman bustled about, leaving Serena standing in the middle of the room, pitcher in hands.

Feeling foolish, Serena wordlessly turned and stomped down the stairs to the water's edge. She scooped out some water, making sure to take it from the icy current, then walked back to the house and up the steps, careful not to spill a drop. When she arrived, she discovered the witch sitting beside the fire, Serena's sketchpad open in her lap.

Fury and violation flooded through Serena as she set the pitcher on the table and reached to snatch it back. "That's mine! I didn't give you permission to touch it!"

The old woman stilled Serena with a burning look. "Not a witch, indeed," she scoffed. "You're a witchling, plain as the nose on your face. Look at this magic. I've never seen such powerful spells from such a young witch." She held up a sketch of Ashton, the one of her soft eyes and strong hands. "Of course you aren't looking for a love spell. You cast your own," she said derisively. She flipped to another page, one of her brother curled up sleeping in bed, his arm around Tinker. "Hmm. Another love spell here, a more powerful one. A protection spell. Even got the dog." The woman chuckled.

Serena's face burned with anger as she snatched back her sketchbook. "Those are my drawings, and they aren't meant for your eyes."

The old woman stared at her, her hazy eyes sharp. "An etching witch. Didn't expect that. If you were smart you'd draw a picture of yourself in there. You've got the people you love protected, but you, foolish girl, you are free game, prey being hunted. You could use a little etching protection yourself."

Serena shook her head, confused and a little frightened by the old woman's words. "I'm no witch. Those are just pictures. My mom was an artist, and she liked to paint. I'd draw with her in her studio."

The old woman nodded, her wrinkled face pensive. "That's where it started. There's power in numbers. Women are much more powerful when they band together. Your mother was your first coven. That's where you learned your magic, where it became so strong."

Serena shook her head, staring down at the closed sketchpad in her hands. "They are just pictures," she said again.

"Bah! And they are just spiders and ravens and trees, too, aren't they?" she scoffed. The old woman's eyes darkened as she leaned forward. "The witch that haunts you was a hedge witch. Before she sold her soul to the devil, she was peaceful and the most powerful midwife of her time. She was strong in her craft, able to engage in spirit flight into the Other World. She could fly into other realms, because hedge witches are connected to birds, the raven in particular. It is their spirit animal. Hedge witches are Night Travelers, or Walkers on the Wind. She was an extremely powerful mediator, communicating between spirits and the living.

"In all my years, I have yet to meet a hedge witch. They are rare, because of their unique ability to connect spirits with humans. But once she offered her soul to the devil, she was no longer a hedge witch. She became something else, something not of this world." The Wise Woman turned quiet, her eyes pensive as she stared into the flames. Serena watched the flames flicker in her cloudy eyes, captivated.

"Your grandma Edith was able to keep the witch dormant for decades, for she was a green witch, much like me," the old woman continued. "She used herbs and properties of the earth for magical and medical value. Edith could retain the source of the crab apple tree's power by binding it in a sacred circle, entrapping the evil spirit . But one night not long ago the circle was broken. My dear friend died that very night, and Alice Lake returned to Korwin Cottage."

Serena gasped, recognizing the name. The picture of the woman in her trunk at Korwin Cottage, the beautiful one with the dark eyes. Her name was Alice Lake. Serena looked up at the woman. "Alice Lake, she was the hedge witch? It's her name you have on your boat."

"Yes. I name my boats *Alice*, after the hedge witch of Conjure Lake. It prevents her from harming me when I am in the water. A simple but potent spell I use for protection. Though you know a thing or two about that." The witch raised her bushy eyebrows at Serena.

"I've seen her," Serena confessed. "I found her picture in a trunk in my room."

The old woman made a face. "Then she's seen you, too. She knows you are there, and she wants you." The old woman sighed. "You didn't even know you were a witch, so I guess I can't blame you for waking her up."

Serena gasped, her eyes wide. "I didn't wake her!"

The woman shrugged, as if it didn't matter. "You, or someone else. But like I said, witches are stronger in numbers, and you sleeping unprotected in that house has increased her powers exponentially. She's feeding off you. Got her teeth there in your neck, and her mark on your hand. Every day you stay by that lake you grow into your power here, and she will get stronger too. Until she eventually devours you and your helpless brother."

Chills ran down the length of Serena's spine, and she shuddered. "How can I stop her? How can I protect Jack?"

The woman slapped both hands down on her knees before standing. "Well, first we have to see what we are up against. Bring me that pitcher of water. We'll have a good old-fashioned scrying."

Serena followed the woman, confused at how quickly the woman's train of thought seemed to shift. "What's a scrying? And what's the water for?"

"Conjure Lake is full of magic and power because of all of our witch sisters who have been drowned in it," the woman said conversationally, as if she weren't chatting about women being killed. "Townsfolk would accuse a woman of being a witch, then drown her in the lake. If she sank, then there's your proof. She was a witch."

"That's ridiculous!" Serena sputtered. "How gruesome and barbaric! Those poor, innocent women!"

"Poor and innocent, my ass!" the old witch cackled. "The townsfolk were right—they were witches—but the only thing they succeeded in doing was making the rest of us more powerful, and giving us an unlimited flow of power from Lake Cauldron."

"Lake Cauldron?" Serena asked, confused, though she recalled the antique map on Ashton's wall. "The giant mythical lake that disappeared?"

The old woman winked. "Disappeared? Or transformed? Nothing is ever destroyed, only changed. It would do you well to remember that, witchling. No, every time they drowned a witch in the water, the lake grew in power. Since we are all connected to the earth, us remaining witches grow in power as well."

Serena studied the witch as she considered her words. The woman's face was long with a pointed chin, and her nose was full and equally long, giving way to small tight lips that revealed her age from the wrinkles that ran above them. Her green eyes complemented her chopped wiry gray hair. She wasn't beautiful, but she had an interesting look that was unique and pleasing.

"You would do well to mind your stare, girl," the witch said without looking up from the collection of items she had spread on the table before her. "It's impolite to gaze at a witch. You never know what hex she might place on you for your intrusive eyes."

Serena blushed and darted her stare to the floor, thinking of the strange librarian with the hand mirror. "I'm sorry," Serena whispered.

"Tell me more about what you found in that old trunk," the old woman demanded.

"I found a sketch in an old chest at the cottage. Inside was a picture of Alice and her baby."

The kitchen witch nodded as she poured the pitcher of water into a large bowl and added various oils and what appeared to be stones and feathers. "It was because of her baby that she sold her soul to the devil. Her youngin' died, like so many infants in that century. Alice was consumed by grief. She used her ability to conjure the baby, visiting her in the spirit realm.

"Townsfolks saw Alice one night in the woods, communing with her dead infant. They declared her a witch and came for her. The same folks who would come to her purple door seeking her prayers, spells, and the delivery of their own babies now hunted her in her own home. But they didn't drown her. Nope, not that one. They dragged her to the crab apple tree in your front garden and took turns throwing stones at her, chanting *witch bitch, hang the witch*, over and over." The old woman looked up at Serena over her bowl. "They bound her hands and hanged her by the neck. But their efforts were futile. Alice was too powerful for those commoners, and she summoned a lightning storm to strike the branch from which she hung, turning the tree black as night. She swore revenge on the villagers. She fled her home and found refuge deep in the woods. She called forth a black cat under a new moon and sacrificed it by boiling the cat alive in a cauldron. She stripped the flesh off the cat and carried its bones to the four corners of Korwin Lane. There she placed the bones in each corner, summoning the devil.

"And to everyone's fright, the devil heard her call. He appeared to her, taking the form of a black ram. He promised Alice immortality, being reunited with her baby for all time. He offered protection from anyone who meant to do her harm by bestowing upon her a dark power that went beyond Wiccan practice. Alice formed a sacred circle and lit it on fire. She entered inside, walking through the flames. There she said the words that I will not repeat, ancient words spoken in the very tongue of Lucifer himself."

The old woman paused, shaking her head. "He accepted her soul and granted her all the foul powers of the night. But in exchange for this new supremacy, Alice must collect more souls for her new master, an endless conquest to appease the devil. So it went, and so it still goes until Alice can finally be laid to rest in this world and sent to hell for all time."

"How do you kill Alice Lake? How do you kill an immortal spirit?" Serena asked, her hands trembling.

"You don't kill her, girl. You vanquish her from this realm, and the only way to do that is to destroy the tree that the devil himself planted."

Serena cupped her hand to her mouth, her chest tight with fear. "Deaken said the tree couldn't be cut down. How do we destroy the tree?" she asked the old woman.

"Well, we ask the spirits, of course!" The old woman cackled, then, quick as a snake, she snatched Serena's hand and pricked her finger. Serena yelped as the woman squeezed a drop of blood into the bowl of water before her. "Sister spirits of Conjure Lake, show us danger. Show us Alice Lake!"

Serena gasped as the water in the bowl swirled and frothed, and the old woman cackled again. "Look at that young magic! Look how our sisters welcome your blood! Now tell me, witchling. What do you see?"

Serena met the witch's cloudy gaze, then leaned over to look into the water. "I see twigs," she said flatly.

"Look closer, foolish girl. And tell me what you see. Tell me what you know."

Serena leaned forward to stare down into the bowl of water. Then it felt as if she were falling, falling, falling into darkness, into death, into sleep, into the lost world in between. She squeezed her eyes shut, and when she opened them again, she was no longer in the cottage. She was outside by the lake, though it was a different season, and the trees were smaller, younger. A different time, then. She knew instinctively she was having a vision. She felt in her whole body that she was no longer in her own body—she was someone else, seeing the world through someone else's eyes. Serena settled her mind, her thoughts, her body. And she watched.

He had met the Wise Woman more than once in his life. He was still a boy back then, no older than sixteen. The boy ventured off alone to visit the Wise Woman when his eye grew cloudy. His eyesight didn't leave him at once. It was a gradual process. One day he woke to find spots blocking his view. The boy flushed his eye with water, thinking he had dirt trapped under the lid, but come midday the spots had spread. He tried steeping tea bags in hot water and placing them over his eye, but that didn't work either.

It continued like that for a few days, the boy slowly getting more spots, and him trying to soothe his eye, convincing himself he was only tired. After a week, the spots formed together, causing a film until he could no longer see clearly out of that eye at all. Everything moved in shadows, and shapes lost their sharpness and edges. Within another week, he lost the ability to distinguish night from day. A blackness was forming, causing the color to disappear from his view. The boy pleaded with his father to take him to the town's doctor, but he refused, spitting on the ground, demanding where his son thought they were going to come up with the money to pay for a doctor.

Desperate, the boy heard in town that there was a Wise Woman in the woods who practiced medicine. She had herbs that could cure gout, and a special tea concocted from vinegar and asparagus that would push out kidney stones. He even heard rumors of the woman brewing a potion that could cause an unborn babe to die inside the mother's womb before anyone would suspect she was even pregnant. The boy was convinced that if the witch could do all that, then surely she could regain his eyesight.

He set off early one morning before the sun rose in the sky. He canoed through the dark waters, searching for the Wise

Woman. He'd been told to bring a gift, but he had nothing of value on his land. No herbs or tasteful produce. His father grew undesirable things like radishes and bitter turnips. Their soil was not lush like the others in town. They could only grow things that were tart and rancorous to the tongue. Still, a gift was required, so the boy had gone out to the garden while the moon still hung in the sky and dug up a bag of each root vegetable to give to the Wise Woman. As the boy made his way to the witch's door, he looked down at his gift, second-guessing his selection. He had considered stealing snap peas and fresh strawberries from Korwin Cottage, but decided against it. He feared the Wise Woman would know they were not from his land and curse his other eye for trying to trick her.

The boy knocked at her purple door as the sun streaked through the inky sky. The Wise Woman looked out from her window and slammed the shutters closed. The boy knocked again, this time trying to peer in through the blocked window.

"Go away!" a voice shouted from inside.

"Please, Wise Woman! I brought you gifts! I need your help!"

The woman snorted. "Nothing but roots. Get out of here. I know what you want, boy, but I can't help your eye. It is diseased. I can smell the rot coming from it."

The boy remained on the witch's doorstep, clutching the bag of vegetables. He stood there rocking on his heels as the heat of the day burned down upon his head. When the moon rose in the sky, he was grateful for its darkness, his skin burned to a deep red from standing all day in the blasted sun. He knocked one more time before the witching hour approached, pleading for the Wise Woman to open her door. The shutters slammed open, and the witch faced him through the window. "Go away, I said!" she screeched at him before *once again slamming the shutters closed, blocking the boy from her sight.*

But he would not give up. He stayed through the night, leaning against the witch's door, clutching his offering. The cold night air burned his raw and sensitive skin, and he shuddered in pain. He thought about giving up and accepting his fate, and returning to his house. But as much discomfort as he was in, nothing compared to the loss of his sight. A roll of thunder traveled above him and he braced himself for the storm that was about to pour down. The heavens opened up, releasing a torrent of rain that continued to flow through the night and continued into the next day. The boy didn't know what was worse, being burned by the blazing sun, or drowning in a pool of rain.

On the second night, the boy once again knocked on the witch's door. "Please. Please help me."

His words were desperate, and the witch again flung open the shutters. "I told you, go away!"

Just as before, the witch slammed the shutters on the boy, leaving him alone in the darkness. On the third day, the rain had stopped and, in its place, hail fell from the sky. Hard balls made from ice and pain and fear landed around the boy, striking him on the head, his back, arms and legs. He fell to his knees, pleading for the witch to help him.

"I have no money. No means to pay for a doctor. There must be something you can do. Please!" the boy begged, exhaustion dragging him to his knees.

Finally, the purple door opened a crack, and the witch appeared. Through his clouded vision the boy saw her approach and lay a hand on his wet and battered hair.

"There is nothing I can do for you, boy," she said again, gently this time. "Your eye is rotting. You contracted a disease, and it's been left untreated for too long. Had you come to me sooner I might have been able to save it."

The boy wept. "I stood here for three nights! You did nothing!" He reached for the witch's arm, clinging to her as he begged her one last time to save his eye.

The witch sighed, for there was nothing she could do. "It was already too late before you came, boy. It's too late, too far gone." She bent down to get a good look at his eye. Covering the eye was a black film. Pus was oozing out of the corner. She chose her next words carefully. "Left untreated, your eye will continue to rot, and you will grow very ill from the disease. I can smell it traveling through your body. It's in your veins, child." The witch stood up to go inside.

The boy clung to her hand. "Please! I'll do anything! Just don't leave me like this," he cried.

"Stay here." The witch sighed before going inside her house. When she returned, she was holding a mug of steeped herbs. "Drink this and in three days your eye will fall out."

He gasped, inching away from the witch. "No! Why would I do that? I don't want it to fall out, I want you to heal me!"

"If that eye doesn't come out, then you will lose your other eye to the same fate, followed by your liver, kidneys and finally your heart. This will stop the root of poison that is inside of you."

"But I will be a freak!" the young boy sobbed. "A monster without my eye."

The witch snorted at his comment. "Vanity. It's what everything boils down to." She handed the boy the mug. "The choice is yours. Lose your eye in three days and have it replaced with a glass one, or lose your life. I cannot decide for you."

"That's no choice at all," the boy wept.

The woman's mouth was a hard line. "That's what everyone says when they don't like their options. But there's always a choice to be made, and this one is yours."

With tears running down his cheeks, the boy snatched the cup from her hands and swallowed the offensive drink in one gulp. It burned all the way down.

True to her word, the boy's eye fell out on the third day, just like she promised. He awoke to find his eye sitting next to him on top of his pillow. He screamed in terror, even though he was prepared for it to happen.

The boy cried for a week over his fate. Some days he thought death would have been better than to walk around life as a one-eyed freak. Losing his eye affected his daily life. He had to readjust his vision to see out of his left eye. His work suffered for the first couple of months. His father was hard on him during those months, cursing him for his lack of accuracy. The boy used an eye patch to cover the vacant socket until he could save enough money to have a glass one inserted. It took him two years of saving to make the trip into the city and have the surgery for a prosthetic eye. Townsfolk said it was a miracle that the witch saved his life when the boy returned with a shiny brown eye that never moved and always stared straight ahead.

The boy, however, never forgot the witch who refused to help him, never forgot the three days and nights of hope and despair on her porch, never forgot the trade he made with the witch that day on her doorstep.

Serena snapped back into her body with a gasp. The Wise Woman stared across the table at her. "What did you see, girl?" she asked urgently. "What dangers of Alice Lake did the waters show you?"

Serena shook her head, confused. "I don't think it worked right. I didn't see Alice. I saw the caretaker, Deaken. I saw him as a young boy right here on your porch. But why would I see him?"

With that, the old woman sat back, another pensive look on her wrinkled face. "Hmm. Curious. Curious, indeed. Yes, I remember the Ward boy. He brought me blighted root vegetables, cursed with the same blight that rotted his eye. I brewed him a tea and it fell out. Fixed him right up and I sent him on his way. I haven't thought about that boy in years." Her mouth was a firm line as she thought. "Strange he'd be in your vision. Caretaker, you say?"

"Yes," Serena answered uneasily. "He has looked after Korwin Cottage, like his father before him. He's the one who told me you'd help me. He drew me a map and is watching my brother right now. Do you think I'm meant to help him?"

"Hmm. Perhaps. Curious," the woman said again before shrugging. "Time will tell. The waters are never wrong. We'll see how he's tied up in all this."

"In all what?" Serena asked, shaking her head. "I don't even understand what is happening." A terrible thought struck Serena. "Do you think Jack is safe with Deaken?"

The woman sighed. "Haven't you been listening? No, of course he isn't safe. And neither are you. I don't know how Deaken Ward is tied up in all this, witchling. That's for you to find out. But the waters are never wrong. Somehow your fate is tied to this caretaker of yours. But how, I don't know." She sat back. "I'll think on it some more. In the meantime, you need to draw yourself in that book. Draw yourself strong and safe and powerful. You can't be what you can't see."

Serena fingered her sketchpad, thinking. "Should I draw Deaken? Would that help?"

The Wise Woman shrugged. "I can't tell you what to do with your own magic."

Serena cupped her mouth. She was worried about Jack being at the cottage without her. "I should be getting back. Jack isn't safe."

"None of you are safe, girl. That is why you must stay here, so I can teach you how to protect yourself. I can help you secure your home, build spiritual borders that no force can penetrate. But you must believe everything I say and do exactly as I tell you. Magic only holds power if the person casting the magic is a believer."

"I keep telling you, I'm not a witch," Serena protested, shaking her head, though her voice was unsure this time. "I am not a witch. How can I protect Jack and myself from Alice?"

"If you pulled your head out of your ass you would have heard me, girl. You have Korwin blood in your veins. You are more of a witch than you realize." She picked up Serena's sketchpad and waved it in her face. "You are a hereditary witch, a witch by birthright, a witchling of your mother's making, her own coven. And you found me, didn't you? Our powers grow in numbers. You will be stronger just for sitting at my table. And so will I. All witches are sisters, you see. We strengthen each other. Once you engage in the art of witchcraft, your true talents will emerge."

The kitchen witch turned to face Serena. "Listen to me, girl, and do what you like with the information I am about to give you. There are choices amongst our kind. We are witches, not the devil's play toys. We make our own fate. You can choose to follow your birthright as a hereditary witch, and all magical gifts that have been inherited to you by genealogy. Or you can walk away now, exit that door and leave this place forever.

"If you choose the latter, you will never further develop your powers into a witch. They began with your mother in her art studio, but they grew stagnant with her death. Your powers will not emerge if you go about your young life as you always have. You will enter womanhood as an ordinary non-magical being. But if you stay and welcome the journey of witchcraft and all it offers, I will be your mentor and teach you the ways of our kind."

Serena hung onto every word the Wise Woman said. She tasted each possibility in her mouth, foreseeing what path her life would hold. She imagined a future away from Conjure Lake with Jack, running, always running, with Jack being dragged from one school to another. No matter where they went, Alice Lake would find them, just like the curse found her parents.

The old woman locked eyes with Serena, her cloudy gaze meeting Serena's dark one. "I will never forsake you, girl, I will never leave you, abandon you or allow you to suffer. I will die to protect you and I will make you my own. Witches are more powerful together. I can share my knowledge with you, my power. All you have to do is accept it, accept yourself. And believe. Magic can only work for those who believe."

The Wise Woman rose. She placed her thumb on Serena's wrist, touching the green markings that tainted Serena's flesh. The markings wiggled and wormed around Serena's arm, and a single leaf rose from the skin, exposing itself in the air. Serena stared in wonder as the old woman plucked the leaf from Serena's flesh. As she chanted, her words grew sonorous, filling the small cottage as if there were a hundred voices speaking at once.

"Come out, tainted one, it must be done.
I reject the poison inside you.
Come out, tainted one, you do not belong.
Discard the home that was given to you.
Come out, tainted one, your day is done.
I shall pluck you from your root like a thorn in a briar.
Come out, tainted one, I shall cast you into my fire."

The old woman then cast the single leaf into the fireplace. It blazed up in a bloom of swirling black smoke, then settled again. Serena noticed another leaf creeping out of her flesh.

"Now you must complete the cycle. Chant those words. Believe in your powers, for it's the belief in the magic that will free you from the wicked poison that was burrowed into your flesh."

"I don't know them," she said softly, her eyes locked on the leaf.

The old woman settled her warm hands on Serena's shoulders. "Yes, you do, witchling. I gift them to you." She breathed over Serena's cheek, and she found she did know the words, as if they were on the tip of her tongue, and they spilled out of her mouth, more of the green leaves lifting and peeling from her skin as she spoke the incantation.

Serena breathed heavily as she placed her trembling thumb over the reed, repeating the words over and over. Each time she chanted the spell, a new leaf would appear, and Serena plucked each one, throwing them into the same flame until all the markings were gone and nothing was left but her own fair skin.

The witch nodded in approval. "So it has begun, girl. I offered my magic to you, and yours answered in kind.

From this point on you are no longer a witchling, my girl. You are my sister witch. My coven — our coven."

Serena stared at the Wise Woman in disbelief, amazed that such things were even possible in this world and within her own spirit. Serena rubbed her naked skin, relieved that the vile mark was finally gone. But something was still troubling her. "You said someone released the raven. Who did that? Was it Alice?"

The Wise Woman glanced out of the window, shaking her head. "I don't know," she answered wearily. "It had to be powerful magic indeed. Perhaps another witch? I can't say." The woman shook her head in frustration. "Believe me, girl, I've tried to identify the culprit. I have visited and revisited that tree countless times, using every spell I know to discover the traitor's name, but whoever they are, they're protected by the tree and Alice herself. I have yet to uncover a way to reveal their identity."

The woman looked over at Serena, then stood from her seat. "But I will. We will, together."

Serena stood as well. "Thank you, Wise Woman. I can't thank you enough. But why would you help me when you didn't help Deaken?"

"I did help that boy," she groused. "He just didn't care for the remedy. But I did my best by him, and I will do my best by you."

"Because we are sister witches," Serena answered.

The old woman smiled. "Yes, we are sister witches. And coven sisters. But that is not all we share. We share blood as well. For I am Yolanda Korwin. Edith Korwin was my sister."

Chapter Eight

The Night Moth

Edith Korwin was loved by everyone who knew her. She was a faithful wife who never strayed from her marriage. A devoted mother who cared for her daughter more than life itself. A loyal sibling who never missed a day without speaking to her baby sister. A treasured friend who always had a pot of tea brewing and a slice of walnut bread, fresh out of the oven, for her visitors.

Many women came to Edith seeking her counsel. She was a kind and soft-spoken woman who chose her words carefully when dealing with a fragile heart. Every visitor who came to Edith's door entered with a heavy heart, a secret problem that needed healing. Edith kept goodies for her visitors, whether it be an herb tea bag filled with lavender, rosemary, and apple blossoms to attract love for the lonely hearts, or a homemade bar of soap made with pure goat's milk and jasmine, a sure way to entice prosperity into one's life. Whatever the ailment was, Edith had a cure, wrapped up in parchment and tied with twine.

The townsfolk all knew that when they were unlucky in life, they visited Edith Korwin, the green witch of Conjure Lake. They would always return with their stomach full of delicious bread and a pocket full of magic.

Yolanda used to consider her sister a fool for not charging the townsfolk for her gifts. She believed that magic shouldn't be given away to the vain and selfish, but Edith never saw it that way. Every person who came to Edith's door seeking help was a person in need and, no matter the circumstance, Edith could never bring herself to ask for compensation.

The day Edith died was a sorrowful day for the small town of Corvin Grove. Her husband had passed unexpectedly, drowned in the very waters that sustained most of their livelihoods. Many of the townsfolk came to her doorstep bearing gifts of comfort, but she turned them all away, her kind eyes hollow, her gaze full of ghosts. A week later when word of her death reached the people of Corvin Grove, none were surprised when they learned she had drowned near the same place her husband's body had been discovered. But talk emerged within the confined walls of the small town. Was it another accident? Or had she drowned on purpose, following her partner into the next life? Many believed she had, but others…others who knew Edith, truly knew her, understood that Edith would never depart this world by her own hand without first saying goodbye to her beloved daughter.

The night of Edith's passing, many women shut their blinds and locked their doors, insisting that evil was outside riding on the wind, for nothing good would steal the soul of such a pure heart. Farmers claimed their pastures had been tainted, the grass turning brown overnight, producing sour milk. Babies cried for an entire week, unable to be soothed by their mothers' touch. Fishermen were unsuccessful, returning home empty-handed, their nets coming up bare, as if the entire lake were depleted of life.

Everyone was affected by the tragic death of Edith Korwin, but no one suffered more than her sister, Yolanda. She refused to leave her cottage, boarding up her windows and front door. She turned countless visitors away, shooing them off her property with a broom from her front steps.

Yolanda feared she couldn't continue living without her sister by her side. She slept downstairs in a chair by the fire. Her eyes sagged, pulled down by the heaviness of exhaustion as she watched the flame flicker, waiting for the raven to claim her life as well. For what others had only guessed at, Yolanda knew to be the truth — Edith's death was no accident. She knew her sister did not take her own life. No. Someone — or something — else had. A dark shadow had fallen over Conjure Lake, invisible, but felt deep in the bones. The grief and fear threatened to overwhelm Yolanda, and her dreams were haunted by a specter of darkness. The raven.

There were times when Yolanda even considered going into the lake and offering her life to the raven. Death seemed the only cure for the pain she was carrying. But in those bleak moments, Yolanda heard her sister's voice speak to her from out of the flames. *I am with you, my sweet sister. You must go on, for there will be a time when I will need you to take care of my own.* Yolanda would weep at Edith's words, for she knew Rose would never return to Conjure Lake.

But it was not Rose who Edith was speaking of — it was her grandchild, Serena, who would appear before

Yolanda's purple door, seeking help. Serena, who wore her mother's face and her father's dark eyes, and carried generations of untapped power in her veins.

* * * *

Serena followed Yolanda out of the cottage. Her mind was spinning. The universe had shifted amongst the stars, changing Serena's fate. A cosmic dance had begun. Serena was a hereditary witch, a witch by birthright. She had the ability to conjure magic to change the course of her life forever.

But what made her balk more than anything was the discovery that she was no longer alone. She had family, a great-aunt who now walked beside her in the woods. To her, that was the pinnacle of all she had witnessed, the greatest gift.

Yolanda led Serena through a copse of evergreens, stopping at a small clearing behind her house. Tall elm trees formed a circle surrounding a lush herb garden. The long tree limbs formed natural shelves that created a barrier wall where flowers bloomed. An impressive array of plants grew wild and tall, rows of herbs stretched forth from the ground like an emerald city on the earth. A pentagram made from bricks sat in the center of the garden.

Serena recognized many of the plants that were carefully tended. Sage, thyme, basil, rosemary, wormwort, mugwort, valerian, echinacea, lemon balm, bee balm and pennyroyal grew inside each corner of the five-point star. The earth inside the star was as crimson as the blood racing through Serena's veins.

Yolanda pointed to the pentagram. "The pentagram is sacred to us," she explained. "The four lower points represent the four aspects of the world — earth, water, air, and fire. The fifth point at the top represents creative spirit over all creation. Mind over matter, girl. The star is always encircled by a wheel, representing the continual flow of life and energy. The pentagram reminds us we can bring Spirit to Earth." Yolanda paused beside the large circle, silent for a moment before looking back up at Serena. "Apply this to every aspect of your daily life. The symbol will help you engage in spiritual thought. Never underestimate the power of symbols, for they are extremely valuable to witches. They not only prepare us for a magical mood, but they aid us to manifest our inner power."

Yolanda bent down to pluck a few mugwort leaves. She shuffled over to a bench made from an elm tree and sank down, gesturing for Serena to join her. She did, and Yolanda dropped her leaves into a waiting mortar. She held it out to Serena. "Now spit," she instructed.

Serena spat into the mortar, feeling silly, but Yolanda seemed satisfied and pointed to a patch of dirt inside the pentagram. "Grab a handful of the blood and dirt and add it to the mixture." Serena bent beside the pentagram with unease and scooped a handful of red earth, wondering if it truly was made from blood, but not wanting to ask in case it was. She returned to her place beside Yolanda and accepted her outstretched mortar.

Yolanda's sharp eyes tracked her movement, missing nothing. "Now repeat after me, girl, and chant these words.

"*With an herb,*
birthed from the earth.
And the spit from a witch.

*Extract poison from
the bite of a bitch."*

Serena repeated each line of Yolanda's spell, the words feeling familiar on her tongue, as though they were the words of a song she used to know and love, though logically she knew she'd never heard anything like it before.

"Good," Yolanda grunted. "Now grind the mixture and say the spell three times, spitting after you complete each chant."

Serena inhaled a bracing breath before she chanted the spell, grinding the mugwort and spitting until it formed a clay. Yolanda took a piece of ivy from a tree and twisted it around the charcoal pencils shoved in Serena's bun, then her long fingers gently pulled the neckline of Serena's shirt down to expose the festering bite on her neck.

"Gather the clay and place it over the bite, making the symbol of the pentagram. As you do, keep chanting the spell and imagine the bite closing its vile wounds, sealing the darkness from your skin forever."

"What's the ivy for?" Serena asked softly, her eyes closed.

Her voice was a hoarse whisper as she placed her bony hands on Serena's shoulders. "To entwine our magic. The plants are my magical instruments, and the pencils are yours."

Serena gathered a handful of clay and shivered as she remembered the feel of Alice's teeth on her flesh as she broke her skin, the sharp pain of poison as it entered her veins, traveling through her blood. Carefully, Serena rubbed the clay on her tender skin, drawing a pentagram with her fingertip as she chanted the strange spell once again.

"Use your mind's eye to visualize the wound closing," Yolanda breathed. "See it, girl. See it, and it shall be. Say it, and it shall close."

The clay soothed her tainted flesh, and a warmth came upon her skin as she concentrated on the bite's poison departing from her body. Three times she chanted the spell, and with each chant the wound sealed itself. Serena blinked, feeling the skin knit back together underneath her probing fingers.

Yolanda plucked seven stems of heather and handed them to Serena. "Wipe the clay off your skin using these heather flowers."

Serena brushed off the clay with the seven heather stems. She ran her finger over the area where the bite once was. Only soft pink flesh remained.

"It worked," Serena whispered.

"Of course, it did!" Yolanda huffed as she settled beside Serena on the bench and pulled her skirts around herself. "This is just the beginning of your abilities, girl. You have much to learn, but you have the gift. And like all gifts, yours will emerge stronger in time."

Yolanda handed Serena a thick black leather book, a crescent moon engraved on the cover. "This is a Book of Shadows. It belonged to your grandmother. I took it after her death and kept it safe all these years. It's yours now."

Serena cradled the strange book in her arms, emotional about this new connection to a grandmother she'd never known. She gazed down at the leatherbound cover.

"The first half of the book contains instructions for the making of amulets, as well as incantations and even invocations, which are used to invoke someone or something. Edith added all her spells in these pages during her life as a green witch," Yolanda told her, her eyes soft. "You will use this book as a reference guide to practice your magical abilities. You'll find everything from simple love spells to growing life from a dead flower, to some of the most powerful protection spells I can offer you. Read it, and learn it. Then make it your own. Edith's spells may guide you, but only you can make them your own."

Serena rubbed her fingers with reverence over the crescent symbol. It was warm, as if it were alive with the life force of her grandmother emanating from the book. She carefully flipped through the first pages, inhaling the aroma of magic from the paper inside. It was a pungent smell of patchouli and cedar. Serena read the first page out loud.

"A sprig of rosemary tucked under your pillow will show you the face of your enemy in a dream. Washing with black soap will pure your body of any impurities and repel curses placed by other witches. Nail the shadow of a witch to the ground with an iron nail to trap her where she stands and prevent her from following you home. Paint a mirror black to see your enemy's weakness and spin around three times under a full moon holding the mirror to have it shown to you." Serena's eyes grew wide at the wealth of knowledge before her.

"A Book of Shadows is a magical tool to be practiced by the witch it is given to. You will collect spells you learn from others, as well as create your own. A Book of Shadows catalogs one's magical journey as a witch.

That sketchpad of yours—you have already begun your own Book of Shadows, even if you didn't realize what you were doing. Magic will find a way to make itself known to those it seeks. You may decorate the pages with the herbs you will use to cast spells, or even drip candle wax onto the pages from spells you have performed."

Her cool fingers wrapped around Serena's hand, turning it over palm up. "I should have known when I saw you on my porch. I sense the gift of art in you. Your ring finger is longer than your middle finger, a classic trademark of an etching witch. Use your talents to record drawings of what you have seen and add them to this book. Include within these pages all ritual tools that aid you in performing magic."

Serena squeezed Yolanda's hand before letting go to run her fingertips over the crisp pages. Black ink swirled in her grandmother's looping handwriting, and she studied the pages, seeing her grandmother's life played out before her, from her first spell as a young girl to the most complicated spell of binding Alice Lake inside her Devil Tree.

Yolanda bustled about the courtyard again, plucking leaves from one place and sprinkling some elsewhere. She lifted a pouch from a basket on a shelf and circled Serena, sprinkling salt as she slowly closed Serena within its center.

"You are far too powerful to be so unprotected at the moment. I am going to leave you inside this circle to connect with the Book of Shadows. Read Edith's life through her spells. You will hear her voice inside the pages as you do. When a witch records her memories inside her Book of Shadows, she is not only writing spells but transferring her soul into the book, preserving her magic for all time."

Tears pricked behind Serena's eyes, overwhelmed with emotion. "I'll hear her voice?" she creaked.

Yolanda's eyes were kind. "Yes, my girl," she said. "You will hear your grandmother. Once you read her words, you will obtain all the spells as your own. You will know each spell by heart and be able to recite them without effort. This is how we share our gifts, our knowledge from generation to generation. She never lost hope that this book would be passed on."

Yolanda's voice grew thick with emotion. "Edith mourned her daughter turning her back on her witching heritage, but she never lost hope. Now I see, child, that you were her hope. To make this book your own, you must open the Book of Shadows to its first blank page, then take a drop of your blood and write, 'My name is Serena Korwin, and this is my Book of Shadows.' Then your grandmother's spells will be your spells."

"But my last name is Bancroft, not Korwin," she whispered.

"No, it isn't," Yolanda insisted. "Claim your book. Claim your heritage. Claim your name in blood."

"My blood?" Serena's voice wavered, uneasy as if Yolanda were asking her to slit her throat. She had never cut herself on purpose before, and felt queasy at the idea of using her own blood to write her name.

"All deep magic begins with a piece of self, girl. For this book to contain your life force, it must hold a bit of you. Blood is the sacred tool of a witch. It's just a drop, not a sacrifice of an animal or a slitting of one's wrist, but merely a drop from your pointer finger on your working hand. Use your charcoal pencil to swirl in the blood and write your name. No magic we perform will ever require a live sacrifice, nor do we inflict pain or harm on any living creature. That is not our way."

Yolanda slipped a pin from her pocket and held it out to Serena. "Are you ready? This blood sacrifice must be freely given. I cannot do it for you." Serena stared at the sharp pin held between Yolanda's long, bony fingers. With a shaking hand, she took the pin from her.

"Very good." Yolanda nodded with satisfaction and abruptly stood. "Nothing more but a prick is required. No pain. I'll leave you to read the book, and if you choose to follow the path of a hereditary witch, then you will write your name within its pages. I'll know when it is done." Yolanda walked into her house, shutting the door behind her.

Serena sat inside the circle of salt, her grandmother's book open in her lap. She flipped it to the first page, and read voraciously, consuming the words like flames consuming a log on a fire. She devoured each spell, internalizing the words as if she already knew them and the page was merely a reminder.

She came from a long line of witches whose blood bled so red it looked black. Words and incantations flowed like water over her, soothing and strengthening her. It was as if each spell was always a part of her, and that she herself had conjured the words and recorded them on the pages, not Edith. She flipped pages, reading spells as if she were reading the autobiography of her grandmother's life. As she read, she saw in her mind's eye her grandmother pregnant with her mother. She witnessed Edith fighting off Alice Lake and binding her within the tree. Moreover, she saw herself in each spell, where she would trace and twist her own magic, her own lines, her own drawings and power in each page.

As she read, she saw. And as she saw, she understood. She saw everything that had ever happened to Edith from the day she became a witch and wrote her name in the Book of Shadows. Serena inhaled the aroma of magic from each dried herb and sprig of flowers pressed onto the parchment. She found strength from her lineage, for she was a part of a strong line of women who could speak to the animals, command the weather to change at their will and light an unlit candle with a delicate blow from their lips. Finally, she came to the first blank page, knowing it marked the end of Edith's knowledge just as surely as the blank page signaled her grandmother's death.

With no hesitancy at all, Serena lifted the sharp pin to her finger and pricked it. A shining drop of deep red blood welled from the mark, and Serena dropped it onto the page and pulled a pencil from her hair. *My name is Serena Korwin and this is my Book of Shadows*, she scrawled through the blood, mixing her blood with the charcoal and crisp paper. Just as she completed the line, a warm wealth of power prickled up her fingertips and down her arms until her entire body tingled with intoxicating strength from head to toe.

Suddenly the birds were louder in the trees, the windchimes more melodious and the chattering waters of Lake Conjure sang, just for her. *Sister*, Serena felt the waters whisper to her. *Sister*, the soft voices of all the witches who came before sang in the lapping waters. Now it was Serena's turn, and unlike her mother, Serena discovered that she desired to be a witch. She felt a longing for the calling, and coveted the delicious taste of witchcraft and all the abilities that came with it. *Yes*, she thought. *I hear you, sisters.*

As if Yolanda had heard the waters whispering as well, the purple door opened and Yolanda descended the stairs, a true smile turning her face into something almost lovely, but not quite. She walked to the far end of the garden, standing in front of the tallest tree where twisty vines grew around the trunk, climbing up to the very top. A glass bottle hung off a vine, filled with herbs and salt.

Serena scanned the trees, noticing more bottles hanging overhead. She somehow knew that each was filled with different properties from nature. Some had spices, salt and sugar, while others had dried herbs and twigs from a hazel tree. The bottles spoke to Serena, singing of love, health, prosperity, peace, happiness and good fortune. With newfound knowledge, Serena felt each positive emotion the bottles held within. She eyed the beauty of their layers inside the glass spheres. Salt sat at the bottom for protection, topped with rose petals for love, juniper berries for health, poppy seeds for prosperity, lavender for peace, oregano for happiness and bay leaves for good fortune. A final layer of sugar rested on top before the cork was added and sealed with white wax. The bottles whispered their well-wishes as they clinked and swung in the tree branches.

Yolanda's eyes followed Serena's gaze. "Those are seven blessing bottles," she said as she gestured to the dancing orbs. "A witch bottle only we can make. Inside lay fundamental ingredients for witches like us. They are taken from nature to bring forth positive energy from the earth and into our homes and lives. The ones I intend for my home are buried in this ground to grow and spread like a seed of blessing." She gestured to the ground around them, then pointed up at the bottles in the trees. "I keep these in the trees for those who come seeking my help. A wife who has a cheating husband, a child who is ill, a husband who lost his job, a daughter with a broken heart. These bottles are intended for those souls."

Serena eyed the clanking orbs. They each overflowed with love and kindness, an extension of the welcome kindness Yolanda extended to those who graced her door. But one bottle in particular caught Serena's eye. Unlike the others, it didn't sparkle and swing. Instead, the branch it was attached to bowed under its weight, as though it were a heavy burden.

Yolanda reached up and grabbed the odd bottle sealed with black wax. She held it up to Serena to see that its contents were unlike the others. A yellow liquid sat at the bottom alongside rusty nails and razor blades. She held it between her fingertips, as if it were a diseased and disgusting thing. "This witch bottle is what you must make. It will keep you protected from Alice Lake. You must gather these items and place them inside a jar of your own from your grandmother's greenhouse."

She held the bottle up so Serena could better see the ingredients inside. "Write this down, girl, on the second blank page in the Book of Shadows. You'll need to remember the instructions I'm about to tell you."

Serena dutifully slid a pencil from her bun and held it expectantly over the blank page. Yolanda shook her head. "Pen. Black ink."

Serena quirked her lips as she threaded the pencil back into her hair and rooted around her messy blonde bun for a pen. She pulled one out and held it up with a flourish to her great-aunt.

Yolanda nodded in satisfaction. "Impressive. First, you draw a pentagram on a white piece of paper with black ink. Then place your jar on top of the pentagram as you add each ingredient. You getting this, girl?" Serena nodded as she furiously copied down Yolanda's instructions. "You must include ten razor blades, a piece of broken glass, rose thorns from one rose, three bent and rusty nails, a tablespoon of sea salt, one egg yolk, rowanwood berries from a mountain ash tree and three drops of your blood pricked from your finger from a thorn of a rose. And, last but not least, fill the jar up with your own piss."

Serena suppressed a shudder as she imagined pissing into a mason jar and hanging it from a tree. *Nothing to see here, Ashton!* she imagined herself saying. *Just hanging up very normal jars of my own urine in this tree over here. Very normal girlfriend stuff.*

Yolanda snorted at Serena's expression. "Ha. You thought magic was all beauty and glamor, girl? It's not. Magic requires a bit of oneself to fight off the evil of another. Blood and urine are required to transform this bottle into a vessel of protection for you and your home. After you seal the bottle, light a black candle and drip its wax onto the lid as you chant this spell." Serena readied her pen as Yolanda's sonorous voice filled her small courtyard.

> *"With nails and razors, and broken glass,*
> *I collect these to cast...*
> *With thorns of pain and blood that spills,*
> *a spell to make out of free will.*
> *From salt of the earth, and yoke of the unborn,*

that no mother will ever mourn.
I take berries from an ash tree
and urine from my own
to claim protection in my land and home."

Serena shuddered as the wind picked up in the trees, and the branches waved as if they too felt the strength of Yolanda's spell. Ignoring the gust of wind, Yolanda continued her instructions. "Once the candle is spent, take the witch bottle and bury it under the crab apple tree. To seal the protection, draw a circle with salt around the perimeter of the tree, just as I have done to you where you stand. This will contain Alice and her raven specter inside the tree circle and prevent Alice from harming you and Jack for the time being. Cast a line of salt along the doorways outside of your house. Make sure you do every door. As you do this, speak the protection spell and visualize a magical seal forming in the salt." She paused, thinking. "Listen to the voice inside of you, girl. Perhaps mark each door. The power inside of you wants to serve you, but it needs direction."

Serena took furious notes. She trusted her great-aunt — they were blood, sisters born from one mother, the mother of witchcraft. Serena could be just like Yolanda. All she had to do was learn from her.

Yolanda craned her neck to face the sun as it traveled to the west, then turned to watch Serena's boat bob in the sunlit waters. "Perform the spell tonight before the moon is full in the sky. It will be enough to keep you safe until you can visit me again. We have much to prepare for, and very little time. But now you need to be on your way. Gather your supplies. You'll find most of these items in your boathouse, but for some ingredients you may have to travel into the woods." Serena started to open her mouth, but Yolanda held up a finger to interrupt. "I am not allowed to collect the ingredients for you. It is more powerful when the witch herself seeks the items and creates the jar alone."

Yolanda reached out to touch her niece's cheek. She saw her sister's features in Serena's pretty face, her expression innocent, afraid, young and eager. Yolanda remembered those days in her own eyes when she first became a witch, and she pulled Serena into a hug. "You will overcome Alice Lake, and I will be at your side every step of the way, girl. You are no longer alone. I promise you."

Serena took her aunt's hand in hers, the power inside her crackling in answer to that which flowed in her great-aunt. She sensed truth from Yolanda's words and welcomed the love that came with her aunt's touch. As Serena turned to trek down to her kayak, Yolanda held up her hand to Serena. "Wait! I have one more thing for you! I'll meet you at the dock."

Yolanda ran inside her house and Serena wondered what was so important. She watched as Yolanda lifted her skirts, running to meet Serena by the stream, swift for a woman her age. Serena settled into her seat, placing her tote bag full of her sketchpad, Book of Shadows and some herbs between her knees.

She reached up to take whatever Yolanda held in her outstretched hand. Serena turned it over, exposing a knotted piece of rope. "Give this to Jack," Yolanda instructed. "Tie it around his neck and make sure it does not come off him. Ever."

Serena closed her hand around the knot of rope, and a vision swam behind her closed eyes, a memory that did not belong to her. A woman was hanging by a noose from a tree. Blood had stained her clothes, turning everything from white to red to black. Her crimson boots swayed back and forth in the grim air. The woman in her vision slowly raised her head, which hung at an awkward angle from her body. Broken. Her neck was broken. But the woman was alive. The blue eyes of the woman locked on Serena and she released a maddening scream as the rope broke, freeing the woman from her death.

Serena's neck snapped back, and she stumbled backward, almost tipping over the side of the kayak. She gasped as her eyes flew open. Yolanda nodded. "You saw her." She bent down toward Serena. "So you know this is a piece of Alice Lake's hanging rope. Keep it on Jack and the raven won't be able to harm him."

Shaking, Serena dropped the length of rope into her tote bag. "Th-Thank you, Aunt Yolanda. I don't know what I'd do without you."

"You'd die, and so would your brother," said Yolanda gruffly. "So let's make sure that doesn't happen. You're not alone anymore, Serena. You have me. And all the witches who came before us. Be smart, and be safe."

* * * *

Yolanda watched as Serena pushed off from the shore and paddled her way through the stream until her figure was obscured from the tall trees guiding her home.

When Serena was a small smudge in the distance, a memory floated unbidden to the front of Yolanda's mind. She remembered when her mother brought her and Edith to their witch garden for the first time.

Yolanda and Edith were consumed by the promise of magic, two small girls eager to develop their skills. Ever since Yolanda could remember, her mother had performed magic, entering their garden during the witching hour to cast her most powerful spells. Edith and Yolanda would sneak out of their room and watch their mother behind a sycamore tree, their eyes locked on her, their hands placed over their mouths to ensure they were silent.

Edith would whisper to her sister, *"That will be us someday. We will be witches."* In her mind's eye, Yolanda saw the first time she stood side by side with her sister, two witches calling forth powers of the earth. The night bowed to them as they held hands, chanting their first spell. She heard the flutter of a Luna moth's wings as it flew above them, its lime wings glowing in the dark sky like fairy lights.

Yolanda opened her hand, welcoming the Luna moth to land on her. She held the moth delicately, feeling its life force tickle her palm. For seven nights, the moth stayed in the garden, waiting for Yolanda. For seven nights, the moth flew into her palm and stayed with her as she practiced spells, whispering a song only Yolanda could hear. On the seventh night the moth died in her hand.

Yolanda had cried over the death of the Luna moth. It was her first lesson that all things must end, and her first experience with having a familiar. Yolanda preserved the lime-green wings inside her Book of Shadows next to her first spell as a way to honor all things pure and beautiful, a tribute to the cycle of life. And to remind her never to take a life.

From time to time, Yolanda would still open her book to that page with the lime-green wings that matched her own eye color. The years had turned Yolanda's memory, and she no longer knew which came first, the Luna moth familiar or her bright green eyes. She'd wondered if perhaps the moth chose her because her eyes shared the same color of the Luna moth's wings, a softly glowing green that could open secrets to life's mysteries.

She wondered what Serena would call to herself, and just what mysteries would be revealed, and she worried for the girl, and whatever fate lay before her. But mostly, she just wanted another cup of tea. So Yolanda tromped back up the steps of her home and slammed her purple door behind her.

Chapter Nine

Light of White

Serena paddled her way downstream, allowing the current to carry her. She craned her neck to get one last look at the cottage. It no longer felt strange, but familiar, as if she had visited it a hundred times in a hundred different lives. Serena leaned back in her kayak to watch the sun sparkle through the trees. Even the forest looked altered. She could hear the crawling of a beetle hiding in a single blade of grass, and feel the beating of a cardinal's wings as it flew above. Her senses had enhanced, connecting her to nature around her. She felt alive, as if there were a lightning storm crackling through her veins.

Jack sat beside Deaken on a bench by the boathouse as Serena coasted her kayak up beside them. Tinker barked as Jack leaped up to meet her. He wore a serious expression behind his smudged glasses.

Serena pulled ashore just in time for Jack to throw his thin arms around her. "Hi, Jack!" Serena said brightly. "Did you catch me any fish?"

"I did, but I let them all go." His words were muffled, his face still pressed into Serena's middle. She raised her eyebrows in surprise. "I couldn't kill them," Jack confessed. "They looked so helpless, flopping inside the bucket. It just didn't seem right to take their life, even if they are just fish."

Deaken cleared his throat as he came up behind them. "The boy's got a tender heart. He's going to be a vegetarian now." Serena looked up at Deaken, surprised by the soft expression on his face as he gazed down at Jack. "Since he can't kill his own food, he also decided to give up meat and become a vegetarian." Deaken adjusted his hat and spit a plug of tobacco on the ground. "It's a good philosophy in my opinion."

Serena brushed her brother's hair from his face. If Deaken was being sweet to Jack, then she'd overlook the tobacco spitting. "Then we shall both be vegetarians together," she said with a soft smile. "I couldn't kill my own food, either." She looked up, catching Deaken's good eye. "Thank you, Deaken, for watching Jack this morning."

"Weren't nothing," he grunted, looking away. "Did you find the visit helpful?"

Serena reached into the kayak, pulling out a bag of blueberries she'd stopped to pick along the banks of Conjure Lake. "Look what I found, Jack. A wild blueberry bush in the woods. I collected some for you. Why don't you take them inside and rinse them off?"

With eager hands Jack snatched the blueberries. "Wild blueberries have twice the antioxidants of farmed blueberries," he said before racing up to the cottage with Tinker barking behind him. Serena again reached inside the kayak, this time taking out her tote bag with her sketchbook and Book of Shadows.

"The visit was more helpful than you'll ever know, Deaken," she said as she tucked the bag underneath her arm.

"So you are a witch." He grunted, nodding as if this confirmed his suspicions. "Like your grandmother before you."

Serena huffed a laugh, taken aback by Deaken's words. "I am, it seems," she confessed. "I never would have known if it hadn't been for your help." Serena straightened her shoulders with a new confidence racing through her. "I will deal with Alice Lake and that tree, but first I have some preparing to do. Thank you again, Deaken. I wouldn't have been able to do this without you. The Wise Woman gave me more than just wisdom today, and I don't think I'll ever be the same."

With a quick nod, Deaken turned on his heel and stomped over to his truck, climbing in and slamming the door behind him. Serena chuckled. She had been so wrong about Deaken when they'd first met. Truly, he'd been nothing but helpful.

As he started up the engine, a thought came to Serena. "Hey, Deaken," she called out. He rolled down his window. "How is Ashton connected to my family?"

Deaken removed his hands from the steering wheel and turned his face toward Serena. "Her momma died from cancer, but not before she went to see the Wise Woman." Deaken spat tobacco out his window. It landed with a splatter on a rock. "But she was turned away and died three days later."

Serena nodded, thinking of how Deaken hadn't been much younger than she was when he had stood on Aunt Yolanda's porch asking for help. She was silent as she watched Deaken's truck disappear down the long road in a cloud of dust. Serena wondered how many times over the decades had Deaken made the trek up and down her drive. In some ways, Korwin Cottage seemed to belong to Deaken as much as it did to her and Jack.

Serena intentionally turned her back to the blighted tree in her yard as she slipped her Book of Shadows from her bag and opened it to the protective witch bottle spell. "Right," she said aloud to herself. "I need to gather these ingredients, and some of the items should be in the boathouse." Serena paced to the boathouse, opening cabinets and rummaging through drawers. The boathouse was as meticulously clean as the house, and she marveled again at Deaken's level of care for the estate. She found a couple of old coffee containers. One tin contained a box of razor blades along with a box cutter. Serena slipped the coffee tin into her tote bag as she ran her hand along the side of the boathouse. Three rusty nails stuck out as old hooks to hang lifejackets. Serena grabbed a hammer off the shelf and used the end to pull out the three nails. She dropped them into the waiting coffee tin and checked her list. "I still need a piece of broken glass." She got on her knees and inspected the far end of the boathouse, where a new window had been replaced. She looked behind a set of cabinets and found a tiny piece of broken glass that Deaken must have missed. "Perfect," she said as she dropped the glass into the tin.

"The egg yolk and salt I can get from the kitchen, but I will still need thorns from a single rose, and rowanwood berries from a mountain ash tree," she said in a long breath. Serena walked out of the boathouse and stared into the woods, wary of attacking ravens, but the trees stood silent and dark. "I'll have to explore the woods for the rowanwood berries." Serena looked inside her Book of Shadows. Her grandmother had glued three rowanwood berries on one page inside. Serena snapped it shut and dropped it into her bag. "The tree can't be far. Nan used fresh berries for a spell. Hopefully the tree is close by."

Serena walked to the side of the cottage where a white climbing rose bush grew tall and feral up the cottage walls. Serena took the box knife and cut a single rose from the bush, dropping it carefully into her bag. She made her way to the back door, entering the kitchen. The container of blueberries lay on the kitchen table, damp and half empty, but Jack and Tinker were nowhere in sight. Serena chuckled as she slipped the blueberries into the fridge and took out an egg. She opened her bag and began to lay out her myriad of ingredients, looking like the most unappetizing cooking show. She lined up all the items along with the salt shaker, and opened her Book of Shadows. A glimpse out of the window told her the sun had begun its descent, and she needed to have the spell completed before nightfall. She grabbed a sachet from one of the baskets by the door and called up the stairs to Jack.

"Jack, I need to go into the woods to find some rowanwood berries. I'm making a scrapbook of the plants here. Do you mind coming with me? Maybe we'll find more wild blueberries."

The thud of his feet on the stairs answered her. "Sure, I love exploring! I'll get a container from the kitchen for the blueberries." Jack shouldered past her as he raced to the kitchen, returning with an empty container and his long wooden stick.

"Are you planning on chopping down the blueberry bush with your mighty sword?" Serena teased.

He looked up at her as he pressed his glasses up the bridge of his nose. "No," he said in mock seriousness. "But I may need to defend you if we run into a dragon, fair sister. You never know when you might need a sword in the woods."

Serena giggled in full agreement. "Come along then, Sir Jack. I want to be back within a couple of hours and I'm not sure how far we have to go to find the berries."

Jack and Tinker dashed by Serena and shot into the woods. Serena followed, pausing at the edge of the tree line, reliving the moment the raven emerged from the trees. She glanced up at her bathroom window, where the glass was still marked in a spiderweb of cracks. She made a mental note to tell Deaken about the window, then she placed her hand on the bark of an evergreen, her eyes searching for the menacing raven. Unbidden, a spell from her grandmother's book rose to her lips, and the incantation spilled forth.

"If it be nearby, show me now
For I disallow.
If it be within
Let its presence be known before
I venture in."

A breeze ruffled through the trees and their branches waved as if in answer. Serena had the distinct feeling that the trees were staring back, as if they were sentinels guarding the woods. A single leaf fell from a tree, landing at her feet. Serena picked up the leaf and, on a whim, placed it on her tongue. The taste was sweet like honey, and Ashton's kind face rose in her mind. Serena wondered if Ashton knew about the raven, Alice Lake or the curse. She closed her eyes, wanting to believe that Ashton didn't know, that she wasn't keeping secrets from her. But what she feared more was that Ashton already knew about the mysterious nature of Korwin Cottage, and didn't care about Serena or Jack enough to protect them or even to warn them.

Her reverie was interrupted by Jack as he ran out of the woods, sword swinging and Tinker following. Serena sighed, knowing that at least for the moment, she and Jack were safe from the raven, and that it was not in the forest waiting for them. *It's safe, at least for the time being, but I must be quick. The raven can appear at any time.*

Jack swatted some tall grass with his makeshift sword. "Are you ready to explore the great unknown?" he asked his sister.

"Lead the way, kind sir," Serena teased. "But first allow this lady to give her knight a favor." Serena reached into her tote bag and pulled out the length of rope that Aunt Yolanda had given her. She knelt down in front of her brother. "I want you to wear this, Sir Jack." Serena's face twisted in concern as she reached her hands around her brother's neck. "It looks silly, I know, but let's pretend it's a hood of mail covered in nails." Serena tied the rope around Jack's neck and muttered a low spell as she did.

> *"Keep him protected*
> *Keep him safe*
> *Unaffected by*
> *Alice Lake."*

Jack ran his fingers over the rope and cocked his head at his sister. "I read that knights wore coifs that had metal hoods as well."

Serena laughed as she leaned over to pinch him. "And knights usually have metal swords, too, but we will work with what we've got." Serena leaned over and kissed the top of his blond hair.

Jack drew back, his dark eyes serious behind his smudged glasses. "I love you, Sissy. If you want me to wear a ratty bit of rope, then I will."

Emotion welled up in Serena's chest, and she reached out to clean Jack's glasses. She handed them back, and Serena and Jack held hands as they ventured into the woods together. The afternoon sun cascaded through the trees, dancing on their faces like gold dust, and it served as a reminder to Serena that time was against them. The grass grew wild, reaching up to their knees. Serena was thankful Jack brought his sword to chop down a path as they walked, Tinker following at their heels. The ground turned to mud beneath their feet and soon they came to a creek.

"It's the creek I told you about!" Jack exclaimed excitedly. He pointed his makeshift sword upstream. "Can we follow it?"

Serena shielded her eyes as she peered upstream to where the creek carved its way through the woods. "Sure, Sir Jack. Just keep your eyes open for a small tree with orange and yellow berries."

He jumped over a log and swatted a low-hanging branch. "Sir Jack to the rescue." He swiped a nearby fern. "Sir Jack to save the day."

"Okay." Serena chuckled. "Lead the way, Sir Jack."

The creek wound around a tight bend, and Serena noticed two fallen trees that formed an arch in the shape of an X in the middle of the creek. Something about it disturbed Serena, and she shivered. Unease crept over her, and the hairs on the back of her neck rose, as if she were being watched.

For some reason the trees frightened her, and she felt the prickling sensation of what could only be the magic inside her, welling up in warning. An ominous sensation came over Serena as she wondered how long those dead trees had been standing there, guarding the entrance to the creek. Jack was busy running ahead, Tinker trailing at his side. Serena opened her mouth to call him back, but no words came to her. She placed each foot carefully, using her newly uncovered senses to feel what she couldn't see or hear.

They continued down the path, using the water to lead them. More fallen trees stuck out of the creek. The day had been clear and lovely, though now an obscure cloud passed over the sun, casting a dark shadow over the ground. Serena quivered as the warmth of the day leached from her body. She jolted as a deer leapt over a fallen tree and slowed as it approached the stream.

"Look at that, Jack," Serena whispered. Jack turned to watch, enchanted. Even Tinker seemed to hold her breath. The deer, a doe, had stopped at the edge of the creek, bending her delicate head into the water for a quick drink. Jack sank to the ground and wrapped his arms around Tinker to keep her quiet. A spell had fallen over them, and Serena's hand fell to Jack's shoulder as they gazed at the majestic deer. As if she felt the weight of their eyes, the deer raised her head in their direction, her ears pointed straight up. She was so close that Serena could see the deer's tongue licking the beads of water off her lip. The deer cocked her head, unafraid of the humans before her.

"She can sense we are not a threat," she whispered in Jack's ear.

He nodded in agreement. A wave of something passed over Serena, an unknowable sense, and she understood instinctively it was her newly awakened witching power, calling out to the deer. Her ear twitched in answer, as if she sensed the wave of Serena's power. The doe took a step forward in their direction. Serena held her breath as she held out her hand. The deer's warm, wet dark eyes met Serena's own dark gaze, and she took a careful step toward them. Gently, carefully, the deer placed one cloven hoof down, then the other. The sense welled in Serena's chest as the deer came closer, and her nose met her outstretched hand.

A dark cloud rolled over the sun, causing the sky to turn black. The deer looked up in a panic, her ears turning in all directions. The deer craned her head toward a whistling sound behind them, her stance now alert.

Too late, Serena wondered if a storm was coming, and looked for a place to find shelter. But it wasn't a storm—something else was coming. A giant shadow swooped down on the deer, encompassing the animal in darkness. The deer shot off into the forest, leaving the shadow behind. Serena looked up, the dread in her stomach already telling her what she would see. The raven hovered above them in the sky, its body silhouetted in the cloud-covered sun.

Serena bared her teeth as she reached down to grab a rock on the banks of the creek and hurled it at the monstrous bird. "Get away!" she screamed as it cawed and circled. The menacing bird flapped its wings before darting off into the grove of trees, taking the darkness with it. Serena stared at the now sunny sky, watching as the clouds receded from the sun, like blood seeping from a wound, allowing light to shine down once again. Jack reached for her hand as Serena squeezed her eyes shut. He watched her carefully, looking up at the now bright sky, and back at his sister worriedly. Feelings of haste washed over her, and Serena knew it was her witching sense speaking to her. They had to hurry. The raven would return. It was just toying with them, letting Serena know it was watching her. Shaking, Serena slowed her breathing into long, even draws.

Jack turned to face his sister. "You all right, Serena?" He tilted his head, examining his sister's blank face. "It was only storm clouds. They're gone now."

Serena took her attention off the sky and focused on her brother. His dark eyes were worried behind his smudged glasses, and his hand gripped hers tightly. She willed her face into a sincere smile and commanded herself not to be afraid of Alice Lake in any form. She squeezed her brother's hand. Looking ahead, she wondered how far they should venture.

"Do you want to go a little farther down? I'd like to find those berries today if we can." Jack nodded as he swung his makeshift sword at the high grass to clear them a path, the earlier lightness of the afternoon forgotten.

In silence, they walked side by side as the creek twisted around another bend, Tinker keeping so close to Jack he nearly tripped with every other step. More obstacles lay in the water—fallen and twisted tree branches broke the surface of the water like crooked arms reaching up to grab them. Serena felt the branches move, inching their way to her on the shore like long-jointed fingers. An old crumbling stone bridge stood ahead inside the creek with three oval openings underneath, each leading further into the unknown.

Serena stepped into the water, curious about the bridge's presence, and reached out with her witching senses. Strong magic was here—other magic, both familiar and foreign, like fruit that had once been sweet but had long since rotted and turned black. Her blood called in answer, and her heart raced in response, sensing the wrongness. The water came up to her calves. It was cool and murky against her skin and her foot sank to the bottom into a bed of weeds and mud. The siblings walked toward the tallest opening in the center of the stone bridge. Jack stopped to examine the stone walls.

"There are markings here, Serena." Jack reached for the cold walls, tracing his finger along the symbols. "They look tribal, like something from another time. Like hieroglyphics from the Egyptians. This one is an X with a diamond above it." Jack looked over at his sister, whose eyes were wide and dark. "What do you think they mean?"

Before Serena could answer, Jack jerked as if he were ripped back by an unseen hand. He tumbled into the creek, and the water turned dark and churning, as if it were boiling. He stumbled to his feet in the swirling water and gripped the stone bridge for support just as enormous spiders poured impossibly from the arching bridge's etchings and covered his hand and arm. He screamed, slinging the spiders into the raging waters as they swirled around him, and he stumbled.

A scream froze in her throat, and Serena splashed into the water, knowing instinctively that if Jack fell under the surface of the dark and churning waters, he would never resurface. Like a wave, more spiders poured forth from the carvings of the bridge and were swept away by the furious current.

"Don't touch the bridge, Jack! There's a horde of spiders in here!" Jack shivered as he stumbled again, and Serena reached him just before he slipped under the water's surface. She hauled him up in her arms, the water clutching him as if it didn't want to let him go. Spiders crawled from Jack onto Serena, and he whimpered in her arms as they crawled up her neck and into her hair. Clenching her teeth to stave off the panic, she gripped Jack in her arms, knowing he detested spiders more than anything, that their creepy long legs and hairy bodies always made his skin crawl with fear. Tinker barked wildly from the banks as Serena hauled her brother to the water's edge. "It's all right, Jack, just close your eyes. I've got you. Hang onto me and I'll walk us out of here. The spiders can't touch us if we are in the water away from the walls of the bridge."

Jack closed his eyes, shaking as he clung to Serena.

Serena fell to her knees as she hit the banks of the water and collapsed beside her brother. Struggling to catch her breath, she eyed the symbols on the wall of the stone bridge. The signs were intended to harm any intruder who came upon the arching bridge, to protect Alice Lake. Her spirit still controls this area and the nightmarish creatures within. Jack lay on the banks of the river, trying to catch his breath as he sobbed. Tinker licked his face.

"Stay here, Jack," Serena breathed. On wavering feet she stood and pressed determinedly into the water again. She approached the bridge, and with a bracing breath she stepped beneath its tallest arch. Stepping underneath the bridge was like switching off the sunlight, and her witching senses tingled as bright and shining figures appeared underneath the old stone bridge. Pressing out her senses, she felt the sinister marks that poisoned the underside of the bridge, making it something menacing and twisted. Serena plunged on, her eyes marking all of the symbols in the tunnel-like underside of the bridge. At the end was a gigantic spider web. Serena felt around her feet underneath the water and pulled out a large stick. She jabbed the stick at the web, trying to tear it down, but its thickness reacted like armor. Serena frantically pulled on the web as a group of spiders raced toward her stick to swarm her arm. She broke off a portion of the web, but the center was still intact.

A spider jumped on her stick, rushing down the base to leap onto her shaking fingers. Serena frantically scooped up the web in one pull of her stick as a mass of spiders clung onto their home. She dropped the fragile twig under the water, lifting it out and dunking it back in. Jack whimpered from the banks, his arm around Tinker, shaking as his sister battled the horde of spiders in the dark, racing against their strength and speed to submerge them under the water. They floated on the surface of the water and attempted to climb her, but the current swept them away. Serena dropped the waterlogged stick in the water along with the spiders she'd drowned.

Breathless, she looked around the tunnel, then stood perfectly still and closed her eyes, searching into the bottom of the water, the top of the stone walls and inside every nook and cranny. Satisfied, she finally opened her eyes, confident there were no survivors. The malevolent force she'd felt before eased.

She felt as though she were a hundred years old as she slogged her way out of the waters to where Jack stood, wet and trembling. She wrapped her arm around Jack's shoulder as they made their way out of the tunnel, her hands shaking.

"I'm sorry, Jack. I should have known there might be spiders in the tunnel. We won't go through it ever again, I promise."

"I think I'd like to just stay on the grass from now on, Serena." His voice shook.

"It's a deal." Serena looked around the woods. "We'll go just a little farther, and if we don't find the rowan berries soon, we can turn around and go home. Sounds good to you?" She hugged her brother to her. "You are so brave, my strong knight."

"I'm not a brave knight." His voice quivered. "I'm scared."

"That's why you are brave," Serena whispered in his ear as she hugged him close. "If you aren't afraid, then you aren't brave. Only those with courage can overcome fear."

Jack nodded, his breathing becoming measured and calm. "Then I am the bravest," he said softly.

Serena's throat felt tight. "Yes, the bravest," she whispered.

With a bracing breath, Jack looked up at her then plunged forward. "Follow me, fair maiden. I will keep you safe," he said, echoing his promise from before. He ran ahead, following a path leading further down the creek.

Still shaking, Serena called out, "Stay on the path, Jack. I'll be right behind you."

She squatted on the earth's floor, placing her palms on the ground. She closed her eyes and inhaled the surrounding forest. Words came to her.

"Guided light, show me the way.
Do not let me go astray.
Lead me to the ash tree
I call upon you
on this day."

The dirt vibrated to her touch, and a deep rumbling sound traveled toward her. She opened her eyes and saw the mountain ash tree's roots surface. She rose to her feet and followed the roots. There behind a group of thorn bushes sat the mountain ash trees, the rowanberries fully ripe. Serena quickly grabbed a handful of berries and secured them in her sachet, which she dropped into her tote bag. She mentally thanked the tree for listening to her plea and turned around to find Jack. He was no more than twenty yards ahead with Tinker close at his heels. Serena ran down the path to catch up to her brother.

The woods became thicker, creating a heavy canopy of leaves blocking out the sun, covering her in darkness. Only a few beams of light shined down on the ground to guide the way. Serena eyed the tall trees, feeling their massive presence. The woods were void of all animals, and silence rang through the forest. There wasn't a bird in the sky, nor a squirrel in a bush. She glanced back at the water. It, too, was silent and unmoving, the churning waters from before settled into a mocking stillness. Not a single croak from a frog nor a flutter of a dragonfly's wing could be heard. Nothing seemed to stir inside the water but patches of oily seaweed. Serena listened intently, hoping to hear some sound coming from nature.

She stood as still as a deer, barely breathing, her eyes closed. She imagined the woods alive with birds and foxes. She willed her surroundings to come back to life, reaching out with her witching senses, but nothing happened. Suddenly, the forest felt dead, an ominous rot of nothingness, as if the entire woods were depleted of life except for her and Jack.

Serena opened her eyes, glancing around. All she saw was darkness and the massive trees that ensnared her within their tall walls. A snapping sound echoed behind her and she spun around, expecting to see a forest animal, but there was nothing. Another snapping sound came from the opposite direction. She turned again, but still there was nothing. The silence expanded as if it were a force weighing on them, and the sky became gray, casting shadows on the ground. A fog emerged from the creek, crawling its way over the grass. Serena stepped backward as the fog reached for her. Cold fingers raked her leg, a sting of pain entered Serena's skin, and claw marks rose on the flesh of her calf. A thin line of blood streamed from the deepest mark. She took a deep, calming breath, and with her pointer finger from her working hand she drew a pentagram on her leg from the blood that seeped out of her skin in deep black drops.

"With my blood I am protected by the power of three.
I call on the witches before me.
I am a Korwin like Edith and Yolanda.
You cannot harm me!"

The cold grip on her leg disappeared, and Serena spun around, scanning the woods, searching for Jack. Shadows danced between the trees, but they were too faint to make out their image. She felt someone—or something—watching her from within the branches. She saw Jack crouched down by an elm tree, his arms wrapped around his chest. Serena stumbled over branches and ground that seemed to reach out to her, ensnaring her legs, and fell beside her brother.

"Jack, we have to go now. Another storm is coming. The sky has gone black and I think we've gone too far into the woods." Serena didn't want to tell her brother the truth, not yet, though he quivered with fear, fear she was aware her intelligent brother knew had no natural source. She didn't even know if she could ever tell him the truth. The poor boy had been through too much already. Serena had never lied to her brother before, but she felt the truth was a heavy burden he didn't deserve to carry.

Jack didn't respond. He kept his head buried in his knees. Tinker cringed between his legs, curled up in a ball.

"Jack, get up," Serena commanded as her eyes scanned the still woods for threats. "We should leave now."

Serena placed her hand on his shoulders, trying to comfort him, but Jack didn't move. Eyes glared out at them from the trees, watching them. Serena tried to pull her brother to his feet, but he was frozen. A branch cracked in the distance. Though she was loath to leave her brother, Serena walked in the direction the noise came from, pleading to herself it would only be an animal scurrying around. Nothing was there.

She turned to Jack. He was no longer sitting. He was standing, looking up at the tree in front of him. He'd extended his arm, pointing to a high branch. Serena followed his hand and there in the tree were two spheres made from twigs hanging like wind chimes. She looked closely at the spheres and gasped as she saw that inside each sphere were twig figures, one of a little boy and one of a girl, both with blond human hair. Serena grabbed Jack by the arm and ran from the elm tree, back through the woods, past the bridge.

The only sounds were their frantic breaths and the crunch of leaves beneath their feet as they sprinted out of the forest. Serena could feel the raven with them, riding on top of them, blackening the sun with its massive wings.

Serena called out to her great-aunt for help. "What do I do? How do I make it out of here?"

Yolanda's voice didn't answer, but something else did. Two bald eagles swooped down, attacking the raven. The three birds battled in the sky. Serena kept running, glimpsing their airborne battle over her shoulder. She gripped Jack's arm like a vise, doggedly pulling him forward, faster. She ran with a feverish speed that pounded into her chest, threatening to stop her heart. Two more eagles charged at the raven, plucking at its head and tearing feathers from its black wings. Serena knew instinctively that Yolanda had sent the eagles to save her, or the sister witches of the water, the ones who had drowned in Conjure Lake. Their voices and strength pushed her onward as she ran, but she had little time to escape. Non-magical birds, no matter how majestic they were, would be no match for the raven. Serena ran until her heart pounded in her ears and her legs threatened to stop moving, forcing

Jack to stumble along beside her. She kept her eyes focused on the clearing, where their cottage was coming into sight. Jack tripped, barely able to keep up. Serena helped him to his feet and willed his body to match her own speed. Jack ran beside his sister, hand in hand, and Tinker frantically followed as the cottage grew closer.

In her mind's eye Serena imagined a ball of white light surrounding the cottage, protecting the house from harm. If they could make it safely inside, they would be shielded from the raven. Serena heard two of the eagles cry as they crashed to the ground, but she did not dare look back. Every second counted, and they were almost to their cottage door. They raced to the yard and fled up the front steps, their feet thundering on the creaking wood. Serena commanded the door to open as they reached the porch and it answered, flying open just as they collapsed inside the door of the cottage. Serena kicked the door shut as she sat on the floor, chanting a spell. She held on to her vision, the ball of white light shielding the house in a bubble.

> *"Light of white,*
> *light of power.*
> *Secure us in this hour.*
> *Keep evil out and protect us within.*
> *Do not let the raven in."*

The raven crashed into the door, releasing a menacing scream. Jack and Serena cowered on the wooden floor of the entryway as they covered their ears. The sound vibrated the cottage. Again, Serena chanted the spell.

"Light of white,
light of power.
Secure us in this hour.
Keep evil out and protect us within.
Do not let the raven in."

Chapter Ten

Change Is Certain

Jack sat with his knees pressed against his chest, his eyes wide as saucers as he watched as his sister rocked back and forth, chanting the spell. The raven crashed repeatedly into the front door, its wings a cataclysm of darkness against the glass, but it couldn't break the impermeable barrier of Serena's white light encircling the cottage. Jack slowly crawled his way to Serena, repeating the words along with his sister as he wrapped his arms around her waist. Tinker crawled into his lap, and the three of them sat huddled against the onslaught of feathers and violence as the hellish bird screamed and hurled itself against the shuddering glass.

Serena took Jack's hands, forcing his panicked gaze to meet hers. "Don't look at her," Serena instructed. "Keep your eyes closed. Focus on my words and imagine the white light surrounding us, keeping us warm and safe."

Jack squeezed his eyes shut as he buried his head in Serena's arm. Over and over they chanted, each time visualizing the white light growing stronger. He huddled in his sister's lap while she stared at the frantic bird that was desperately trying to get in. With a final furious caw, the raven flew into the sky to block out the sun, its immense wings casting a heavy shadow across the house. The windows of the cottage rattled and the floorboards shook underneath their feet.

"Believe in the words, Jack," Serena whispered before she rose to her feet and pressed her hands against the door.

"Hear me now, raven," Serena commanded in a voice that was not her own. "You will not enter. Leave us and go back to the Devil Tree where your wickedness was birthed. I will not let you enter this house!"

In response, the raven renewed its scrabbling attack against the door, and a scrambled message appeared backward on the glass in a smear of blood. Jack was unable to make out the words. Serena's breath fogged the other side of the glass as she lifted her hands to press against the icy window panes of the door and repeated the chant one last time.

"Light of white,
light of power.
Secure us in this hour.
Keep evil out and protect us within.
Do not let the raven in."

A glowing light poured out of Serena's hands and spread over the porch, stretching to encircle the entire cottage. With a final, panicked caw, the raven was driven from the house and was pulled, struggling, into the heart of the cursed crab apple tree. The tree opened from its center like a gaping wound to engulf the raven, and black ooze seeped from the opening as the tree's scaly bark rejoined, closing the wound and trapping the raven inside.

Jack stared in open-mouthed wonder at his sister. She leaned back against the front door, out of breath, and Jack crawled to her side and wrapped his arms around her. Serena hugged him back. For a long moment they were quiet.

Finally, Serena spoke. "Do you want to talk about what just happened?" she asked.

Jack squeezed her almost painfully. "There isn't a book in the world that could explain what just happened," he said finally. "But I was looking for one back at the library. I had my suspicions that Conjure Lake was home to witches. I just didn't have the proof." Jack shrugged his shoulders. "Until now."

Serena touched her hand to the underside of his chin, forcing him to look at her. "I don't know how to explain it, but maybe I can show you," she said softly. Jack nodded. Serena pressed her forehead against her little brother's. Jack jerked immediately, feeling the thoughts nudge against his own. He hardly breathed as images flowed over his mind, as Serena fed her knowledge of the recent events into Jack.

In mental images that were not his own, Jack saw in his mind's eye his sister in the woods meeting their great-aunt, the Wise Woman of Conjure Lake. He saw Serena extracting the seaweed from her wrist, a spell on her lips. Jack could feel the raven as it flew into Serena, ripping hair from the top of her head. The bitter metallic taste of blood filled his mouth as Serena bit into the tainted apple. He knew of their grandmother and felt the warm and golden magical inheritance that

Serena now carried, the power of generations of witches flowing in her veins. He looked into his sister's tired eyes and inhaled her exhaustion. Without a word spoken, Jack understood the magnificent power of Conjure Lake that also flowed through his sister, the bond of their great-aunt and the sinister and malevolent force that now hunted their bloodline.

Jack drew back, his eyes serious behind his smudged glasses. "You won't have to do this alone, Serena." Jack nodded earnestly as he looked up into his sister's face. "I know what you are, and I'm going to help you fight the raven."

Serena bent her head toward her little brother as silent tears streaked her cheeks. "Jack, I'm so sorry all this is happening. But I promise you I will defeat Alice Lake. It's my job to protect you." Serena wiped her tears with the back of her hand and stared into Jack's face. "I'm going to send that raven back to hell."

Jack nodded, his fingers listless on the length of rope around his neck. "I believe you, Serena. You can do anything, and I know you can do this." Serena smiled as a tear rolled down her cheek. Jack took a deep breath before continuing. "But it's not your job to protect me. Mom and Dad left us both alone. It's up to us to look out for each other. Whatever happens, Sissy, we are in this together." Jack rose to his feet to look out of the window to Conjure Lake beyond. The wind danced through the trees as a blue heron flew to the edge of the shore. Everything had become peaceful again, as if the raven had never fought to get through their door. Silver fish broke the water's surface, jumping into the warm air, then crashed back under the waves.

Serena's chest gave a painful squeeze as she watched her serious brother silhouetted against the glass, the world wild and beautiful beyond. Life had changed so much for Jack for both of them, really. It had become a continuous calendar of tragic events over the past twelve months. And at the tender age of seven, Jack had discovered that the only certainty in life was change itself. Serena marveled at the strength in his little body, at his faith and courage. She knew Jack missed their parents, but the pain was bearable now.

He looked decades older than his mere seven years as his dark eyes took in the view, now that he was aware of the intoxicating magic and choking darkness that encompassed Korwin Cottage. With a hollowing ache, Serena thought back to how their mother Rose would enter Jack's room every night, a book in hand and her skin smelling of lemons and lavender. Not once did their mother miss a bedtime story. She always came to tuck Jack in when the moon hung low in the evening sky. She remembered how Jack always looked forward to their bedtime routine. Their mother would sit on the edge of the duvet as the stars twinkled outside his window, and she would slip her cool hand inside his small, warm one.

Sometimes their dad would wait by the bedroom door, listening as Rose read to Jack, a magical and wondrous story escaping her lips. When Rose was finished, their dad would saunter over to him with a gentle smile on his face and place a goodnight kiss upon Jack's head. Serena realized that Rose was unconsciously performing her own magic on Jack through books, a protection that had kept Jack safe and capable beyond his years. His love of books was more than just a hobby or passion—it was magic spun from the strong bloodline of Korwin woman.

Jack's spine was straight, his hands steady, his eyes fearless as he watched the world beyond. *He's right.* They had each other to lean on. Serena wasn't alone, and no matter how much she wished to protect Jack from the dangers that lurked all around them, she knew his mind was strong and his heart courageous. Serena stepped to the door and pulled him close into a side hug. In silence, they watched as the heron ducked its elegant neck into the water, resurfacing with a small silver fish. The blue heron glanced over at the cottage before taking flight into the lake. Jack wished he had wings so he could fly with the heron.

"Herons eat up to a pound of fish a day," he said absently.

Serena studied his profile. "Do you know what I am, Jack?" she whispered as they both stared through the glass.

"You are a witch," he answered, no trace of fear in his tone.

She nodded, though he wasn't looking at her. "Now that you know what I am, Jack, and what must be done, I need you to promise me you will keep our secret safe. Don't tell anyone what I am or what lives inside that tree."

Jack glanced at his shoes, biting his bottom lip. "Not even Ashton?" he asked.

"No, Jack, no one. People won't believe us, and as much as I like Ashton, I don't know if she would accept me if she knew I was a witch."

Jack crossed his arms as he turned to face his sister, his young face angry. "Then she's an idiot, because what you are is incredible."

Serena chuckled. "Jack, you are an old soul." She stroked her brother's face. "You are so wise for being only seven, wiser than most adults. You are going to grow up to be a very kind and sensitive person someday."

He nodded as he turned back to the glass. "I know," he said resolutely. He paused, thinking. "What about Deaken?" he asked. "Does Deaken know?"

Serena never failed to be impressed by her observant and intuitive brother. "Yes, Deaken knows."

Serena placed her hand on the doorknob. "Stay inside, Jack. I'll only be a moment." She opened the front door and stepped onto the porch, turning to examine the door. From this vantage point she could see the words that had appeared in a violent scrawl on the glass as the raven fought to get in. They were not English, though Serena didn't recognize the language. She heard a knocking on the glass and looked up at her brother's face behind the window pane. *Latin*, he mouthed to her through the glass.

Serena sighed. Latin. Of course her little brother would know. She sounded out the bloody words that now stained the door written in blood. *Eram quod es, eris quod sum.* Serena slipped her Book of Shadows from her ever-present tote bag and pulled a pen from her bun to jot down the Latin phrase, then paced inside to sit at the kitchen table. Her supplies for her protective charm were still laid out from before their disastrous trek through the woods. Jack slipped into the chair beside her, looking down at the book with avid interest.

"What's the matter, Serena? What did the raven write? Do you know what it means?"

She shook her head. "No, silly, I don't speak Latin. Do you?" she asked, only mildly joking. Her brother never ceased to surprise her.

He shook his head in disappointment. "I don't speak Latin yet," he said.

Serena gave a small smile at the word *yet*. Always the professor. "I'll need to research this later." She placed the book on the table, looking over at Jack. "I need to work a protection spell. The raven is only trapped for a moment, but soon it will return." Serena surveyed the ingredients she collected for the witch bottle.

"Can I stay?" Jack asked. He wanted to be with his sister, to help her, even if it was just observing her new powers.

"Of course you can." Serena nodded to an empty chair. "Just sit right there and we will do this together."

Jack sat motionless, his eyes bright and his clothes mostly dry as he watched his sister draw a pentagram on a white piece of paper. Serena placed an empty glass jar on top, following each instruction accurately. Jack remained perfectly silent, his face studious as he listened to his sister explain each of the ingredients on the table—nails, razors, broken glass, thorns from a rose, salt, yolk from an egg, berries from the ash tree and a small cup of her own urine. At that one Jack looked up at her in disbelief, and Serena blushed. "Yes, it's really my pee!" she answered. Jack howled in laughter, but made sure to keep his hands firmly in his lap.

Serena read the spell from the Book of Shadows as she placed each item inside the jar. She took out a box of matches from one of the baskets and lit a black candle.

Rebecca Henry

"Here goes nothing," she said to her brother as she threw in the three bent rusty nails. They made a clinging noise as they hit the bottom of the jar. Serena carefully handled the ten sharp razor blades, releasing them one by one inside the jar. Next, she picked up the piece of broken glass she found in the boathouse and dropped it in.

"With nails and razors, and broken glass,
I collect these to cast..."

Serena broke each of the thorns off the white rose she had collected from their trellis and placed those in next. She saved the last thorn to prick her finger so a drop of blood fell into the jar. Jack's eyes were wide as eggs, but he was silent.

"With thorns of pain and blood that spills,
a spell to make out of free will."

Serena reached for the sea salt and added a pinch to the ingredients, then added the golden yolk from an egg. She opened the sachet that held the rowan berries they'd gathered from the mountain ash tree as images of the day replayed in her mind.

"From salt of the earth,
and yolk of the unborn,
that no mother will ever mourn.
I take berries from an ash tree."

Serena looked over at Jack as she held the cup of urine in her right hand. Jack watched, spellbound.

"And urine from my own
to claim protection in my land and home."

She emptied the cup into the jar, then screwed the lid on tightly. She held the black candle over the jar, and ebony wax dripped along the edge of the lid, forming a magical seal. Serena repeated the spell as the wax continued to drip onto the bottle.

For a long moment nothing happened. Jack and Serena looked at each other. "Is it working?" Jack asked, his voice small. Suddenly, the contents inside the jar swirled together, creating a tornado, a cyclone of metal. The deeper Serena chanted, the stronger the tornado became, until it was a raging cyclone held within the small glass. Jack's lips formed the words with her in silence.

"With nails and razors, and broken glass,
I collect these to cast…
With thorns of pain and blood that spills,
a spell to make out of free will.
From salt of the earth, and yolk of the unborn,
that no mother will ever mourn.
I take berries from an ash tree
and urine from my own
to claim protection in my land and home."

The melting of the candle sped up, dripping faster onto the jar, as if time were moving ahead of them, or the candle was now burning hotter. The wax hardened around the glass, forming a protective shield around the jar, and soon Serena couldn't see the ingredients inside, only the hard black shell that now secured the witch bottle. Within seconds, the candle was spent, and its blazing light flickered out. Jack held his breath as

Serena placed both hands around the jar, her dark eyes focused as she charged the bottle with the wild energy surging through her bloodstream. She could feel heat emanating from the wax. Satisfied the spell had worked, she picked up the jar and headed out through the back door.

Jack followed close on her heels, Tinker in his arms. "What do we do now?" he asked.

"Now we get a shovel and bury it," she answered.

Jack ran ahead to the boathouse and came back, dragging the shovel along behind him. Serena passed him the bottle as she took the shovel from him and began to dig at the base of the cursed tree. He held the bottle up to the sky, examining its contents. A shadow of the ingredients inside glowed in the evening sky. "It looks like fireflies," he said in wonder.

"Not fireflies, but protection," Serena corrected him as she worked the shovel into the hard soil. She swiped at the sweat on her brow. "Once we bury the witch bottle, Alice Lake cannot harm us." Serena paused. "At least for a little while."

Jack watched her. "Want me to dig?" he asked. Serena shook her head, panting with effort. The ground was rocky and hardscrabble underneath the black and twisting crab apple tree. Motion caught her eye, and she looked up in time to see faint lights on the road at the end of Korwin Lane. She couldn't imagine who would be on the road right now. She could feel the menace emanating from the tree, and she dug in her spade with renewed effort.

Serena dug until she hit the deepest part of the tree's roots. Its black scales moved as she exposed its vulnerability, undulating like a snake. Wordlessly Jack handed his sister the witch bottle, kneeling beside her next to the fresh bed of earth. It looked like a grave. Serena charged the bottle one final time with her hands, imagining it full of strength and powerful protection before placing it in the ground. She nodded at Jack, and together they threw dirt on top of the jar. "Believe, Jack," she whispered. They chanted the spell one final time.

> *"With nails and razors, and broken glass,*
> *I collect these to cast...*
> *With thorns of pain and blood that spills,*
> *a spell to make out of free will.*
> *From salt of the earth, and yoke of the unborn,*
> *that no mother will ever mourn.*
> *I take berries from an ash tree*
> *and urine from my own*
> *to claim protection in my land and home."*

Serena patted the last bit of dirt, assuring the witch bottle was completely covered. "Do your magic and keep us safe," she whispered.

Night had come, and darkness surrounded them. The moon shined down on their faces as dark clouds drifted by. No stars shone in the sky, just the heaviness of thick clouds and the brightness of the white full moon. Jack slipped his hand into Serena's. Together they made their way back to the cottage steps. Serena walked over to the back door to retrieve a canister of salt.

"Last step," she informed Jack. "Then it should be done. You wait here."

Serena crossed the lawn and poured the salt around the tree, visualizing a sacred circle trapping Alice Lake inside. Serena stood outside the circle she had created, and Jack appeared beside her.

"I told you to wait on the porch." She elbowed him.

He ignored her as he pressed his glasses up his nose and leaned into her. "Think it worked?"

Shrugging, Serena placed her hand on the cool ground. Only peace and harmony spoke to her. Serena then placed her hand inside the circle. A wind picked up, swirling around the Devil Tree. She could feel the raven stirring within.

"It worked," she whispered to Jack. "She's trapped inside. We are safe for the night." Serena sighed a heavy relief. "Just one last thing to do before we go inside."

"What?" asked Jack

"I have to mark all the doors with salt."

Jack followed behind his sister with Tinker in his arms and studiously watched as Serena poured salt in a straight line over the threshold of all the doors leading inside the house. Serena imagined a protective line repelling evil from entering their home. Once she had spread salt across each doorframe, she stepped back and sighed, exhausted. "I think we are done. I just need a few minutes alone to work on something in the greenhouse. You stay inside. I'll be up in a sec to draw you a bath."

Jack nodded, and his steps were heavy as he slogged up the stairs. It had been a long day, not just for Serena, and her heart filled with love and pride for her strong, brave and brilliant little brother. She felt an overwhelming sense of love for Jack. Serena found it unbelievable that only a year ago she was a college student and now she was an orphaned witch, with a little brother whom she loved like a son.

Like Jack, Serena realized that change was the only certainty in life.

Chapter Eleven

Eram Quod Es, Eris Quod Sum

Serena waited until her brother reached the top of the stairs before she found her laptop and carried it into the greenhouse off the kitchen. The sun had finally sunk below the horizon, and moonlight streamed through the windows. She laid her Book of Shadows and sketchpad on the worn and well-loved work table before sitting down and cracking open her laptop. Gathering her long blonde hair, she began to wind it round and round in a tight bun, securing it with several pencils and pens as her laptop booted up.

"Okay, time for some answers," she said aloud to herself while she opened Google and did a search for the strange words that had appeared in blood on her front door. She made a mental note to ask Deaken for help getting it cleaned up, knowing it would probably upset Jack to see it in the light of day. *Eram quod es, eris quod sum.* The search quickly popped up with Latin sayings. Translated, the message read – *I was what you are, you will be what I am.*

Serena closed her laptop, and a shiver escaped her body. *I was what you are, you will be what I am. Well, that's creepy and ominous*, she thought to herself. Thinking, Serena lit a white candle, welcoming its warmth and glow. The words disturbed her, and she wondered at their meaning.

"I was what you are. You will be what I am." She repeated the words as she wrote down the translation in the Book of Shadows. "I could never be what Alice Lake has become," she said aloud, as if to convince herself. Serena thought about the message, and about Alice. Other than their dark eyes and powers of witchcraft, they had little in common. Serena had lost her parents just like Alice had lost her child, but the loss hadn't driven her to madness and rage the way it had Alice Lake. True, Serena still had her brother, but she knew even if she had been alone, she'd never turn to black magic the way Alice had. Serena stared into the candle's flickering, solitary flame. "She's just trying to scare me. She knows I'm a witch. She's attempting to throw me off my path."

Serena flipped to the page where she had written her name in blood. *My name is Serena and this is my Book of Shadows.* She pressed a hand to a fingerprint of her blood that darkened the page. "I will never become like Alice Lake," Serena said aloud. "I vow to protect myself and my brother from her and any harm that comes our way. I swear on my Book of Shadows that I will not run away in fear of Alice Lake. I will meet the raven in a match of magic, and I will send her soul back to hell. This is my promise as a witch."

As if in answer, the white candle on the tabletop flickered three times, and Serena took it as a sign that the Book of Shadows would guide her in her journey as a witch. Serena flipped through the pages of her book, scanning the collection of spells her grandmother had accumulated over the years. Serena jotted down notes, adding small revisions to a couple that spoke to her, and sketched in the margins whatever visions arose in her mind as she reflected on the words. Serena sensed the spells shaping themselves to her, as if the Book of Shadows were claiming her as well. By reading the book, Serena understood that she had the ability to not only use already made spells, but to also revise and compose her own. Where this knowledge came from, she didn't know. Perhaps the blood of the generations of other witches that sang in her own blood guided her.

Incantations were like baking a cake for a witch like Serena. She could modify any existing enchantment and form it to her own personal needs or desires. She drew images beside each spell, binding their power to her etchings, or perhaps the other way around. Serena wasn't sure how it worked, but she felt the certainty of it.

As Serena ventured further into her Book of Shadows, she noticed another chapter dedicated to love spells. *For lonely hearts*, the chapter read.

"Hmm, Nan was busy working love charms for all the lonely souls in this town," Serena muttered to herself. It was odd for Serena to imagine anyone wanting to cast a spell to secure the heart of someone who didn't love them back. It saddened her to think of the innocent victims that were tricked into loving a person who was not meant for them.

Serena's thoughts immediately focused on Ashton, and she opened her sketchpad to the portrait she had sketched. Her soft, warm eyes stared back at her. She couldn't deny the intense attraction she had for her, and how comforted she felt when she was near. Ashton had come to her rescue, but more than that, she was a friend. Someone to listen, someone to care. A lump rose in Serena's throat and she swallowed it away. There weren't a lot of people left who cared about Serena, and that made Ashton someone special to her.

She traced the long line of Ashton's neck and her mischievous smile. Those ridiculous dimples that made her stomach do flip flops. She understood the temptation of love enchantments, but she could not sympathize with witches who bestowed them on the desperate. In Serena's opinion, it was unethical. Love was uncontrollable, unexplainable, unbearable and unmanageable. She had seen her fair share of girls give up their own self-worth just to catch the eye of their desired one. Serena could not support witches who would tilt the balance of ethics to make someone love a person outside of free will, and she vowed she never would cast one.

Serena gazed into the steady rhythm of the candle's flame, her spellbook open to love spells on one side, her sketch of Ashton on the other. She concentrated on Ashton's face, her gray eyes that sparkled like the northern star. She thought about the way her gentle touch heated Serena's skin when Ashton's hand found hers, and a longing grew inside her.

Serena couldn't remember the last time she wanted someone to comfort her. For the past year, it had been Serena comforting her brother, putting everything she had into Jack's emotional needs. It wasn't until that moment, looking into the candle flame, that she realized she wanted Ashton to love her. As this realization washed over her, the white candle flickered, and the flame turned black, and an ominous color scorched the air with a charcoaled streak. Gazing into the black flames, Serena saw Ashton within its flickering, this time underneath the shadowy wings of the raven.

Serena wondered what it meant, why the flame had turned black with her thoughts of Ashton. Something was wrong. She typed "black flame" into the search bar and leaned over her laptop, devouring the words. Curling black smoke represented negative energy, conflict and bad luck, and it signaled opposing forces.

What did it mean? Serena closed her eyes, listening to the voice inside her, the intuition to guide her. Somehow Ashton was connected with conflict and opposing forces. A warning, then. The image of Ashton underneath the outstretched wings of the raven continued to haunt her. Perhaps…perhaps Ashton had been the one to release the raven from the Devil Tree? She shook her head. That didn't feel right, but she couldn't shake the image of Ashton standing underneath the black wings.

Tears rose unbidden and she shook her head, fighting back the tears that threatened to fall like rain during a heavy storm. She thought that perhaps she'd found a friend in Ashton, or maybe something more. The flame continued to flicker its warning. The raven, Ashton and Serena. Ashton and the raven. *My God, she must have released the raven!* There were too many coincidences. That had to be it.

Serena felt so foolish, so naïve for believing Ashton cared. Perhaps it wasn't a coincidence after all that Ashton had shown up when she had to rescue Serena. She thought about how her house and tree were visible from Ashton's cabin with a sinking feeling. Perhaps not a coincidence at all. Rage welled up inside her, quick and hot. At that moment, Serena wanted revenge.

She shook the thought from her mind. Where had that thought come from? That wasn't like her. Again she flipped to the Latin words and their translation. *I was what you are, you will be what I am.* Unease filled her, but she didn't have time to think of her own emotional desires — Alice's raven was only momentarily trapped inside the tree. Jack needed extra protection. Any other form of security would help them, and Ashton was only a distraction. Serena clenched her fist as she swore under her breath, irritated that she had allowed her mind to wander off into a daydream about Ashton when she had real issues that needed to be resolved. Perhaps the warning meant she should stay away from Ashton. She understood how dangerous love was, and promised to never allow her heart to lead before her head ever again. Alice Lake was the perfect example of how love could turn a witch to darkness, and Serena didn't want to follow that path.

Serena flipped through the book's thick pages, landing on a protection spell for the bath. She read the instructions out loud, her pencil scratching out a corresponding shorthand image of the spell, imbibing it with power as she spoke.

It seemed pretty straightforward, and Serena stood with confidence as she began to gather her witching supplies. She plucked a bay leaf from her herb garden and wrote *Alice Lake* on it with a pen from her hair bun. In the kitchen she found a small cast-iron pot and filled it with water. She lit the gas stove, and when the water was at a boil, she crushed the bay leaf and added it to the pot, along with rosemary, mint and salt. She watched as the ingredients brewed in the pot, turning the water brown. Satisfied, Serena removed the pot from the stove and went upstairs to draw Jack a bath, careful not to spill a drop of her potion. Serena bent beside the grand tub, filling it with warm water. She glanced through the cracked glass window to the world beyond. The trees were calm and the air was still, and the moon filled the bathroom with a soft glow. She sighed, secure that Alice would not be becoming for them, and that Jack wouldn't have a repeat of the nightmare bath Serena had taken the day before. Just as Serena was going to pour in her mixture, she was startled by a knock at the front door. Her blood humming with warning and discomfort, she turned off the water and went downstairs.

Ashton was on the front porch, her face harried as her eyes met Serena's through the leaded glass. Serena's heart skipped a beat. She willed herself to contain her emotions. Desire and warning warred within her, and she forced her breathing to steady as she opened the front door. The candle had warned Serena about Ashton, and while she didn't understand the reason, she knew it meant to be careful. *Tread with caution. Do not trust.*

Ashton's gray eyes met Serena's cold gaze. Serena curled her hands into fists so she wouldn't reach out to Ashton, reminding herself how Ashton had already betrayed her by not disclosing the truth about the curse on Korwin Cottage. Rage take over. Out of everyone that had come into her life, Ashton was the one Serena wanted, but the candle warned her that she was also the one Serena couldn't trust. She opened the door, crossing her arms as she stared coldly at Ashton's perfect face, her red cap, her messy dark hair.

"Ashton, I didn't expect you to be here," Serena said in a sardonic tone.

Ashton grabbed Serena by the hand, pulling her outside. Her feet skidded over the doorway, grains of salt scattering under their feet.

Ashton's face was pale and fearful. "Why is this written on your door? Is that blood? Who did that? And what is all this around your door? Salt?" She scanned Serena's face. "Are you in trouble? Have some local teens been out here playing a prank on you?"

Before Serena could answer, Ashton reached for Serena's hand. "You should have called me. I would have come right away. What's going on here?"

Serena released her hand from Ashton's and took a step away from her. "Why? So you could inform Alice that I know everything now?"

Ashton's face creased in confusion, and she shook her head, bewildered. "Serena, what are you talking about? Who's Alice?" Ashton turned her head, scanning the dark garden beyond. "Is there someone here, Serena? Did Alice do this to your house?"

Ashton took a step closer to Serena, closing the gap between them. Her eyes were filled with worry. "Serena, if something is going on, please tell me. I want to help you."

Serena cocked her head at Ashton, her eyes glaring as she remembered the flame's warning. Danger. Conflict. Opposing forces. The raven and Ashton. "Do you? Do you really want to help me, Ashton?"

Ashton raised her eyebrows at Serena's snarky comment and took a step back. "Whoa, Serena. What has gotten into you?"

Serena crossed her arms, nodding sarcastically as she spoke. "Well let me see... I arrived at this freakish house not knowing a soul, only to be bit by some demon witch my first night here, and guess who comes riding in on her white boat to save me? You told me it was just a spider, but it wasn't, was it?"

Serena pointed her finger in Ashton's face and she took a step back. "And when I tried to explain that something unnatural was going on, you dismissed me, said it was just superstitious nonsense. But you went on to inform me the next day about Miss Yolanda. Ironically, you failed to mention that my own land had been cursed by a witch." Serena's voice rose as she pieced together Ashton's betrayal. "I had to hear the truth from Deaken Ward, and that's when I realized you knew. You always knew and you didn't tell me."

Serena took a step closer to Ashton, her presence filling the space that separated them. Ashton's face was pale. "Knew what, Serena? What do you think I know?"

"You can't be trusted," Serena hissed through clenched teeth. "You didn't tell me! I almost drowned in my bathtub, my brother could have been killed and you just allowed me to go on thinking it was nothing more than a case of bad luck. That it was in my head. That the isolation was getting to me. That everything was just fine and good and safe. That you were good and safe. That you liked me, but this must be a big joke to you."

Ashton wrapped her arms around herself. "Wait, you almost drowned in your tub? I don't know what you're talking about Serena, but you're scaring me."

Serena threw her head back and laughed. The sound was strange even to her own ears. "I'm scaring you. I'm scaring you? Oh, that's rich. Don't you think it's the other way around?"

Ashton's eyes went wide, and she retreated a step down the porch stairs as she stared at Serena. "I'm the one who's scared!" Serena raged. "I'm the one who is up against the raven and trying to protect my baby brother from powers I can't even begin to comprehend, but I'm trying! I'll do anything to break this curse and make sure Jack and I are free from the same fate my parents and my grandparents faced."

Ashton held her hands up. "Raven? Serena, what are you talking about? What did you do?"

Serena lifted her chin as she sneered. "What I needed to do to end the curse. I became a witch." Serena turned facing the crab apple tree where it stood in the darkness, the salt ring around it glowing in the moonlight. Footprints marred the ground where the salt ring stood, salt scattered across the dirt.

Ashton's eyes darted toward the tree, her hand cupped her gaping mouth, then her gaze jumped back to Serena. "Witches, ravens and curses? That's insanity, Serena. You're talking about that old nursery rhyme, aren't you? It isn't real—it's just something little kids jump rope to. I'm worried about you. Both of you." Ashton shook her head. "I shouldn't have left you alone here. I should have known the isolation would get to you. I'm so sorry, Serena. You're right. I didn't keep you safe."

Serena advanced on Ashton's retreating form. "You are worried about me? Oh, that's rich." Serena cut Ashton off and blocked her path. "You can stop with the games and all the lies, Ashton. I figured it out. I saw a vision of you with the raven. I know you released the raven and had my gran killed. You're the reason I'm here. You're the one who summoned me."

Ashton backed away from Serena, her eyes closed as she shook her head. "I could never hurt you, Serena. Are you saying you think the curse is real?" She opened her eyes, spinning around the garden, desperately searching for something or someone. "Is Alice here? Is the raven here, Serena? Help me understand," she pleaded.

They now stood underneath the branches of the cursed tree, and its branches waved in the dark night tauntingly. Serena looked at Ashton with a chill permeating her bones. "You blame my great-aunt for your mother's death, and you're seeking revenge by coming after me and my brother." Serena pointed at Ashton, whose face was stunned. Serena spun on her heel and headed back toward her house. "You will say anything to trick me. But I know I'm right. I saw it in the flame. Stay away from me and my brother."

Ashton stood in the shadow of the crab apple tree, frozen and silent, and before Ashton could say another word, Serena slammed the front door behind her.

Serena stomped up the stairs to the bathroom to where her cast-iron pot still steamed with her protective brew. A sharp pain entered her heart, like a thorn pricking her skin. If Serena had not closed the door, she knew her desire for Ashton would overcome her logic and she would once again be a victim to Ashton's deceit.

Jack stood in the bathroom doorway, watching as Serena emptied the brew into the bath. "Was that Ashton?" he asked cautiously.

Serena shook her head. "It was nothing. Don't worry about her. She's gone now." She sat on the edge of the tub, placing her finger in the water as she spoke the incantation.

"Let the rays of light enter in.
Guard this home day and night.
Protect us with your shield of white.
The semblance left by herb and spell
I ask you now to safely seal this entrance well."

Her finger flared with warmth, and the water began to swirl. Jack watched in open-mouthed amazement as the spell brewed inside the tub.

"Wow. That's incredible, Serena." He placed his hand in the tub, the feel of magic washing over his skin.

Serena smiled, thankful Jack accepted her new abilities. "All right then. Hop in and take a nice long soak. I'll be downstairs in the greenhouse looking through my book. I'll come back up when you're done and tuck you into bed."

Jack took off his glasses and placed them beside the sink. "Okay, Serena. What happened with Ashton?"

"Nothing." She pasted on a false smile, though Jack looked unconvinced. "She's not going to bother us again. Take a bath, Professor. Okay, sweetie?" With that, Serena closed the door behind her, relieved that her magic could help protect Jack. She glanced at her reflection in the hall mirror. Her fair complexion, round, dark eyes and golden hair stared back at her. She was angry at herself for not controlling her emotions with Ashton sooner. What had she been thinking? There was no room for romance in her new life, and there were too many uncertainties here that she had to work out before she could even begin to think about a relationship. Besides, the candle had warned her that Ashton couldn't be trusted. Right?

Exhaustion threatened to overwhelm Serena as she padded down the stairs. Serena passed the front door. She would have to do something about the words left from the raven. Her, not Deaken. Yolanda had a purple door, a door for witches. Yolanda said everything had a purpose in magic, that even the color of her door served a purpose. Serena made a mental note to look through the Book of Shadows searching for a passage on colors. But first, she needed to undo her feelings for Ashton.

Serena didn't allow herself to feel anything as she sat in the greenhouse and the moon filled the room with a brilliant glow. She found a chapter on reversing love spells, for it certainly felt like Ashton had cast a spell over her. She must have, for she knew she felt a spark of magic the first time they had kissed. Her heart welled in pain, and she pushed down the feeling. She forced herself not to think of the expression in Ashton's hurt eyes, of her strong hands and kind smile. Serena lit a black candle and filled a silver spoon with salt with resolve. She placed the spoon over the flame, looking up into the night sky as she chanted,

"Salt, my white friend, protector of unwanted magic,
remove the feelings and break the bond.
Release me from Ashton's con.
Bring forth only true desires.
Those that are pure
and cannot burn away in a fire."

Serena watched the spoon as the salt sizzled and popped inside, then tore the page of Ashton's face from her sketchbook. She fed the paper to the candle's flames, watching as they licked and consumed

Ashton's beautiful face. Serena imagined the magic leaving her body, escaping through the greenhouse windows, through the night sky and out into the lake. She sighed, her heart aching. She rubbed at the ache in her chest. She didn't feel any different. Perhaps some spells took more time to take hold.

Serena placed the spoon on the table and blew out the black candle, the ash from the burned paper blowing on an unseen breeze. Even though she was relieved she would no longer desire Ashton—surely the spell would kick in soon—she struggled with feelings of guilt and loss. Serena hadn't realized until then how desperate she wanted to be loved by Ashton and how deeply she wanted to love her in return. She ordered the emptiness in her heart to go silent. Love and witches did not mix—Alice Lake was proof of that. She would not—could not—become like Alice. The words on the front door mocked her. She did not have the time or energy to waste on her own loss. Love was the human condition that could break you, and Serena needed her strength to fight the raven. She turned her back on her aching heart, pushing away thoughts of Ashton as she flipped through the Book of Shadows for information on colors, and before long she discovered a chapter that proved useful. Her grandmother Edith had described in great detail the meaning of a purple door.

Serena read with deep interest about the many properties the color purple represented to witches. "I never knew a purple door meant open-mindedness and is practiced in feng shui as a color that you can place in any direction," she said to herself. Her eyebrows rose as she kept devouring the words. "This is fascinating" she said, a whistle escaping between her lips. "When painting a door purple, you are sending out a message that you're versatile to life's possibilities."

She paused, exhaling a long breath. "Wow, who knew? Come to think of it, I've never seen a purple door before now." She scanned over the page, pausing once again to read out loud to herself. "In medieval times, peasants would seek out white witches by their purple doors. It was a calling sign that a good witch dwelled within."

Serena's toes tingled. She took it as an omen. She stood up, wiggling them inside her damp shoes. She looked out of the window to the dark night beyond, deciding that even though she was tired, this couldn't wait. "Looks like I'm going to paint my front door purple." The idea that magic could communicate to Serena through her body, earth, air, water and fire was energizing. It gave her a desire to learn more, be more and grow more as a witch. She wanted to be connected to the life force that now surrounded her. She didn't want to think about her aching heart. About Ashton under raven's wings.

Serena remembered seeing paint in the boathouse earlier that day, and she walked out the back door, careful to step over the line of salt. Heavy clouds covered the full moon, securing her in darkness. The night was quiet — too quiet. Not a bird or a frog stirred. A snapping sound came from the woods, a tree branch cracking underneath someone's step. Serena turned around scanning the woods behind her. She didn't see anyone in the darkness.

Serena shook her head. It must be a fox or other nocturnal creature out for their evening hunt. Alice was trapped in her tree. Serena headed for the boathouse, wishing the moon would break free from the dark clouds. She felt along the side of the wall for the interior light and switched it on, bathing the clean and pleasant boathouse in warm light. Serena opened the bottom cabinet to rummage through paint jars. There amongst the half-empty cans was a canister of purple paint. She used a screwdriver to open it. Good — it was still fresh. She replaced the lid before grabbing a paintbrush and rag.

Another snap came from outside in the still darkness, and Serena jumped to her feet. She stood perfectly still as she concentrated on the noise stirring outside. She walked to the window, peering out into the woods. Nothing was there. She bit her bottom lip, willing her mind to remain clear, but she gave in to the fear that began to invade her.

Something was not right. The night was turning — evil was rising — she could feel it pricking her thumbs. She thought back to the footprints in the salt around the base of the evil tree, and a chill crept up her spine. She'd been fighting with Ashton. Had they disturbed the circle?

Serena grabbed a hammer on her way outside. She turned out of the boathouse, looking over the lake. The water was motionless, as if all life inside was dead. The trees stood before her still and stiff, depleted of energy. Cautiously she moved toward the cottage, turning side to side. She knew something was out there with her, waiting for Serena to let down her guard. She felt it in her blood, in her bones. *Danger. Warning. Ashton. Raven.*

The moon was barely visible. The sky had become one dark blanket of clouds. Serena placed each foot carefully, as she was unable to see the path in front of her. A hand touched her shoulder in the darkness, and Serena screamed as she turned around, swinging the hammer. Ashton yelped as she leapt back, barely missing the hammer's blow.

Serena's heart raced as she saw Ashton standing before her. "What are you doing? I almost killed you!"

Ashton placed her hands up in the air. "Serena! You almost killed me!" she said at the same time. "You almost took my head off with that hammer!"

"I told you to go home." Serena's voice shook from the near-hit. She really could have killed Ashton, and she was shaken to the core. "Why are you still here?"

"I know you did, but I couldn't leave you." Tears were in her eyes as she placed her hand on the hammer, gently lowering it. Serena hadn't realized she still held it toward Ashton's face, and it slipped from her fingers to thump on the ground. "I don't want to scare you, but I have a bad feeling." Ashton's voice wavered. "I'm worried about you—about both of you. I know you don't want me here, and I know you don't want to hear what I have to say, but something is wrong, Serena."

She took a step toward Serena, but stopped when she saw the expression on Serena's face. "I saw headlights down Korwin Lane and I couldn't leave you and Jack all alone. I thought I would wait by my boat for a while, just until I knew you were both in bed." Ashton looked back at her boat. "If you don't want me here, I'll leave. I don't understand, but I'll go. Just, just maybe call Deaken to stay with you."

A whistling sound came from the edge of the woods. Serena spun around, scanning the trees. Ashton stood beside her. A twig snapped behind them, Ashton flung Serena behind her as she spun around to face the noise. "Get inside, Serena. It could be a bear."

Serena clung to Ashton's arm. She knew it wasn't a bear lurking in the shadows. She sensed the wickedness growing in the dirt pushing up through the weeds. The tree, the broken line of salt. It was Alice — it had to be. There was no one else. Just then, a scream rang through the dark night. It came from the cottage.

"Jack!" Serena shrieked, running to the house. Ashton ran behind her as they raced up the flight of stairs to the bathroom. The lights inside the cottage flickered on and off, frantic and fast. Serena turned the knob of the bathroom door, but it was locked. Serena banged her hip against the wooden door, but it refused to budge. Ashton came up next to Serena and together they smashed their bodies repeatedly into the door.

Jack's screams grew louder, more frantic, and water coursed underneath the door to puddle at their feet. Serena could feel his terror rushing through her veins. Still, he screamed on and on in one endless wail. "He's scared, Ashton! We need to break down the door! Now!"

Together, Ashton and Serena slammed their shoulders into the door. On their third try it flung open, and they tumbled into a pile on the wet bathroom floor. Serena stared in open-mouthed horror as long strips of seaweed reached up from the drain of the tub to slither over the side and onto the wet tile. Wet tentacles of seaweed wrapped around Jack's face and head, smothering him, and his screaming sputtered as he choked on the rotten weeds. The length of rope, the one meant to protect him, was slung over the side of the sink. Oh no. He'd taken it off to bathe. Serena screamed, slipping in the water as she raced to her brother. Just as her hand closed over his arm, he was jerked back, dragged into the overflowing tub by the serpentine seaweed. The reeds yanked Jack under the water, and Serena reached inside the tub, trying to pull Jack out of the bath. Jack's body went limp, and Serena feared the worst as she yanked and pulled at the seaweed encircling him. She clutched a piece, snapping it off from the stem, freeing Jack from its oily grasp. Ashton fell to her knees beside Serena, and together they dragged Jack onto the bathroom floor. His eyes rolled into the back of his head, and he was no longer breathing. Serena pressed her fingers to Jack's neck, searching for a pulse.

"He's alive," she whispered to Ashton. Jack was motionless except for the slight rise and fall of his chest.

"Why isn't he moving, Serena?" Ashton's voice shook. "Why isn't he responding? What is happening?"

Serena opened the palm of her hand to reveal a piece of broken seaweed that wiggled manically in her hand. It writhed and twisted like an angry snake looking to strike. Ashton shook her head, backing away from Serena.

"That's not possible," she whispered as Serena looked down at the reed. Tears burned on Ashton's cheeks. Serena blinked at her, and the reed vanished. In its place lay a severed finger in the palm of Serena's hand. Ashton screamed, but Serena only considered it, then closed her fist around it, clutching it in her hand until her knuckles turned white.

Chapter Twelve

The Face in the Mirror

Ashton helped Serena lift Jack's wet, still body from the cold tile floor. His glasses lay discarded on the wet tile, and Ashton slipped them into her pocket so they wouldn't be stepped on. Serena cradled Jack to her chest as she carried him to his bed. Tinker slunk underneath the bed and huddled in the corner, shaking. The professor was still, so still.

Serena's worst fears had come true. Jack was gone, taken by Alice Lake. Even though his body was in her arms, her witching sense told her his spirit was gone, another victim to the raven, and to the cursed tree that hungered for blood and revenge. Tear after tear slipped down her cheek to fall on her brother, his face still frozen in terror, his skin in welts from the tangle of choking seaweed.

Like the phantom pain of a severed limb, Serena had felt his spirit leave their world, sucked out of his body and plummeted to a realm of darkness that Serena couldn't follow. Serena knew she couldn't find Jack on her own.

Ashton sank beside Serena on the bed and stared down at Jack's frail form. He seemed so much smaller, so vulnerable, without the spark of life lighting his dark and curious eyes. "What just happened, Serena?" Ashton asked as she laid a tentative hand on Serena's shoulder. Serena was still, as if frozen. Ashton slid her hand from Serena's shoulder to Jack's forehead. His body was cold, so cold, and his breath came in short gasps. Ashton smoothed her hand down his cheek, willing Jack to wake up. "What happened to Jack, Serena?" Ashton pleaded again.

"She took him, Ashton." Serena's voice was toneless, wooden. "She took my Jack." Serena leaned over to place a kiss on Jack's head. She drew a throw blanket from a nearby chair and spread it over her brother's small body, tucking the sides in around him just like their mother used to do. With a final kiss on his cool cheek, Serena spun on her heel and marched out of the bedroom, heading for the front door. "I have to go." Serena's voice was calm, like a sea after a storm.

Ashton followed a step or two behind Serena, her face stricken with confusion and fear. "Go where? Jack was just attacked by some diabolical seaweed creature, and part of it broke off and transformed into a flipping finger!" Ashton stepped into Serena's path, blocking the front door. "And all you're going to say to tell me is you have to go?" Ashton grabbed Serena by the shoulders and searched her face. It was like staring into the face of a stranger. "Tell me what is going on!"

Serena shrugged off Ashton's grip, staring her dead in the eyes. "My brother's soul was taken by an ancient spirit named Alice Lake." Serena's voice was hollow and resigned, and Ashton shuddered as she took a step closer to Serena.

"The Alice from the nursery rhyme?" she breathed.

Serena nodded. "Alice has been tormenting us since the day we arrived in this cursed place, and it's all because I'm a hereditary witch, something I just discovered about myself. And the only person who can help me get my brother's soul back—if that is even possible—is Yolanda." Serena shouldered past Ashton and turned before descending down the porch steps. The porch light overhead cast her face in ghostly shadows. "That is, unless you are ready to tell me the truth."

Her knees weak, Ashton leaned against the door frame of the front door, careful not to touch the bloody words still scrawled threateningly across the wood. "The truth about what, Serena?" she asked slowly.

Serena bared her teeth in a twisted snarl. "Tell me what you know about the crab apple tree. Explain to me why you never warned me, never mentioned anything about it, and why you never said your mother went to see my great-aunt for a spell to cure her cancer. Why didn't you tell me any of this when we met?"

Ashton hung her head and took a deep breath, her gaze locked on the floor. "Because I never believed any of it, Serena. It was just spooky nonsense about some lonely old ladies in the woods. I didn't believe Miss Yolanda or your grandmother were witches, and I certainly never believed your ugly tree was cursed." She looked up, her gray eyes sparkling with tears. "I knew about the nursery rhyme. I used to jump rope to it in the schoolyard with the other kids. But it wasn't real, Serena. None of it. I thought they were just grifters offering desperate hope for desperate people. My mom believed in the folklore so intensely she made my dad go with her to see Miss Yolanda to cast a spell that would save her life, but Yolanda isn't some voodoo swamp doctor. She's just a person like you or me. She can't do magic. Yes, my mom died shortly after she visited Miss Yolanda. That's not Yolanda's fault. That's just life. And sometimes it hurts."

Ashton scrubbed at her eyes with the back of her hand before she continued. "Miss Yolanda sat next to me at mom's funeral, and she told me if she could have, she would have done anything to save my mother's life. And I believed her. And because I believed her, that also meant I didn't believe she was a witch. She's just a lonely, superstitious spinster who lives alone in the woods."

Ashton gave a nervous giggle edging on hysteria as she tried to hold back her tears. "I didn't tell you any of this, Serena, because I like you. I wanted you to like me. I see something in you, something in us. I've never had a real relationship, but with you, I feel like it's possible. I didn't want to scare you away with some superstitious talk from a bunch of backward mountain folks." Ashton reached out to clasp Serena's hand. When she didn't pull away, Ashton drew her close, squeezing her fingers with both of her hands. "If I thought any of it was real, I would have told you. Serena." She shook her head, her eyes pleading. "I couldn't bear it if you or Jack were hurt." The tears that threatened to fall now slid freely down Ashton's cheeks. "And now, Jack..." She squeezed her eyes shut, shaking her head. "I don't even understand what's going on, Serena. Where did the finger come from, Serena? Whose finger is that?"

The wall Serena was trying to build around her heart to keep Ashton out collapsed, and Serena fell into Ashton's arms. Ashton wrapped her arms around her, squeezing her tight. Serena pressed her face into the curve of her neck. "I'm sorry, Ashton," Serena whispered, her words muffled. "I shouldn't have accused you. I'm so confused and scared, and I thought the candle flame was warning me about you. It told me of a threat, of danger." She paused, thinking. "I don't know." She leaned back to look up into Ashton's gray eyes. "I don't know whose finger this belongs to, but I'm certain that whoever it is, they are the one responsible for all this. They are the one who released Alice Lake and killed my family."

Ashton ran a comforting hand up and down Serena's spine. "Serena, what are you talking about?"

Serena brushed away Ashton's tears with her free hand. "Close your eyes, Ashton," she ordered softly. "It's easier if you see my memories." Serena placed a hand on Ashton's cheek.

Before Ashton could protest, Serena led her through the beginning. Visual images flew into Ashton's mind. She saw Serena being taunted by the raven. She watched as Deaken drew a map of the stream and handed it to Serena. She saw Serena waiting at the purple door of the Wise Woman's cottage, and watched as she gave Serena her grandmother's Book of Shadows. She watched as Serena pricked her finger and scrawled her name on the page in blood. Ashton witnessed Jack examining the strange symbols written on the stone bridge. She felt Jack's panic as the spiders attacked him. Ashton felt Serena's magic as she buried the witch bottle, calling forth protection to guard their home deep within the earth under the crab apple tree. She saw her portrait being burned over a candle flame, and she saw her own face looking through the cottage window that evening, scared and worried.

Ashton stumbled back, retching, breathless from the onslaught of thoughts and feelings that weren't her own, but she felt them as though they were. She had never believed in magic, witches or the supernatural. Serena had given her an alternate view of reality, one dark and mysterious, that she was only now awake to. She stumbled, her knees weak, and Serena grasped her arm to steady her, then wrapped her arms around herself.

Fear flared through Ashton, and she took a step away from Serena. But Serena looked so lost, so alone, so hopeless with her arms wrapped around herself, as if she were trying to keep from falling apart. Ashton's heart broke at the sight, and she stepped close again to gather Serena in her arms and pressed a kiss to her temple. Together. Whatever was happening to Serena, they'd face it together. No matter what perilous entity Serena was up against, Ashton wouldn't let her fight it alone.

For a long moment they stood still in the porchlight, each holding the other up. Serena sniffed as she broke apart from their embrace. She stared down at her feet, then, puzzled, looked down at the line of salt at the doorway. Or rather, where the line of salt had been; now there was only a dusty scattering of white where the protective line of salt used to be. Serena turned to stomp down the porch steps.

"Where are you going?" Ashton called warily before following. Serena stopped before the twisted crab apple tree, her hands on her hips. the severed finger still clutched in her fist. She stared down at the disturbed ground—a fresh bed of open earth lay in a small mound. Serena remembered the scattered circle of salt, the footprints in the soil. The salt circle surrounding the tree had been broken, shattering her protective spell.

Falling to her knees, Serena clawed the ground, her nailbeds filled with soil. The witch bottle was gone. Someone—or something—had dug it up. "Ashton, run inside and get my tote bag from the kitchen—the one with my book and jars."

In a flash Ashton was gone, and she returned with the bag in tow. She fell to her knees beside Serena. "Let me know what I can do to help," she murmured.

Serena grabbed a handful of dirt and dropped it into one of the glass jars. Using her fingernails, she peeled back three scales from the bark of the cursed tree. She added them to the jar of dirt, along with the severed finger. It was fat and bloated, as if left in water far too long. It was too deteriorated, too waterlogged to identify the gender of the owner to whom the finger came from and no clues were visibly left on it.

"I'll find your name and I will hunt you down," she promised softly. The person was close by—she could feel them. And so was Alice. She could feel her, too. She pushed out with her witching senses. The deception lingered in the air, like something sour and rotten. Rising, she stood resolutely before the sinuous Devil Tree. The bark undulated like scales on a serpent slithering up the tree, mocking her. Mocking them. She wanted to rip away the bark, peeling back its layers, reveal the black heart of the tree and tear it out, to rend and destroy. Her brother's soul was inside. She could feel him, sense his presence, his fear, yet she could not reach him.

Helpless, Serena stumbled to the boathouse. She untied the kayak from the dock and placed her tote bag with the jar and Book of Shadows by the seat. She felt around the bag for her cell phone. The battery was nearly dead—she had minutes left, if that. She scrolled down to Deaken's name and hit the call button. It rang twice, then went to voicemail. "Dammit," Serena cursed. "Deaken, as soon as you get this message, go to my house. Jack is in trouble. I've got to go see the Wise Woman. I'll explain everything when I get back." She looked down at the phone in her hand. The screen went black, and she only hoped she got her message out in time. She dropped her cell phone on a worktable in the boathouse as she stepped into the rocking boat.

Serena didn't know if she could find Yolanda's house in the dark without Deaken's map, but she hoped her new witch senses would be enough to guide her there. "Ashton, I have to go. I need to see Yolanda. She is the only one who can help me get my brother back."

Spurred to action, Ashton grabbed hold of the side of the kayak. "I'll come with you. You shouldn't go alone, Serena. I can help you find the place in the dark."

Serena looked up to see the full moon slip behind a silver cloud, and she knew instinctively it was a sign, a sign that the power of two was needed. "Thank you," Serena said as she placed a hand on Ashton's arm. Ashton nodded, then turned to tie a flashlight to the front of the kayak while Serena settled into the back seat. Together, they paddled off into the emptiness of the night.

The night air was still. The only sound was their oars slicing through the surface of the placid water. It was easy to believe they were the only two living things left in the silent world. Ashton kept her eyes trained on where the water curved up ahead, though she could have found the place with her eyes closed. She had grown up on these waters, and they were as much a part of her as her own bones.

Her soft voice was low in the night. "I was happy before you arrived, Serena." Her voice was soft, though Serena heard every word. "I was content to be a shipwright, work side by side with my father. I wasn't looking for love, and I certainly didn't believe in magic."

Perhaps it was the quiet night that seemed to swallow her words. The truth flowed from her like waters along Conjure Lake. "Growing up, I heard the rumors in town about Miss Yolanda, the Wise Woman of Conjure Lake. You can't live here without hearing the warnings—don't step on her garden and trample her vegetables or she will hex you, or cause a plague of warts upon your face. Don't go to her without bearing a gift, or you will leave her cottage cursed in love, unable to find your soulmate. Don't stare her directly in the eyes, or you will go blind for three days, unable to find your way back home. Yolanda was feared amongst the town people, and they'd whisper about her whenever their children suddenly fell ill with chickenpox, or when the flu came through town. 'It was Yolanda who sent the pox,' everybody would say." Ashton turned her body to glance at Serena. Her dark eyes met Ashton's, and she nodded for her to continue.

Ashton faced forward again, confessing her truths to the dark trees beyond the rippling water. "If a red ring surrounded the moon, fishermen would not go out on their boats for fear of drowning. Blood on the moon, they called it. The fishermen would stare at the moon from the dock, gossiping to one another. 'The witch has cast a ring around the moon. We can't go out into the lake, or we will be sucked up by the water drowning to our death.' They say your grandmother killed your grandfather—got mad at him and drowned him in Conjure Lake. I never believed it. She seemed like a sweet old lady to me, always offered me cookies if she saw me out on the kayak. I thought the rumors were mean-spirited. I was sad to hear she died—sad to hear they both died."

Their paddles sluiced through the waters, and Ashton used her oar to guide them past a jutting tree branch in the water. "I used to mock the superstitions, honestly," Ashton confessed. "I never believed Yolanda had powers. I thought she was a lonely old woman, living like a hermit in the woods. I always figured Yolanda was nothing more than a sad old lady who lived alone without love. Now I'm not sure of anything anymore. Maybe there was a curse placed on the town, maybe Alice Lake was to blame for all the misfortunes that have taken place in Corvin Grove." Ashton shook her head. "Magic is real. There's no way to explain what I saw happen to Jack." Her voice caught on his name, and she swallowed before continuing. "But I think I started to feel something was different when I met you, Serena. I think magic entered my heart the moment I fell for you. I don't know what made me get in my boat and go to your place tonight. I just knew you were in trouble. I could feel it—I could feel that you needed me."

Serena closed her eyes and drew a deep breath, realizing she wasn't the only victim of Alice Lake. Ashton had been drawn to the magic of Korwin Cottage and the curse that was now Serena's reality.

But what of the candle's warning? She had seen Ashton in the shadow of the raven.

They stirred the kayak through the dark waters in silence, as a heavy fog grew quietly on the lake. Dense fingers of fog thickened around them, tangling through the dark trees. Serena turned around, watching as the fog crept toward them. "Do you see that fog, Ashton?" she breathed. "Don't let it touch you. It draws blood. I know, it got my leg earlier." She placed her hand on the surface of the black water, calling the power of her sister witches before her, commanding the lake to guide her.

"Let the fire from my soul
fester in the water like burning coal.
Ignite the flames to guide.
I will follow what you provide.
Carry me on to the Wise Woman I seek.
Be my eyes through the dark and bleak."

Small reeds under the water grew taller, an answer to her call, and they formed a path ahead of her. The reeds burned with a flame that held no fire, illuminating a path through the snaking creek, leading her on to Yolanda's cottage. Serena paddled faster, trying to outrun the dense, reaching fog, but it was steady and gaining speed, reaching toward them like tentacles. The burning reeds shone under the lake like flames trapped under the surface. The fog crept up beside her kayak, reaching for Serena. She bared her teeth as she blew on the fog, forcing it back.

"Out of my mouth and into the air.
You cannot touch me.

All you can do is stare."

The fog hovered around the kayak and Serena, but did not consume her, did not touch them. Ashton held her breath, watching. "Don't touch the fog, Ashton," Serena commanded again calmly. "No matter what happens. I'm a new witch—I can only hold it back for a few minutes.

Serena stretched up in her seat, craning her neck to try to see ahead in the dense fog. She called out to Yolanda. "Help me, Yolanda! She's coming!"

Ashton swiped at the sweat pouring down her brow as she looked behind them. Ashton looked as if her blood had chilled as she watched the fog roll toward them, taking the form of a large raven. "Serena!" she breathed. "It's coming! Paddle quick!"

Over the creek and through the dark waters and past the guardian trees, up the cottage steps and into Yolanda's home, Serena's voice flew. Yolanda heard Serena's cry, and ran to her fireplace, dropping a white owl feather into the burning flame.

"Wings of the night take flight.
Soar through the dark.
Stir up a wind.
Carry my niece on the speed of a sprite.
Bring her to my home.
Outrun the blight!"

The owl feather burned into a white smoke rising out of her chimney. The smoke darted through the black sky, streaking the night like angel wings.

The smoke raced toward Serena, aiming for the fog. The smoke formed into two massive wings, like a large white dove, engulfing the kayak. The fog reached for the wings, its mist turning into two large hands. The wings opened their feathers wide and thrust the fog back in drifts.

"Paddle, Serena! Hurry!" Ashton's voice was frantic as she took command of the kayak, thrusting them through the water with all her strength. No longer calm, the waters churned furiously around them. Serena closed her eyes, not looking back as the owl wings swiped once again at the fog, bashing it away from their kayak.

Ashton navigated the kayak through the burning water, following the amber glow of the reeds beneath the surface of the dark waters as she dashed around tree branches and broken logs in their path. The fog was winning. Ashton leapt out of the kayak and splashed in the waist-deep water, grabbing the nose of the kayak to guide it through the tangled twists of branches that seemed to reach out at them like probing skeletal fingers.

"Ashton!" Serena called out, frantic. "What are you doing? Get back in the boat!" Ahead, a barrier lay, blocking the path to Yolanda's cottage. Vines, seaweed and dead tree branches rose from the water to twist into a dam of thick thorns and briars.

"Serena, we'll never get through this. We have to go around," Ashton called through the howling wind. She stood waist-deep in the dark and swirling waters, guiding the nose of the kayak through the meandering path. Serena half-stood to drop into the water beside her, but Ashton protested, urging Serena to sit back down in her seat.

"No, Serena, stay here. I'll guide you through." Ashton continued to pull the kayak's nose and zigzagged her way through the thorny branches that reached and raked at her arms, cutting through her shirt like razors and leaving long, thin lines of blood down each arm.

"Ashton, be careful!" Serena called, terrified that she might be slashed in half by the unnatural thorns that shot out of the water like swords. Too late, too late she remembered the portrait she had burned, the one Aunt Yolanda had called powerful magic. A love spell—a spell of protection—and Serena had burned it, leaving Ashton completely defenseless against the onslaught of dark magic.

The raven specter hung in the air above Ashton, and Serena's heart twisted. It was her vision: the raven's wings stretched wide over Ashton. This was the warning from the candle. Ashton was in danger, and Serena destroyed her only protection. Ashton's foot slipped into a sinking pile of mud and she stumbled, her head almost dropping below the water's surface. A branch moved and sliced Ashton's face like a knife. Serena screamed, reaching for her. Ashton was defenseless against the raven, and it was all Serena's fault.

"I'm okay," Ashton called out as she fought to get her feet under her, blood sliding down her cheek to drip into the hungry water. "Stay in the boat, Serena. I'm okay." Ashton got back up on her feet, though when she went to take a step forward, her foot was trapped in the mud. Ashton bared her teeth as she pulled her leg out of the water with all her might. As though the mud were loath to release her, her foot eventually gave, her Converse lost to the sucking mud and black water.

Her face was a mask of calm as she looked back at Serena and gave a reassuring nod as she continued to navigate the kayak through the dam of thorns. Serena felt something stir underneath the kayak, and the boat rolled gently, as if lifted by a giant wave. There was something below them — something big — and it was headed right for Ashton. A scraping sound ran along the bottom of the boat, sending shivers up Serena's spine.

"There's something here!" Serena called out just as a row of thorns stabbed out of the boat and into the air, creeping and jerking its way to Serena. She gripped the sides of the boat, searching her mind for a spell just as she felt Ashton's arms encircle her waist and hoist her out of the kayak. Serena clutched the tote bag containing her spellbook and jar to her chest as she gripped Ashton's hand. Together they stumbled through the shallow water, thorny limbs catching their legs and tearing at their flesh. Ashton limped beside Serena, pulling her ahead to where a light shone through the dark night, revealing Yolanda's purple door.

Yolanda was outside waiting for Serena, her arms extended wide. "Hurry, Serena! Quick, come inside! The fog is right behind you. It will be here soon!"

Serena ran hand in hand with Ashton, too afraid to look behind them as the wind whistled and screamed in their ears. Yolanda raced to Serena's side, moving the girls inside the house.

"We must get inside. The wings will protect us when the fog comes, but only if we are inside the realm of safety." Yolanda ushered Serena and Ashton to the purple door, pushing them inside. Yolanda stood on the porch, her wizened face grim as she stared down the fog riding on the surface of the water. She raised her arms in the air, a broom in one hand, a lighter in her other. Yolanda held the lighter to the broom bristles, and they erupted in a glorious halo of white flames. She drew a line over the threshold of her house with the fire-blazing broom.

"Light of white
protect us through the night.
Do not let the fog entire in.
Fight it with a fire that's bright."

White flames exploded around her, bathing the porch in brilliance. Yolanda stepped through the doorway and slammed it shut behind her. Moving to the window, she stared out into the dark night, watching as the fog hissed and popped against the protective flames. Satisfied that they were safe, Yolanda crossed the small space to where Ashton and Serena stood by the hearth fire. She calmly took the bag containing the jar that Serena clutched to her chest. Yolanda gently peeled Serena's fingers back until she released the bag, and she carried it to her work table. Serena leaned into Ashton as they watched in silence as Yolanda lifted the jar from the bag and squinted at its contents.

"Hmmm. Who you got here?" she asked as she turned the jar this way and that in the dim light, examining the severed finger encased in glass and dirt. "Somebody nasty, I'm sure. Let's find out who." Yolanda emptied the dirt and bark pieces into a bowl. She separated the finger from the bark and dirt, then smothered the finger with oil. Next, she coated the finger in salt.

Ashton sank into a seat on the other side of the table, her sharp gray eyes missing nothing. Serena moved to her aunt's side, watching her work. Yolanda nodded her head to Ashton knowingly. "Not looking for love, yet here she is at your side, risking her life to keep you safe," she said, nudging Serena with her elbow.

"Stop that," Serena murmured, and the corners of the Wise Woman's eyes crinkled with mirth. Her face became serious again as she leaned over to gently blow the excess salt from the thick finger. Then she stabbed the finger violently with a fork, causing both Serena and Ashton to jump. Yolanda placed the finger on a cooking sheet, then carried it over to the fire to bake. The Wise Woman moved quickly for a woman her age, her nimble fingers pinching off a bit of dried herbs here, and gathering handfuls of basil, galangal and anise.

With practiced movements she added a scoop of each herb to the bowl, stirring as she went. Yolanda opened a small vial, holding it up for Serena's inspection. It was labeled dragon's blood. She tipped the vial over the bowl and added a single drop to the herbs. Next, Yolanda took her pestle and mortar and crunched the mixture of herbs and bark until it was just a sifting pile of black powder. This she scooped into a tea strainer and dipped it in a cup of boiling water.

Serena watched intently as Yolanda prepared the spells. A popping sound came from the fire, and Yolanda placed the tea in front of Serena before removing the finger from the baking sheet.

"It's ready," Yolanda said, holding the fork with an oven mitt. Ashton made a face. It looked like a burnt hot dog roasting on a spit. Yolanda took the finger off

Rebecca Henry

the fork and tied a piece of twine around it, then handed it to Ashton. "Why don't you make yourself useful and tie that to the chandelier over there?"

Ashton's face was green as she stretched to loop the twine around the ancient chandelier, her wet hoodie riding up to reveal her belly-button ring. Serena looked away, her cheeks heating. The finger now dangled on a long string over the floor. Yolanda grabbed a piece of white chalk and squatted down to draw a cross with two arrows pointing at the end, she then enclosed the arrows in a magic circle. Yolanda stood up, and with open arms she stood outside the circle.

"I call forth the direction of evil, who intentionally did harm to my niece. Point the finger to the one who dug up the earth and set free the raven from the Devil Tree."

Nothing happened at first. The finger dangled from the string over the chalk lines on the floor. Then the finger twitched, making Serena and Ashton jump. Slowly it rotated, faster and faster, until the finger was spinning around wildly. Goosebumps rose on Ashton's arms, and she scooted closer to Serena, who stood still, watching, as it slowed and stopped, landing on the arrow pointing east. Yolanda immediately bent down to place a small hand mirror on the arrow, careful not to step inside the circle.

"Serena, go to the mantel and take the jar that's labeled sage," the old woman commanded in a low voice. Serena did as she was told, then took her place between Yolanda and Ashton. She snuck a peek at Ashton, whose eyes were glued to the finger dangling over the mirror.

"Now sprinkle the sage on the mirror and take my hand," Yolanda ordered.

Serena dusted the mirror with the sage, the finger still quivering as it pointed east. The two witches held hands, creating a magical bond. "You, girl." Yolanda nodded her head at Ashton. "Come, take Serena's hand. There is strength in the power of three." Ashton threaded her fingers through Serena's, her grip strong and warm. She squeezed Serena's hand, and she squeezed hers back in response.

Ashton looked over at Yolanda. "But I'm not a witch. How can I help the spell?"

Yolanda snorted. "There's witch blood in all of us Conjure Lake girls. All you need to do is call it forth." Yolanda turned her gaze to the mirror. Ashton met Serena's gaze and she shrugged.

"Now, repeat after me." Yolanda raised her hands in the air, lifting Serena's with hers. On her other side Ashton did the same.

"Face of destruction, come to me.
You have been detected by the power of three.
I call forth your reflection.
It is time to make the connection."

Yolanda cut a glare to the girls, and they repeated the words to Yolanda's satisfaction.

"Good. Now we chant together. All of us."

Serena looked at Ashton, and Ashton nodded as she squeezed her hand again. *Together*, she mouthed to Serena. Warmth filled her chest, and Serena nodded as they closed their eyes, calling upon the higher powers of the earth.

"Face of destruction, come to me.
You have been detected by the power of three.

I call forth your reflection.
It is time to make the connection."

The sage scattered on the mirror, creating a human face. The mirror absorbed the sage, and slowly an image formed on the glass. The two-dimensional image deepened and transformed, and Serena craned her neck to see the face coming to form. The glass swirled with smoke, then cleared to reflect a face of hard lines, a face Serena knew. Deaken Ward.

"No," Serena breathed as she lunged toward the mirror, her hands shaking in rage. Yolanda and Ashton gripped her hands, holding her back.

"Don't be foolish, girl!" Yolanda ordered. "Keep our bond together." Yolanda narrowed her eyes as she bent down to retrieve the mirror, not letting go of Serena's hand.

"So, the traitor has a face. Deaken Ward, you imprudent lost soul. You will suffer for all time in hellfire for the crimes you have committed."

Something loosened in Serena's chest, and she nearly fell to her knees. Ashton's strong arms caught her and held her tight. "I called him," Serena moaned. "I told him Jack needed help. This is my fault." Fury rose in place of the despair, threatening to pull Serena under. "I trusted him. I thought he…" Her words broke off, and Ashton sank to the ground with Serena in her arms.

"This isn't your fault, Serena," she whispered in her ear. "There was no way of knowing. I've got you, and we will get Deaken. Jack will be okay. Everything will be okay." She looked up at Yolanda, her eyes hard. "Right, *Wise Woman*?"

Yolanda snorted at Ashton as she stared down at Deaken's sneering image on the mirrored glass. "I know you, you weak little man. I see you — all of you — now. I won't underestimate you again."

The image of Deaken moved, and Serena and Ashton both jumped when he spoke, the words clear as day. "You dumb cow. It's too late. The raven has what it came for, and we both know how this will end for Serena."

Chill bumps raised on her skin. "Can he see us now?" she breathed to Yolanda.

She shrugged. "He can feel us. He can hear us. Think of it like a witchy telephone. Or FaceTime."

Serena clenched her jaw at her aunt's triviality, then blew into Deaken's face, causing a wind to slap him across the cheek. He started, his eyes full of hate as he glared back at Serena.

"How could you do this to us? Because of you, Jack is in danger! How could you do this to a little boy?"

Deaken's eyes were slits of anger. "You think you are special," he sneered, "entitled to the magical heritage of the Korwins, but it does not belong to you. These lands belonged to my family. For generations, my family was forced into serving the Korwins. Your family took away our name and birthright and stripped us of everything that we are entitled to. But no more. I will end your reign of terror and power. Me. I will destroy you all and your curse on our lands. Conjure Lake will belong to the good people of Corvin Grove again, and Korwin Cottage will belong to me. As it should have been. The house, land and inheritance should be mine, but instead, it went to you. But no more. I will destroy you, and end your evil bloodline once and for all."

Serena looked at Yolanda, confusion spreading on her face. "What is he talking about?"

Yolanda looked at Deaken, her eyes blazing with fire. "Explain, traitor," Yolanda commanded. "Korwin Cottage was never yours, you one-eyed fool. You were just the caretaker. An assistant to Edith's husband."

"He was my friend," Deaken roared, his face turning purple. "He didn't drown. That witch sister of yours killed him, I'm sure of it."

"He was drinking and fell out of the boat," Yolanda scoffed. "He drowned. It was an accident."

"I don't believe that," Deaken seethed. "He fished those waters every day of his life. She killed him. I know it. Everyone knows it. So I freed Alice Lake from the crab apple tree to finally eradicate the evil witches from this land, so no one else will ever suffer at their hands again, and I can reclaim what is rightfully mine."

"Rightfully yours?" Yolanda sneered mockingly. "And what would that be?"

"Who built Korwin Cottage?" His face curled in fury. "Whose family farmed that land? You see, before we were known as Ward, we went by a different name. We were the Lakes, and everything the water touched belonged to us. A great-grandfather of mine was bewitched by Alice Lake. But then she was known as Alice Korwin. He married her and gave her his name. And his baby. And she was an abomination—a witch, just like you. God punished her by taking her baby. My bloodline's baby. My great-grandfather was so heartbroken, that when Alice Lake sold her soul to the devil, it was my brave, courageous, self-sacrificing great-grandfather who gathered the posse and hanged that bitch from the tree. It wouldn't bring his child back, but Alice wouldn't hurt anyone else."

His voice quivered with righteous indignation, sending chills down Serena's spine. "But she was tricky. She escaped and cursed the land. He went on to marry a good, God-fearing woman, and changed his name to Ward to distance himself from that evil bitch. He chose the name Ward because it means protector. And that is our family duty. To watch over and protect the people of Conjure Lake from the threat of witches. But all my life I've known it was my duty, my legacy, to release Alice Lake from the cursed tree and destroy all you witches once and for all, and to finally claim Korwin Cottage for righteousness. For my family. For *me*."

Serena's face was pale as she turned to Yolanda. "Is that true?" she asked hoarsely. "Did his relative have a baby with Alice Lake?"

Yolanda only shrugged. "Sounds about right. Babies don't just appear on their own. We're magic, but we still need a man around for some things." She elbowed Ashton. "But not everything, am I right?" she asked suggestively as she wagged her eyebrows.

Ashton made a face of distaste and stepped away from Yolanda. "What's wrong with you? Now isn't a time for jokes, Wise Woman."

"Bah, so serious," Yolanda groused. "This is the most exciting thing to happen in decades."

Serena ignored their bickering as she stared down at the mirror with hate. "You seem to think of yourself as some kind of hero, Deaken. But you aren't a martyr — you are a monster, just like Alice Lake. And if any harm comes to Jack in any way, you will see what a true monster is. I promise you that."

"I have no desire to hurt that boy." Deaken's eye shone with a fanatical gleam. "He is tainted by your blood, but I can help him. If he survives, I will take him in as my own. He is a victim in all this. When Alice Lake kills you and the old woman just like she killed your parents and grandmother, Korwin Cottage will go to Jack. He will be a Ward, and I will raise him in decency and goodness. Never again will he be subjected to the corrupt influence of the Korwin witches. He will have a chance. A chance at goodness. At righteousness.

"But if he doesn't survive" — Deaken's eye turned dark as an evil smile twisted on his lips — "his blood will be on your hands. He will be a fitting sacrifice to destroy the demon's magic that runs in your bloodline."

Yolanda raised her voice, causing the house to shake in fury. "Silence, you snake. That boy is a Korwin. There is power in his blood, even if he cannot manifest its magic. Alice had the privilege of being a Korwin. She perverted her birthright the moment she used her magic for evil. Her bloodline was stripped of Korwin magic and only destruction and perversion can flow from her powers. You will accomplish nothing. You will claim nothing. Everything you wish to sow, you will reap tenfold. Korwin Cottage will never be yours, you will never harm the Korwin witches, Alice Lake will be banished once and for all and that boy will be freed. It is you who are the abomination, Deaken. I felt it when you stood on my porch all those years ago. I knew only poison and rot came from your spirit, and only hate and destruction will be your legacy. All of this will be for nothing, and you will die with no one to mourn or miss your name."

Deaken sneered, his face twisted with hate. He held up his bandaged hand. "There is nothing I won't sacrifice to destroy you all. I gave my finger to free

Alice again. A willing blood sacrifice." Violence and hate spread through him like a plague. "Jack's soul is bound to the tree, allowing Alice to be free once again, just like I set her free when your sister tried to contain her. I am the reason why your evil sister and her spawn are dead. And I will end the both of you, too."

Yolanda's body trembled like an earthquake and Serena could sense the fury rising inside her like a volcano. She raised her hand holding the mirror high in the air. Serena felt the power rising in Yolanda, threatening to spill out in hate. She grabbed her aunt's arm, tugging the mirror down.

"Yolanda, no! Don't allow him to taunt you. He wants you to strike out in hate. Don't you see? That's how Alice gets her power! She feeds off ours! Deaken is trying to force you to strengthen Alice! He wants to corrupt your power."

The moment Serena spoke the words, she knew them to be true. All magic required balance. Light and dark. But there was no light in Alice. Not since she bound her soul to the devil. Hate would not drive out Alice Lake — it would only increase her power. But how did they fight pure evil without succumbing to it?

Yolanda ignored Serena's words. Her rage was consuming, and she panted as her fists shook with fury. "He killed my sister." Her voice wavered with emotion. "He destroyed the only love I've ever truly known. My Edith." The name caught on a sob.

With her hand on her Aunt Yolanda, Serena could feel the emotions threatening to overwhelm her, and she saw flitting images that were not from her own mind. She felt the hot, searing pain Yolanda felt the day her sister drowned. Yolanda wanted revenge. She wanted to reach inside the mirror and tear out Deaken's tongue. Serena could feel her intentions. Could feel her sliding into malice and revenge. The place where Alice had bitten her neck pulsed with ice. This was just what she wanted. Yolanda was playing right into Alice's hands.

Serena threw her arms around her aunt, holding her tight against her as she whispered in her ear. "Yolanda, no! This is what he wants! What Alice wants. The moment you avenge your sister in evil is the moment I will lose you, too! And Alice will be all the more stronger for it. You can't do this! This is not our way. Please! Dark magic corrupts absolutely. We are witches of light, Aunt Yolanda. We will defeat Alice in our own way."

Yolanda struggled against Serena, and Ashton stepped close to wrap her arms around them both, lending Serena her quiet strength. She said nothing, just held them, waiting for whatever Serena decided. "I want him dead," Yolanda moaned. "My sister was pure. She was light and love. The very essence of good, and they killed her! She is dead because of him!"

Deaken smirked. "Was she? Is that why her daughter fled, never to return home? Rose saw the both of you for what you truly were and rejected her heritage. She wanted her babies to grow up away from you and your sister."

Yolanda's nostrils flared, and the hand holding the mirror shook with rage. "You do not know what you are talking about, Deaken Ward. Rose was tempted by Alice. The raven came to her and offered her the world in exchange for her soul. Rose saw a glimpse of the unholy power being offered to her, and it terrified her, for she was too innocent for this fight. That is why she left. But you hear me now, you foul worm. Rose never stopped loving her mother. She may have turned her back on her magical heritage, but not on her parents. She loved them and did what she thought was best for her own family. I felt it — the love she had. I felt it every day of her life until her last day."

Tears streaked Serena's face. The thought of her mother being haunted by the raven hurt her heart, for Yolanda was right. Rose was the purest soul who had ever lived. She ached to think of her mother facing such darkness, and how courageous she must have been to escape the alluring power of Conjure Lake and the evil witch who threatened to use her to destroy it all.

Deaken smirked in the small mirror, his hateful eyes bright, looking like he'd already won. He was enjoying hurting Yolanda, the witch who took his eye so many years ago.

Serena reached for the mirror, taking it out of Yolanda's hand. Yolanda made a small sound of protest, and Ashton shushed, holding her. Not holding her back, but holding her up, and lending her strength. Yolanda sagged in her arms as she relinquished the mirror to Serena.

Gently, Serena placed it back inside the chalk-lined circle on the ground.

"I will not destroy you, Deaken. You think you are controlling Alice because you cut off your finger and released her again, but you aren't. She is the one pulling your strings. I won't hate you, Deaken. I feel sorry for you. I feel sorry for that little boy who lost his eye, and I feel sorry for the pathetic and hateful man he grew up to be. You are no guardian of the lake, Deaken Ward. You are a sad, lonely man who loves no one, and no one loves you. And I won't let you hurt anyone else."

Deaken snarled, but his expression was unsure. Whatever he expected, it obviously wasn't this.

"I'm not going to kill you, Deaken. That isn't our way. Hate fuels hate. Darkness empowers darkness. And like my mother before me, I reject that path. I choose light. I choose love. I feel sorry for you, Deaken. And I won't let you harm anyone else ever again." Serena took a deep breath, and she felt the weight of Ashton's eyes, offering strength and warmth. "So I bind you, Deaken. I bind you in light, and my light is more powerful than your darkness. Your darkness, your hate, will not touch anyone ever again."

Serena held up her hands, and they glowed with a white light, a blinding white light that emanated from her palms and filled the small cottage with light.

*"Let the past be the past.
Let the evil end."*

Yolanda stared at Serena. "What are you doing?" she breathed.

Serena ignored her aunt and continued.

*"From this day to your last,
you will never hear, see or speak the name Korwin.
Let it be stripped from your memory."*

A look of horror rose on Deaken's face, and he bared his teeth at Serena.

"Girl!" her aunt hissed. "What are you doing?"

Serena raised her hand to Yolanda, silencing her. "The right thing, Aunt Yolanda."

Serena knelt beside the chalk circle, careful to keep her toes from crossing the white lines. She placed her glowing hands on the mirror, covering Deaken's eyes and mouth.

"I send you out into the world, Deaken, not as a corrupted Lake, not as a false-guardian Ward, but as a man with no evil intentions. You will never return to Korwin Lane, for you do not know it exists. For you, witches will no longer exist. I contain you. I bind you. I encircle you in light. Your hands will no longer be stained in blood."

Deaken tried to scream, but no words could escape his lips, and his remaining eye bulged at the effort, the other dead and staring.

"I vanquish you from my sight, Deaken Ward, and from this town. You're free, there is no more bad blood in your veins. I release you from Alice Lake's hold, from your own poisonous memories, and I free you from the binds of hate. You are free. Free to walk the path of light."

Yolanda fell to the floor as Deaken's face faded from the mirror. Serena sat back on her heels, spent. She looked up to find Ashton staring at her. Ashton gave her a soft smile, and pride shone in her gray eyes.

"He killed my sister, your grandmother!" Yolanda wept. "He killed your parents! And you set him free?"

Serena moved to her aunt's side and wrapped her arms around her bony shoulders.

"No, Aunt Yolanda. You're the one I set free."

Chapter Thirteen

How to End It

Yolanda stared at her niece. She seemed different, though it would be difficult to explain exactly what had changed. Her young face had matured overnight. There was a gravitas that perhaps hadn't been there before. Yes, that was it. Serena seemed settled, strong. She was no longer an insecure girl from the city who had lost her way in life. She wasn't crippled by fear or lost inside an abyss of sorrow. Serena was secure and confident in her new abilities as a witch. Yolanda saw wisdom where confusion used to be. Serena had been reborn in Yolanda's cottage with the purple door, like a phoenix rising out of the ashes of death, and with that change, a rebirth of new strength and insight took its place. Morality rested inside Serena, the mark of a white witch.

Ashton stood behind Serena, and she leaned into her as she wound her fingers through Ashton's. For a long moment no one spoke.

Yolanda cleared her throat and pointed to the mason jar that contained the concoction Serena had made from the dirt and bark of the Devil Tree. "Well, no point standing around all day. Take that and follow me. It's time you end this."

Yolanda led Serena through the back door entering her garden. Serena turned behind her, still holding Ashton's hand. Ashton smiled at Serena, following her into the garden.

"Is it safe to go outside?" Serena questioned before stepping out through the back door. Her worried eyes scanned the garden for signs of the diabolical fog.

"My fire protects us," Yolanda answered as she shuffled down the steps of her cottage. "The fog cannot reach us here."

Yolanda walked to an ancient oak tree that stood firm and solid, its roots secured deep in the ground. Witch bottles clinked in its branches.

"You had it right, girl. Everything in this world requires balance. An ask and an answer. And like everything in this world, there are twins, good and evil, yin and yang. The Devil Tree on your property is the evil in Conjure Lake." Yolanda stopped beneath the sprawling branches of the oak tree and looked up. "This oak on my property is its answer—its sister, if you will. This oak tree contains the spirits of our white witch sisters who came before. This oak tree is powered by the best in all of us." She turned to Serena, her eyes grave. "I can't follow you to where you must venture, Serena, but I will remain here, as a guardian to protect you as you go through to the other realm."

"What do you mean, other realm?" Ashton asked.

Yolanda put her hands on her hips. "Was I talking to you, girl? Jack's soul is trapped in the Devil Tree. Serena's gotta go get him."

Ashton drew in a breath, her eyes on Serena. Serena felt faint. She understood what was expected of her. Since the moment Serena laid eyes on the crab apple tree, she'd feared it, sensed its darkness, its otherness. She thought back to the sketch she'd done that first night, of the twisted black branches that seemed to spear the sky, and the bark that reminded her of the skin of poisonous snakes. The tainted fruit that bore dead embryos, the twisty branches that reached for her when she walked by.

Serena couldn't imagine what darkness lingered inside such an evil tree, and the thought of Jack's soul being trapped inside such wickedness filled her with despair. Was he hurt? Did he think she'd abandoned him? She pictured Jack hiding, finding a cold, dark corner to crawl into and vanish among the shadows.

Jack always hid when he was afraid. When Serena came home after the accident, Jack was in his closet, hiding under a blanket, shaking and silent. That was how Serena found him, scared, broken and lost under a security blanket with Tinker in his arms. She broke down crying, seeing her little brother as a huddled mass of blankets on the floor, all alone in the dark. That day she'd knelt beside him on the closet floor, wrapping her arms around his small frame. "I will never leave you," she'd whispered to him, promising Jack would never be alone.

But even a child knew that was a promise no one could make.

"What if you die, too?" Jack had whispered beneath his blanket.

Serena had gently pulled the blanket off of Jack's head and lifted his chin to meet her eyes. "I'm not going to die. I promise death won't take me because I won't go anywhere that you're not." She reached out her pinky to seal the deal.

Jack had stared at Serena's outstretched hand, and with a deep breath, he reached out and linked pinkies with her, then allowed her to pull him out of the closet and into her arms. Serena never broke a promise. Death wouldn't be coming for her. "How many days until the full moon, Jack?" she asked in a soft whisper. Jack kept a calendar on his nightstand by the bed. He'd written "full moon in twenty-eight days," at the top of the month.

"Twenty-eight days," he replied.

"That's right and that's a certainty, isn't it?" Jack nodded yes.

"Then trust in that, okay? Trust that some things in life are certain. And I'm one of them."

The blanket had fallen away from Jack's shoulders and his hand found his sister's. "Let's go for a walk outside," she'd said. Together, they'd walked out of the dark closet and into the sunlight.

Serena clutched the mason jar of Yolanda's concoction to her chest, the earth and tree bark swirling in a black liquid. She had kept her promise. Death didn't come for her — it had come for Jack instead.

"Drink the potion and I will open the portal to the other realm," Yolanda ordered. "You will find yourself on the other side of the Devil Tree. Jack will be there. His soul is still close by. You will have to find him and bring him back to our realm."

Serena's eyes were wide with trepidation, but her hands were steady, and she gave her aunt a quick nod. For Jack, she'd do it. For Jack, she'd do anything.

Yolanda placed her hands on Serena's face. "If I could, I would follow you. I would stay with you until the very end of time itself, but I am not allowed. Only you can go. You bear the mark of the raven on your neck. The raven has claimed you. Only you can enter."

Ashton clutched Serena's hand and squeezed it three times. "I'll be here, Serena. I'll wait for you. You'll find him and you'll bring him back to us."

Serena flung herself into Ashton's arms, and Ashton made soft, indistinguishable sounds as she smoothed her hands over Serena's hair and down her back, pressing kisses to her cheek and ear.

"I'll be back, Ashton," Serena mumbled into her neck. "I'll end this."

"I know you will," Ashton whispered as she pressed a kiss to Serena's temple, then cheek. Serena turned her face toward Ashton in invitation, and slowly the space between their mouths closed. Separated by a hair's breadth, they breathed into each other before their lips met. Ashton closed her eyes, allowing Serena's lips to find hers as she wrapped her arms around Serena's hips, pulling her closer into their embrace. "You taste like cinnamon and magic," Ashton whispered.

Serena giggled, the sound as soft as Ashton's lips, as she brought her fingers to her mouth. "Honey. You taste like honey," Serena whispered back. Their foreheads touched one last time as they gripped each other's hands. They stayed like that for a precious moment under the full moon, both knowing that a moment was all they could spare.

Too soon, Serena stepped back and cracked open the mason jar. It hissed and bubbled. Serena gave it a sniff and wrinkled her nose. Disgusting. With one last glance to Yolanda and Ashton, she tipped the jar back and swallowed. Her body immediately rebelled, and she swallowed again, forcing the vile contents to stay down. It churned in her stomach, the bitter, acrid taste of hate and vengeance and fear.

Yolanda watched, nodding grimly. "All of it, girl. You have to drink all of it."

Everything she loathed in this world was before her in a single cup of death and destruction. She tipped back the jar, allowing the hot fluid to coat her throat, clawing and burning as she swallowed. Eyes watering, Serena passed the now empty jar to Ashton.

Yolanda took the jar from Ashton's hand and set it on the steps of her porch. Next, she drew a piece of white chalk from her dress pocket and traced a large circle on the center of the oak tree.

"Are you ready, girl?" she asked in a hushed voice. Serena drew her shoulders back and nodded. Yolanda knelt down and closed her eyes as she raised her hands in the air, speaking the incantation to open the portal. A white light glowed from her palms as she chanted.

"I ask on my knees
for the circle to open to me.
Unlock your secret door.
Allow Serena to walk through and finish the score.
Guide her on to the other side
where death and evil reside."

The bleached circle of chalk on the trunk of the tree glowed a soft white light, and as Yolanda chanted, the glow swirled and brightened until Serena had to squint to see it. The circle slowly sank inside the bark like a snake eating its own tail while drowning in quicksand. The tree swallowed the circle whole, leaving a vast hollow opening that stretched and gaped like an open mouth. A piercing chill escaped the circle, engulfing Serena's body and ruffling her messy bun. She shivered from the touch of death, turning her face away from the tree.

"It's not the tree that is haunting you, but the raven who is waiting for you on the other side," Yolanda said gravely. "This tree leads to a passage where the Devil Tree connects. You will be safe until you reach the Devil Tree. Once there, the protection of my white magic will leave you and you will be on your own." Yolanda's voice broke. "My own niece, blood of my blood, my sister witch. I'd lasso the moon and take its place in the night sky, forced to live in solitude forever, banished from this world if it meant I could change places with you, Serena. So young and new in your powers…"

"I know," Serena said softly as she laid a hand on the Wise Woman's arm. "I know you would. But this is my duty, my brother. This is what I am meant to do."

"You are a brave witch," Yolanda said, the words tight in her throat.

Serena turned to face the tree. Its gaping hole was ominous and dark. She paused and turned back to her aunt. "How will I find Jack?"

"You have his glasses, don't you? Hold them tight in your hand, and they will be your eyes in the spirit realm. Use them to help you find Jack. He will know it's you because you'll have a piece of him. They will help him find you as well."

Serena's face paled. "I don't have them. I left them at the cottage."

"I didn't," Ashton spoke, her voice ragged. "I put them in my pocket for safe-keeping." She reached into the pocket of her damp pants and pulled them out. One of the smudged lenses had a crack. "But I don't know if I did a very good job of that."

Yolanda gave Ashton a rare look of approval. "You did well enough. Give them to Serena and they will guide them to each other."

With a grateful look, Serena accepted the glasses from Ashton's outstretched hand. "I couldn't do this without you, Ashton."

Ashton smiled. "You don't have to."

With a deep breath and Jack's glasses clutched in her fist, Serena turned to Yolanda. "What do I do once I find Jack?"

"You run, girl. You run straight back to me, and you don't let anything get in your way."

"But what about the raven?" Serena asked. "She will follow me."

"You worry about finding your brother. Leave that part to me. The raven will not be able to come through this tree, I will make sure of it."

Serena had too many questions. How would they kill Alice Lake? How would they banish the raven from coming after her and Jack once the tree was sealed up, and what if the siblings were trapped inside?

"Just return with Jack," Yolanda instructed. "Your light will guide you to him. You will feel him, hear him, but you may not see him. He's on another plane — that world does not work like ours. It's the spirit realm. Trust your heart. It will guide you. Listen to your intuition. The power in your blood will guide you to safety, as long as you follow the path of light and use the glasses, they can see things you won't be able to."

Serena's eye found the stained and empty jar sitting on the porch steps. A wave of dizziness passed over her. She could feel her very soul slipping out of her body, escaping her chest without permission. Another wave of dizziness passed over her, stronger than before, and her knees felt weak. As she sank to the ground, Ashton slipped to her side and pulled her into her arms.

"So c-c-cold," Serena stammered, her teeth chattering. "It's getting dark." Ashton held her close, burying her face in Serena's neck. "Am I dying?" Serena croaked. Choking darkness threatened the edges of her vision, and her breath came in pants. Was this how it ended? Poisoned by her own concoction? Was this her fate? To die before she could save her brother?

"What's happening to her?" Ashton narrowed her eyes on Yolanda as Serena went limp in her arms, her knuckles white where she held onto Ashton.

"Hush, girl. You aren't dying. You are spirit walking. Your body will stay here with us, like Jack at Korwin Cottage. Your soul will depart. I promise I will guard you while you are on your journey. I will not leave you, not for one moment, not for anything in this world."

"I've got you, too, Serena," Ashton whispered in her ear. "I'll be here with you the whole time. I promise I won't let you go."

Serena's eyes fluttered shut. She took one last breath, and her body stilled. Ashton's face was the last thing she saw before the world went black.

"Serena?" Ashton asked tentatively as she shifted her grip on Serena's limp form. She pressed her fingertips to Serena's jaw. "There's no pulse." Ashton looked up at Yolanda accusingly. "She's dead. She's gone, just like Jack." Ashton cradled Serena's lifeless body in her arms, tears rolling down her cheeks. She bent, pressing her ear to Serena's chest.

Ashton turned to face Yolanda. "Jack still had a pulse when the raven took his soul." Tears fell faster, dripping onto Serena's upturned face. "Serena has no pulse. She's dead." Her voice wavered as panic set in. "Please tell me she is not dead!"

"Enough with the hysterics, girl! She's not dead! I told you both — she's spirit walking. Her body must hibernate so her soul can move on to the next realm. It's the only way for her to bring back Jack."

Ashton carefully laid Serena down and sat cross-legged, Serena's head in her lap. She pulled out the pencils in her bun and stroked her long, tangled hair. "But Jack had a pulse. I know — I checked myself. Serena doesn't." She stroked Serena's cheek. It was cool to the touch.

Yolanda loomed over Ashton and Serena and crossed her arms, her face stern. "Now you listen to me, girl. There's a reason God gave you two ears and one mouth. So you can hear more than you should speak! Like I told you, Serena is not dead — only her body is dead, but this is temporary. As long as her soul is in the other realm, she can return to her body and will be very much alive once again. Think of it this way — her spark of life moved out of its earthly vehicle and is now traveling, or spirit walking, through the realm. But Jack isn't spirit walking. Jack's soul was taken."

Yolanda sighed as she settled herself beside Ashton and Serena's prone form on the grass. She looked down at her niece, her face grave. "Jack's body can remain in a comatose state for three days without his soul, but when the sun rises on the third day, if Jack is still trapped in the other realm, his soul will belong to the night kingdom and he can never return to his body. His heart will stop beating and he will die before the rooster crows."

"Three days?" Ashton asked in disbelief. "Will Serena be gone that long?"

Yolanda shook her head. "I don't know, girl. I hope not. This is her battle now. It is her role to fight. It is our role to sit vigil. Women have been comforting women at their bedsides since the beginning of time. Now we sit. We watch. And we wait."

Ashton squeezed her eyes shut, but when she opened them, her tears were gone. "Okay," she said softly. "We wait."

Yolanda's gnarled hand found Ashton's, and she squeezed it as she looked down at her niece. "We are two people sharing a love for one person," Yolanda whispered. "You have no idea how powerful that is. Power and strength that Serena needs right now." Her green eyes met Ashton's clear gray ones. "You must be very brave to come here and very strong of heart to outrun that fog."

Ashton looked up at the night sky, which was void of stars. Slowly she shook her head. "No, I'm not. It was Serena. She did everything. I just tried to keep her safe. Obviously I didn't do a very good job." Ashton looked over at Yolanda. Her green eyes glowed in the darkness, like the wings of a Luna moth.

Yolanda shook her head. "That's where you are wrong, girl. You saved Serena from Alice the first night you met. She drew your picture in her book. You two were meant to find each other. You see, the love of a witch protects those in her heart. And witches tend to love other witches most of all. There's a reason we seek covens and female companions."

"But I'm not a witch." Ashton's fingers trailed down Serena's cool arm. "I'm not anything special."

Yolanda bent her head at Ashton. "Maybe. Maybe not. You were able to outrun the fog. You were able to treat Serena's wounds. You were able to make her love you. There's magic in that. Like I said, there's a little witchiness in all the women of Conjure Lake. The love between two witches is cosmic and beautiful, in all its forms. Platonic, familial or romantic. It's deep, girl, and it's pure. You being here strengthens her, even if it seems you aren't doing anything. Loving her makes her stronger. You can do that, right?"

Ashton looked up at the starless night as she let out a long breath. "I can do that. What happens now? What do we do while we wait for her?"

Yolanda sighed. She knew the answer would not satisfy Ashton. "It's up to her now. She will need to walk among all the lost souls the raven has claimed, and without using her eyes, she will have to find Jack."

Ashton processed Yolanda's words as she stroked Serena's cheek. "And once she finds Jack?"

Yolanda looked out over the dark waters of Lake Conjure. The night was still. "Then we go to the Devil Tree and reunite Jack with his body. That tree, girl, is where we end it."

"But how? Cut it down?" she asked.

Yolanda huffed a humorless laugh. "No, that would be too easy. Alice Lake is an ancient witch who has possessed the body of a raven. It has become her opus for evil, and it will not go down without a fight. No, we will need to kill the raven before we can banish Alice. We must take a picture of Alice Lake and nail it to the tree. Then we'll need to pluck one feather from the raven itself. Serena will need to open the tree to retrieve

Jack's soul. His glasses will guide her through the darkness. Once his soul is safely through, we will thrust the feather inside the entrance and seal the hole back up. You with me so far?"

Ashton nodded, her face determined. "What happens then?"

"We will need to work quickly and make a sacred circle surrounding the tree and call forth the four corners — earth, water, fire and air. All the elements combined will cause a storm unlike anything you've ever witnessed. As long as the circle isn't disturbed, the storm will be contained within its lines. Then, we simply order lighting to strike the tree, call forth fire to set the tree ablaze and rain to wash away the evil," she said, ticking them off on each finger. "Finally, we call the earth to swallow the tree and take it back to hell."

Ashton shook her head, sighing heavily. "Well, when you put it that way, you make it sound so easy." Her words were teasing, but her heavy tone belied her fear. She looked down at the lifeless body of the girl she loved — or something close to it, something that felt warm and kind and good, something that would turn into love if they nurtured it. And Ashton hoped they'd get that chance. Ashton gently kissed Serena once more time as she wound a strand of Serena's white-blonde hair in her fingertips. She brought the strand to her face, stroking its softness over her cheek and inhaling Serena's soft scent. She smelled like blueberries and pancakes, like childhood memories, like the woman she was in love with but had only just met.

Ashton stared off into the garden, visualizing the road ahead of them. "Then that's how we will end it," she said. "I'll follow your lead. I'll do whatever it takes." Ashton raked her long fingers through Serena's hair, smoothing her hands over her face and arms, either to comfort Serena, or to comfort herself.

Yolanda paced back and forth before the proud oak tree, muttering incantations under her breath. She would not allow one tinge of evil to escape. Yolanda could feel Serena moving further away from their world and deeper into the other realm, like an invisible string stretched taut between them. If Serena got into trouble, she'd know it. She'd feel the line between them snap, just like it had the day the raven had claimed her sister Edith and drowned her in Conjure Lake.

A heavy sense of inevitability fell over Yolanda. When Yolanda and Edith were young, they knew the raven would come. The rotten tree grew in their yard, and they knew never to approach it, never to let its twisted black branches tangle in their hair or pull at their clothes. The tree was a constant reminder of the threat that hung over their heads, should Alice Lake ever be released. Their mother put all her energy into preparing the sisters, teaching them to be ever vigilant of signs of the raven's appearance.

Their earliest lessons in the garden were protection spells, their mother instructing them to hold hands as they cast lines of salt on the earth. The young sisters ran barefoot in the woods, feeling the cold ground for the raven. They drank loose leaf tea under a sycamore tree, scanning their empty cups for the symbol of the raven. They kept watch for the coming of the black omen of death.

Yolanda and Edith had been schooled on the history of Alice Lake since they were children, and warned of their duty to guard her. The raven was sneaky, and would appear when the girls found themselves alone, to torment, taunt and tempt them. To turn to the darkness, the promise of unlimited power dangling before them, striving to turn the girls evil, as Alice Lake herself once did centuries ago. It wasn't clear which sister the raven had set its sights on until the night before Edith's eighteenth birthday.

Yolanda had not always been a solitary witch in the woods. Long before she became the Wise Woman, she was just Yolanda Korwin, a simple girl of Conjure Lake. Yolanda had fallen in love with a boy named Callum. He was the son of a traveling sales agent who was passing through town on his way to Rochester. The salesman had stopped at Korwin Cottage for a tarot card reading, and he had his son with him. But Yolanda and Edith's parents had been away that day. Their parents traveled often to neighboring towns, selling their produce at various markets, and offering what concoctions and comforts their witch mother could to the area.

Edith had stood on the porch of Korwin Cottage as she explained to the man their mother was away. But Yolanda paid no attention to the older man. She only saw the boy with him.

As was the way with witches, Yolanda had fallen in love with the boy the very instant she laid eyes on him. Callum was tall and lean, with chocolate-colored hair and almond-shaped eyes. Yolanda had watched Callum from behind a rosebush, creeping through the flowerbeds like a fox on a hunt. Callum had spied her, and pretended not to notice the feral young witch stalking him. She'd crept up behind him, and he'd turned at the last minute and shouted, "Boo!"

Yolanda had fallen back on her ass in shock, then they'd both howled with laughter.

Yolanda could remember the sound of his warm laugh. It had brought a tingling sensation on her arms, causing goosebumps to rise on her skin. Callum was just as affected. The city boy had been enamored with the wild young witch of Conjure Lake, and he wanted her just as badly as she wanted him.

All her life Yolanda had been instructed to stay with her sister, to never leave her alone at Korwin Cottage. There was strength in numbers, and it was their duty to look out for one another, for the threat of the raven hung over them always, and they had to be ever vigilant for trouble.

It had been just one night. But it had been enough. Yolanda closed her eyes to the painful memories that threatened to overwhelm her. She had failed her sister once. She would not fail Serena.

The memories flooded Yolanda like an unwelcome ocean wave. Callum would have stayed with Yolanda forever if she had let him. Yolanda was instructed not to leave Edith alone at Korwin Cottage.

The next day had been Edith's eighteenth birthday, and their parents still had not returned from their travels. A woman was in labor, and it was a difficult one. Their mother was needed to serve as a midwife. So Yolanda had baked a birthday cake for her sister. They were going to celebrate that night, just the two of them. The two sisters had sat cross-legged on the porch, laughing as they sliced the cake, and eating it piece by piece until they had stomachaches. Edith decided to go to bed early after a warm cup of tea to settle her tummy.

When Callum emerged from the darkness to appear on their porch, he pleaded with Yolanda to go for a walk with him in the woods. He and his father were departing the next day, and he begged to have a few

Rebecca Henry

hours with the beautiful green-eyed Yolanda. She knew she shouldn't, but Yolanda imagined Edith safely tucked in bed, asleep. And so she'd left her. Left to steal kisses in the darkness with Callum.

Yolanda pressed a fist to her chest. This part of her memory always hurt the most, and was the part she always returned to, like poking a bruise to make sure it still hurt.

Yolanda met Callum at the edge of town by the old cemetery. As Yolanda lay with Callum in the cool cemetery grass, lost in his kisses, she felt her sister's fear like an icy blade in her back. With a gasp, she'd sat up. *Edith.*

Yolanda had sprinted through the night as Callum called to her. Yolanda flew over the familiar ground barefoot, hardly noticing the stones cutting her feet, and she felt her sister's fear and panic. *"I'm coming, sister!"* Yolanda had screamed into the dark night.

She thundered up the porch steps and to the bedroom she shared with her sister. Edith had been huddled in her closet, wrapped in a blanket. Two bite marks marred the soft skin of her neck. Alice had found her alone, and without the protective power of two sister witches, she had been able to strike. The raven had claimed Edith as its victim.

From that day forward, the raven had haunted Edith, filling her dreams with darkness and fear, stalking her, hoping to catch her alone, never relenting. Until the day it finally succeeded, and Edith drowned alone in the same waters that had sustained and strengthened the witches of Conjure Lake.

Yolanda never forgave herself for leaving Edith alone that day. She punished herself with guilt, wondering if she wasn't so selfish, maybe her sister might not have been chosen by Alice to face the raven. And she never saw Callum again. He lived only in her memories, his face hurt and longing as she left him in the cemetery.

Yolanda never spoke the boy's name again. How could she be with him when her selfishness had allowed the raven to claim her sweet sister? With a broken heart, she cursed her own selfishness as she burned each letter he sent, three a week for an entire year. She thought if she rejected his love, then somehow, she could correct the raven selecting Edith and distance herself from her own selfish longings. In penance, Yolanda never took a lover, for it was her own selfish heart that had allowed her sweet sister to be claimed by Alice Lake.

Where Yolanda was hard, Edith was soft. When Yolanda was impatient, it was Edith who soothed her nerves. Edith had been all lightness. There was so much of her in Serena, it pained Yolanda. Yolanda knew she was not Edith's equal. Where Edith found grace in the sarcasm of others, Yolanda found spite. Edith blessed those who did her harm and turned the other cheek. Yolanda faced her enemies head-on, determined to stand her ground.

As the seasons turned, so did her bitterness, and the hate she felt for herself bled into the world around her. Yolanda turned inward, and moved to the cottage deep in the woods, distancing herself from others with their superstitious fears and baseless hate. Edith would tell her sister to forgive the fearful townspeople who whispered about Yolanda and called her the swamp witch behind her back. They were just scared, uneducated souls who didn't know any better, Edith would say. Yolanda would only snort, waving her hands in the air. She believed in the worst in people and expected nothing less.

Yolanda knew it was her black-hearted selfishness that saved her from being targeted by the raven. The raven only sought the pure of heart. Edith was a gift of compassion, a bleeding heart who sacrificed her needs for those around her. Yolanda wished she could have been as good as Edith, if only to protect her dear sister from the fate that came for her.

Edith never blamed her, and Yolanda suffered from the guilt of that as well. She would have to punish herself for the two of them, for her sweet sister would never condemn her selfish heart. Instead, Edith took on the brunt of containing the Devil Tree, turning to her powers for protection. Yolanda swore she would dedicate her life to help strengthen her sister's defenses, and would protect her for the rest of her days.

But Yolanda had failed that as well. Failed to protect her sister, and failed to protect Edith's daughter, Rose. Rose knew the raven would search for her on her eighteenth birthday, just as it had sought out and marked her mother. The morning of Rose's eighteenth birthday, she visited her Aunt Yolanda one last time to explain why she was leaving and why she would never return. The curse would end with her, she'd said, and she'd never return to the place of her birth so the raven would never be able to reach her.

Yolanda knew this was her fault as well. If only she had been better, if only she could have been the one the raven wanted, both Edith and Rose would have been spared. Then the raven claimed Rose as well, and her husband, leaving two kids orphaned and alone.

So much guilt. So many failures. So many sister witches who had suffered from Yolanda's failures. She would not allow herself to fail Serena. Yolanda waited by Serena's body, her heart heavy with guilt, her mind thick with sorrow. She would not watch another Korwin die. She wouldn't allow the raven to take her sweet niece the way it claimed her dear sister and niece.

She had to protect Edith's grandchildren. She wouldn't fail her sister, not again.

Chapter Fourteen

Within

Serena sat up and looked around. She could see Ashton and Aunt Yolanda leaning over her, their faces creased with worry. Puzzled, she got to her feet and looked down. Of course. She was spirit walking. That was her body they were leaning over. It was her, but not. It was a strange sensation, watching Ashton stroke her blonde hair back from her slack face. She felt as though she were intruding on a private moment, though she was the one the private moment was with, technically. Her heart filled with warmth for the two brave women watching over her still silent body on the ground. She needed to be brave, too.

Serena looked down at her hand where she still clutched Jack's glasses. Ahead, the portal within the oak tree loomed. In this realm, the chalk-lined edges of the circle Yolanda had made on the trunk of the tree swirled in iridescent colors, making the gaping blackness of the hole within the tree all the more ominous.

"I guess I just fall in, like Alice in Wonderland?" She looked over her shoulder to her aunt and Ashton, but of course they hadn't heard her. Couldn't hear her. Right. She was on her own. "Okay, here goes nothing," she said through gritted teeth as she laid a hand on the swirling edges of the tree and pressed herself to the darkness.

Then she was inside. Serena walked through a narrow passage inside the Tree of Life. The walls were close, made of twisted roots and bark that brushed her shoulders as she made her way through the dark and winding tunnel. A soft glow surrounded her as she moved onward. She realized the glow was fireflies gathering together to guide her through the passage. "Thank you," she breathed, and the fireflies pulsed in response. Sister witches long dead, perhaps by Alice's hand, showing her a way. The ground was hard, also made from gnarled roots, which lay before her as a path.

Serena could tell the moment when she moved beyond the root line of the Tree of Life. The air became cold, or not cold exactly, as she couldn't feel anything without her body, but chilled nonetheless. Her eyes were vailed in a sheet of blackness. She didn't know what was waiting ahead, but she could sense the despair thickening the air, coating the passage in sorrow. As she neared the spirit realm to the Devil Tree, Serena was consumed with sadness, and one by one, the light of each firefly winked out. All the lost hope and tragedy from the souls captured within were forming a black aura. The air grew thick with despair and hopelessness.

Serena couldn't see her hand in front of her face. Serena understood why she could not rely on her eyes.

The blackness was all-consuming, covering the realm in a sheet of despair made from the broken-hearted. Mothers who lost their infants, twins who were separated from their siblings—all screamed out to Serena inside the tree. She clenched her teeth, trying to block out their cries, though they tore at her heart. One foot in front of the other. She had to get to the other tree. The space around her opened up, and an icy breeze blew around her, though she was still blind to her surroundings. She put on Jack's cracked glasses, and suddenly she could see. Everything was still dark, still black, but she could see shadow forms within the darkness. *This must be Jack's spark of light showing me the way.* She turned a wide circle, then stumbled. Something was on the ground. No, someone.

It was a body, a boy. *Jack.* With her heart in her throat she dropped to her knees and reached out, but when she turned the body over to examine the face, she was horrified to discover the boy had no features—only a smooth surface of pale skin covered where his face should be. "Jack?" she asked, and she jumped when the body twitched.

Serena gasped. "Jack, is that you?" she asked. She shook the boy and his non-face twitched again, but the boy could not speak, for his mouth was gone. No eyes, no nose, no mouth. Only smooth, twitching skin. He could hear her. She placed her hands over the boy's eyes, channeling his life memories. Images flowed over and through her, of a young boy on vacation with his family. He was around Jack's age, perhaps a little older. He was on a boat, sandwiched between two smiling people. His mom and dad. She could feel the love they had for him, and the trust and love he felt for them. She experienced his fear and panic as a storm rose from nowhere, toppling the boat. The raven had collected him, bringing him here to this terrible shadow place of limbo while it left his parents to drown in Conjure Lake.

Serena choked back tears. She grieved for his young life that was taken abruptly before his life fully began. She hung her head, unable to help the boy. It was unfair how the boy's fate was a thousand times worse than what his parents endured. She wondered how long he'd been trapped here, alone and cold, mute and forgotten. He still had ears, and she leaned down to whisper in one.

"I will help you," she promised to the boy. "I will kill the raven, and I will set you free, or die trying." As she started to stand, he reached for her, dragging his body toward her retreating voice. Serena took his hand in hers and placed it on her cheek. "You've been so brave. Just hold on a little longer. I'll free you. Once the raven is dead, I will summon your soul to be free. I promise."

Serena walked on, unsure of which direction to go in. She remembered her aunt's words — to follow her light, that it would lead her to Jack — but Serena couldn't see her light within the blackness which engulfed her. The glasses allowed only a sliver of flickering light, casting long and threatening shadows that seemed to twist and move like serpents. Huddled bodies littered the ground, and bits of smoldering ash fell from the sky as though the night were on fire and the stars themselves had died. She was in a clearing of sorts, and scorched trees hung low, crooked branches depleted of leaves. Everything was charred, including the moon, which hung dead in the black sky. The air was cloying and smelled of choking death. She was close to the Devil Tree.

Serena pressed her fingers to the smudged and cracked lenses of Jack's glasses as she concentrated on him. She imagined his sweet little voice, his broad, happy smile. His golden hair that always looked like sunlight and honey, that shone like their mother's. More forms tensed and twitched on the ground, more victims of the raven, and Serena stepped carefully to avoid treading on one. One by one they'd lift their heads, each one as faceless as the last, and reach toward her with outstretched hands. They could hear her. With horror, she realized Alice had left their ears so they could hear others' cries of torment. She avoided the poor souls' outstretched grasps. With her mind's eye, she reached out with her witching sense, searching this terrible place for her brother. Serena called to Jack as she visualized him spinning in circles in their front yard in the city, back when their parents were alive, when life was good and free of misery. *Sissy.* A light pulsed just beyond Serena's vision, and she whipped her head around. Jack was close. She felt him calling out to her from beyond the woods.

Serena ran as if the ground was hot with embers burning her feet, hurdling over the husks of Alice's victims that lay scattered like discarded trash. She ran toward the woods, toward his voice. She knew he was close, that Jack could sense her as well. She pressed Jack's glasses further up her nose and looked around the vast darkness. With a gasp, she saw him, lit like a Christmas tree. Her presence in the other realm was a blinding beacon of light shining bright in the dark, and with his glasses Serena could see Jack hidden amongst the branches of a black and twisted sycamore tree. She stumbled to his side and dropped to her knees, cradling his head in her hands as she pressed her forehead to his. She'd found him.

Like the others, his eyes were gone, the skin smooth and flat where his nose should be. His mouth had disappeared, but his ears remained, and he could hear his sister calling to him. "I've got you, little brother," Serena whispered as she pulled Jack into her lap.

Even blind, he knew it was his sister. He would know her anywhere. His arms went around her and Jack pressed his featureless face into her chest. Serena stroked his back.

Jack knew his sister would come for him. Just as sure as the sun rises every morning no matter the weather, he knew Serena would come find him. Jack understood he was in the Devil Tree, and that she was beside him. He could feel her arms and hear her voice. Jack responded to her calls in his mind. He said her name over and over in his heart. He willed her to find him with every fiber of his soul. And she did.

Jack couldn't see, but he could feel and sense. He could detect shadows lurking in the corners of the trees, other lost souls hiding from the raven. He always knew when the raven was approaching the way one knew death was prowling at their door. Jack could sense it coming now, and his hands found Serena's arms and squeezed. He had to warn her. It was coming. It was almost here. Around them, other forms shifted and moved as if they also felt its approach. The raven. Serena's presence had woken the raven, and it would be here soon.

Jack knew it wasn't him that the raven wanted—it was Serena. Jack was merely the worm dangling on the raven's hook. Even without eyes, Jack could detect the force of light and love that shone from Serena, and he knew it was this light that the raven craved. Not to steal, but to consume and conquer. To absorb and destroy and feed upon.

Jack had never been brave like his big sister. He was always the scared one, the one who was afraid of spiders and shadows. He hated the dark, and had begged his dad to keep a nightlight on in his bedroom, a sliver of light to ease his fear in the dark.

But now the darkness was alive, and it would give chase. Jack pulled back from his sister's arms and blindly stumbled to his feet. "Jack?" Serena probed as she rose to her feet as well and reached for his hand. She didn't know what was flying on death's wings. She hadn't seen the raven in its full form in this realm. She didn't know its terrible touch that burned and killed inside the tree. But Jack did, and he was afraid. In his mind he screamed one word over and over — *Run*.

Serena heard his frantic cries through their mental connection that linked them, and she gripped Jack's small hand in hers and ran, dragging Jack behind her, careful to steer his blind run around the reaching bodies that littered the root-twisted ground below them.

With her witching sense Serena felt the shadow of the raven pass over them like a cool whisper of silk. The raven was close now. Its massive wings whistled as it approached the siblings. Serena dared to cast a glimpse over her shoulder, and through the cracked lenses of Jack's glasses, she saw the raven's bloody beak open in a screeching cry. The bodies on the ground writhed and huddled as they pressed their hands over their tortured ears.

Serena paused long enough to gather Jack in her arms. "I've got you now, Jack," she assured him. "We are going to get out of here." Jack clung to his sister.

The helpless souls on the ground sensed Serena's light and reached out their hands to grasp her ankles as they lifted their eerie, faceless visages to them. Still, Serena ran on. She spared only a glance for the raven, so close she could see her own light reflected in its dark and soulless eyes. It shrieked as it dove for them, and Serena tucked Jack's head under her chin as she hit her knees and rolled. She felt its beak tear at the hair that had come loose from her bun, and she screamed. They weren't going to make it back to the Tree of Life. It was almost upon them. Serena was too slow with her brother in her arms. A sob caught in her throat, knowing they couldn't outrun the raven.

Her scream sent a shockwave through the huddled and broken faceless bodies on the ground. Almost as one they rose to their feet and turned toward the raven, their pale, blank faces turned to the approaching dark. As if they sensed her presence, they stepped aside, clearing a path for her to run through, showing her the way back. As they passed, the faceless bodies closed rank behind them, and they lifted their hands to the raven, waving their arms to block it. The raven cawed furiously and beat its wings against the wave of bodies that pressed forward toward it. They were buying her time, she realized. They were helping her.

She whispered her thanks as one by one the fireflies returned, their dim light blinking on in the winding darkness. Serena's heart was pounding inside her chest, and her ears were ringing as her body struggled to run faster and faster. They were getting closer to the Tree of Life. Serena could see the opening to their realm, the swirling chalk-lined circle of light on the trunk of the Tree of Life just up ahead.

Just then, a root lifted and twisted around her ankle, and Serena stumbled to her knees with Jack in her arms, the glasses flying off her face into the dark beyond. They wouldn't make it. The raven was so close Serena could feel the wind from its wings slapping her in the back, and she curled her body protectively around her small brother. He curled up in a ball as Serena wrapped her arms around him and pressed his featureless face into her neck. She closed her eyes, accepting their fate. She'd tried her best. And failed. If she couldn't save Jack, at least he wouldn't be alone in that world. At least they would be together. No matter what world Jack was sentenced to, Serena would stay with him and they'd face it together. With a sense of finality, Serena kissed her brother's head. Jack wouldn't be lost amongst the other faceless souls who were bound to that realm for all time, for Serena would be there to protect him. Together, the way their parents would have wanted.

Something touched Serena's face, and she flinched back, a sob in her throat. Prying her eyes open, she saw a pale outstretched hand. Serena skittered back with Jack in her arms. Another hand reached out to her. The bodies—Alice's victims. One of them held Jack's glasses out to her, and with a shaking hand, Serena reached out to accept them. The other souls stood around them, forming a circle of protection.

Alice's victims surrounded the siblings, forming a barricade, a wall of faceless bodies ready to do war with the raven. The bodies reached for the raven as it came soaring down, its talons opened wide. The raven grabbed a faceless body and flung it against a crippled tree, but another one was there to take its place. The raven grabbed two more, flinging them across the ground, but more came to replace the two that were taken.

Serena stood up, helping Jack to his feet. Searching the ground, she spied a feather one of the faceless lost souls had pulled from the attacking raven's wings. With the black feather clutched in one hand, Jack's glasses in the other, she pulled Jack to her side and tucked him under her arm.

"Now we run, Jack," she told him as she surged forward. "Run, Jack!" she gasped as the lost souls parted to make way for them. Ahead she could see the shimmering opening of the Tree of Life, and Serena could see her Aunt Yolanda in the far distance, as if viewed through a telescope. She gripped her brother's arms and pressed his glasses to his face. "Wear these," she commanded. "They'll let you see the way to safety." He put them on and turned his featureless face up to Serena. Though he still had no eyes, no nose or mouth, she knew with the glasses he could see her. She pointed through a twisting passageway to where the light shimmered on the chalk-lined circle in the tree. "Keep going, Jack. Keep going until you reach Ashton and Aunt Yolanda." Jack pressed forward, his hands raised in front of him as he stumbled through the twisting portal to safety. Through the distance Serena saw him collapse through the gaping hole to where Aunt Yolanda waited.

Serena followed behind Jack, turning back to glance at the battle that had broken out behind them. She shuddered at the horrific carnage — dozens of bodies stood before the raven, and it beat its wings wildly at the wall of bodies that tore at the bird with clawing fingers. They fought hard, tearing out feathers, clawing at the raven's eyes. The ground was littered with broken bodies, but still more surged over their blind forms. The raven fought madly, tearing limbs from its victims, but still they came, relentless. The raven charged through the crowd, plucking off arms, clawing at the bodies, shredding them in pieces.

Serena kept running, and the tunnel seemed to telescope, the twisted roots of the walls urging her onward. She could hear her aunt yelling for her to be quick, to hurry. The walls narrowed, and she had to turn sideways as she ran through the narrowing corridor of the tree. Roots lifted from the ground to trip her, slicing at her ankles like razor blades, yet still she ran. Branches moved, reaching for her like blades of a sword, one reaching and leaving a long line of blood across her cheek.

Serena saw the light from the Tree of Life shimmering as she approached. The tree was calling for her, pleading for her to make it through. The raven screamed in fury, spitting the blood of the innocents who tried to hold it back. Serena ran until her chest felt like it might break into pieces. The portal swallowed her, moving her quickly through its womb. With shaking hands she reached toward the shimmering circle of light, and she tumbled through the Tree of Life's opening. She emerged as a glowing ball of blinding white light, and she floated past her Aunt Yolanda to her own body that lay in Ashton's arms, still and frozen in the grass. Ashton held onto Serena's body as her spirit slipped back inside her chest, bringing life once more to her silent heart.

Serena gasped as she opened her eyes. Ashton's arms went around her, and Ashton sobbed into her hair as she hugged her, kissing her forehead, tears streaking her face. Serena sat up and opened her hand — a black feather rested in her palm. Yolanda stood beside them, holding a glass jar with a tiny light inside. Serena reached for the jar, rubbing her thumb over the glass. The light mimicked the movement of her thumb. The mason jar held the spark of Jack's soul.

"We will get you back to your body, Jack," Serena whispered. "I love you so much." Serena kissed the jar and cradled it to her chest.

Ashton helped Serena to her feet. Her body felt so heavy after the lightness of traveling through the tree, and she sagged against Ashton. "Serena...I'm so sorry. I wish I could have been there with you."

"You waited for me, Ashton," Serena rasped as she stole her arms around Ashton, and Ashton held her up. She pressed their foreheads together and Serena smiled. Ashton smelled of cedar and lily pads and everything that was good, and Serena took a deep breath, inhaling her scent. She wanted to drink her aroma and feel it trickle down the back of her throat, which still felt raw from her screams inside the tree, even though her body had stayed here the entire time. She reached up and felt wetness on her cheek. Somehow the injuries from inside the tree must have been reflected in her frozen body. She felt humbled by the terror that Ashton must have felt, and honored that she'd stayed, that she'd come with her on this hellish journey at all. So many words bubbled up in Serena's throat, so many she couldn't speak. Instead, Serena took Ashton by the hand, giving it three gentle squeezes. Ashton smiled gently, understanding, no words needed.

Yolanda looked up to the sky. The fog had lifted. "Okay, lovebirds, break it up. We must go," Yolanda said. "The raven is weakened, but it is not dead. We have an advantage, but it won't last long." Yolanda ushered Serena and Ashton out of the garden as she passed Serena her tote bag with her spellbook and the jar containing the soul of her brother. "Hurry. Get to the boat. We need to end this tonight."

Serena placed the glass jar gently in the bag then set it between her legs as she steered the boat out of the dock. Yolanda was in the front holding a flashlight while Ashton sat in the back, a paddle across her knees. Serena had no way of knowing how much time had passed, but full dark had fallen and no stars winked between the black tree branches. The lake was quiet. Not a toad croaked, nor a cricket chirped. Bats stayed hidden inside trees, while fish hid among the seaweed at the bottom of the lake. The moon peeked out from the dark clouds and shone brightly on the glimmering water of Conjure Lake as they traveled back to Korwin Cottage. A red ring circled the moon, a sign of blood and death. Yolanda aimed the flashlight at the calm water, but nothing emerged to drag them below the dark water's surface. It felt as if the whole world were holding its breath, waiting to see what would come next.

Serena wondered, too. "Aunt Yolanda...how do we join Jack's soul back to his body?" Her whisper echoed over the still night air.

"By ripping out the raven from the tree that took him," Yolanda answered without turning around. "That's how."

Serena and Ashton cut silently through the water to draw the boat up to Serena's dock. Ashton jumped out first, then turned to help Yolanda. "Get your hands off me," Yolanda groused as she climbed onto the dock. "I'm not long in the tooth, girl. I've been getting in and out of boats without assistance since your daddy's daddy was knee high to a grasshopper and I'll be doing this well until I'm dead."

Ashton's lips formed a tight line as she looked over at Serena, and despite the danger, Serena laughed. Ashton shook her head as she found Serena's hand, and together they faced the Devil Tree. If Deaken had been here, he was obviously long gone now, and Serena smiled with grim satisfaction that her binding and banishment spell had worked.

The cursed tree looked contorted in the moonlight. Its branches twisted and writhed in pain. The leaves rustled, then turned black and glowed like armor. As they drew closer to the tree, Serena could feel with her witching sense the raven stirring inside the tree, fighting against the souls it had claimed. It was desperate to escape.

She didn't have much time. There would be no room for errors. Everyone knew what part they must play. Everything had to go just right. Ashton would stuff the raven feather inside the hole, and Yolanda would form the circle around the tree in salt, ready with the dagger and jar of light. Serena would nail the photo of Alice Lake from the old sketch she'd found in the trunk. Before they called the corners, Serena would need to position Jack's body within the circle so his spirit could return to him.

Serena went up the creaking stairs of the cottage, first to the trunk in her room, then to Jack's bedside, where he lay still as death, only the faintest motion of his chest to indicate he was still alive. Serena cradled

Jack's body in her arms, hugging him close to her chest, then gathered his limp body in his arms and carried him down the stairs and out into the night, the picture of Alice Lake tucked away in her back pocket.

Serena passed Jack to Ashton's open arms, then stepped up to the festering trunk of the Devil Tree. The bark twisted and writhed, as if alive and angry. Without hesitating, Serena drew a white circle on the center part of the tree's trunk, just like Yolanda had done with the Tree of Life. She pulled Alice Lake's picture from her pocket and held it in her right hand. Around her, Yolanda busied herself by working her way around the tree's circumference, casting a circle with salt. Ashton placed Jack's body inside the circle and stood next to Serena, slipping her hand into Serena's free one. Serena closed her eyes and concentrated on Jack, his tiny light glowing in the glass jar cradled against her aunt's chest. The small light flickered and danced. *Soon*, Serena cast her thoughts to her brother. *Soon*.

With her witching sense, Serena reached into the Devil Tree. Serena saw a vision of the raven inside the tree. She needed to pull out the raven's body and stab it in the heart with a dagger in order to return Jack's soul to his body and free all the lost souls trapped inside the tree. Serena took a deep breath as she extended her arms wide.

"Tree of Death, I summon thee.
You took a life away from me.
You have no claim on the boy I love.
Release my beloved Jack to me.
I order you now to set him free."

The center of the tree sank inward, its hard, twisting bark closing in on itself, black blood flowing like a wound. Gritting her teeth, Serena reached inside the swirling mass of splintered wood and stinking blood. A soft glow emitted from her hand, encasing it in light and protecting her skin from the tangle of blackened gore that blocked her way. Feeling around, her hand closed on a mass of stiff and sticky feathers. She gave a hard yank, and a wing draped out of the ungodly tree. Serena gripped the wing tightly and pulled with all her might, feathers sticking to the mess of stinking black blood that coated her arm. Her fingers pressed along the line of the wing until she found the bird's shoulder. The bird was stiff and still, perhaps dead, perhaps frozen. Either way, Serena had to act quickly. Methodically, she twisted and tugged, drawing the body of the monstrous bird from the body of the tree.

Sweat ran down the side of Serena's face, but Ashton made no move to help her. Serena had to do this alone. Ashton stood grounded next to her, a hand on her back for silent support. She used her body as an anchor for Serena to lean on as Serena dragged the raven's corpse through the opening. The tree clung to the body, attaching its roots to the raven like tendons around a muscle. The head came through the tree. Its beak and head covered in the blood of the faceless souls it had torn through on its way to Serena. Another hard yank revealed the bird's chest, followed by his back and finally the legs. Serena quickly dragged the blood-covered body within the circle where Yolanda was waiting with Jack's soul. With a nod to Serena, Yolanda held Jack up by his shoulders and opened the lid to the jar.

*"What was separated in death
will now be rejoined in life.
Soul to body be reunited.
Jack awaken by taking life's first breath."*

Serena reached for the dagger in Yolanda's outstretched hand. She held the body of the bird against the grass with one hand and the blade above her. Moonlight glinted off the sharpened blade. "This is for my mother, you beast from hell!" The blade fell in a swoop and sank deep into the raven's chest, spearing it through the heart as Ashton twisted loose the lid of the glass jar. The tiny bead of twinkling light rose from the mouth of the jar and soared into the night air. It twinkled as it hovered over Jack's body. Then, with a fluid movement, the light entered his open mouth, slipping inside Jack's lips.

Yolanda brushed Jack's hair as she whispered to him. "Breathe, little one," she commanded softly. "Take your first breath. Come back to us."

Jack obeyed his aunt's command and took a deep breath. Yolanda lowered her head to his chest, listening. "That's it, boy, breathe. Keep breathing. Another breath. Good job, son."

His heart stuttered a beat, then another before it began to beat steadily. His middle finger gently twitched. Yolanda stayed with him, aiding his spirit to keep her nephew alive.

The three women stood within the circle of salt, watching and waiting. Finally, Jack opened his dark eyes, smiling up at his great-aunt. Yolanda hugged him. "What a brave boy you are," she breathed, tears trickling down her wizened face as she pulled his glasses from her pocket. She murmured to him how no other boy alive could fight death and come back. He was truly a living miracle. With strength Serena didn't know her aunt had, Yolanda lifted Jack and carried him to the safety outside the ring of salt.

Serena wanted more than anything to run to him, to hear his heart beating and wrap her arms around him, but Alice Lake's soul was approaching through the opening. It sounded like a scream on the wind, like rusty nails and white-hot hate. Ashton shoved the oily black raven feather through the stinking mass of the wounded tree while Serena hammered a nail through the photo of Alice Lake.

Like an animal in pain, the Devil Tree screamed and shook, its blackened leaves rattling like broken glass, raining rotten crab apples down on them. Black ooze spit from the center of the gaping hole, splattering Serena and Ashton in stinking gore. Serena placed her hand over the opening and chanted a spell to seal the bleeding opening.

"Passage to hell, you are no longer needed.
Close up your pores scale by scale
and trap the feather
inside your well
for soon you will be banished and dead like a nail."

Serena and Ashton ran outside of the circle, careful to avoid disturbing the salt as they joined hands with Yolanda.

"Jack, run inside the house with Tinker and wait for me there," she ordered over her shoulder. "No matter what happens, do not come outside."

"I want to help." Jack pressed his cracked glasses up his nose.

Serena saw his desire to help in her brother's dark eyes that matched her own, and she smiled at him. "One day you will, Jack. You are growing up so fast and before you know it" — she shook her head — "before I'll know it! You will be a man. But today, today you must hide. I can't lose you again, Jack."

Jack lingered only a moment before he swallowed and dashed up the steps of Korwin Cottage. With one last glance to her brother, Serena turned to face the tree and prayed calling the corners would work. The tree shook, and the ground beneath them rumbled. The roots writhed and twisted beneath their feet, making standing difficult on the uneven ground. The branches grew longer, reaching like fingers into the night sky, the leaves transforming into daggers, seeming to pierce the moon.

Serena looked over at Yolanda, knowing they had to call the corners now. "Go, Jack, hurry! Get inside!" Jack stood in the doorway on the porch, pausing a moment before ducking inside.

Two long arms reached out of the tree, their hands shaped like grasping talons. Sharp nails capped the bony, reaching fingers. It slithered out of the bleeding bark as if its body were oozing out from a fresh wound. With crippling movements, its head contorted through the opening. Whatever it was, Alice no longer was human. Its black hair was plastered over its pale face and Serena watched as Alice slowly emerged out of the tree, crouching on the ground inside the circle. With a serpentine grace Alice slowly rose, rolling its body up to a standing pose. Its shoulders popped with jerky movements as its back straightened and its joints snapped into place. It stood tall before the witches, casting a black shadow over them.

Alice's glowing eyes were fixed on Serena, and it released a deafening scream shaking the land, causing tree branches to cleave from the Devil Tree and crash like firewood on the witches. "Stay where you are!" barked Yolanda. "Be strong! Hold the line!"

Alice charged toward Serena, its nightmare face twisted in fury, but was flung backward when it hit the salt barrier. It landed hard on the ground and hissed. Alice rose to its feet and pressed its toes to the line of salt. It drew its blackened lips back in a snarl and spat on Serena's face, burning her flesh. Serena ignored the pain and turned to face east with her hands raised high in the air.

"Guardians of the East, I call upon you to bless this rite and guard this circle. Bring air to cause wind." A high wind swirled within the circle, rising from the dirt, trapping Alice in the tornado.

Without losing a moment of time, Serena faced south. "Guardians of the South, I call upon you to bless this rite and guard this circle. Bring lightning to set fire to this tree."

A storm cloud formed overhead, positioned above the circle. Lightning came streaking down, repeatedly hitting the Devil Tree. In fury, Alice howled and scratched at the invisible barrier of magic holding it to the circle. It plucked out its long onyx hair as feathers scattered around the circle, each one curled up and twisted. Long limbs formed from the black feathers, tall, sleek bodies without faces or features. Lightning struck, and the tree caught ablaze. With a scream, the leaves on the tree turned into arrows and fired at Serena, not contained within the circle of salt. Serena fell to her knees as an arrow sliced her calf. Without a word, Ashton tore a piece of her shirt and tied it around Serena's leg, binding it tight.

Yolanda raised her hands to face west. "Guardians of the West, I call upon you to bless this rite and guard this circle. Bring water to cause rain to wash away this evil!"

The thin black bodies crawled closer to Serena. They stopped, reaching their hands out to her, clinging to the air, writhing and twisting, desperate to reach Serena's flesh. The beings contorted as they clawed at the salt, digging away grain by grain to remove the barrier.

More arrows rained down from the tree, crosscutting Ashton's arm. She screamed, clamping her hand over the cuts. Arrows flew at the witches, slicing Yolanda across her back. Rain fell, hard and heavy, like nails drilling into the ground. Alice raised its arm over its body as feathers sprouted from its skin, creating a shield. The tree was now smoldering ash, branches cracking and falling into dust. The twisted bodies kept digging in the ground, trying to break through the salt circle. Serena leaned against Ashton, accepting her help as she rose to her feet.

Serena faced north and raised both hands. "Guardians of the North, I call upon you to bless this rite and guard this circle. Bring Earth to cause a sinkhole and swallow this tree and the darkness inside." She limped closer to the circle, her arms still stretched wide. "Let the innocent souls be spared and fly free to the afterlife." Serena stared into Alice's pale face, its mouth open in a silent scream. "May this tree never resurface and be the raven's tomb for all time."

The earth rumbled, the storm above spiraling into a violent tornado, sucking up the fallen branches and leaves. A line formed under the tree, a crack that quickly spread across the earth. The ground split open, swallowing the thin black bodies first. In a frenzy, they tried to climb out, reaching over each other for grass and bits of roots to cling to, but bit by bit they were torn apart and fell into the gaping hole. The tree was being dragged down to hell, and it twisted and groaned as the earth slowly swallowed it. As the tree sank further down, Alice scampered up the branches to the top of the tree, looking down at its fate below. Alice's hair wrapped around its body like a cocoon of feathers, transforming it into a raven. The bird spread its wings wide, trying to fly into the sky, but was shot down by the storm, landing back with a sickening crunch. Its body smoldered and burned in the smoking aftermath of the lightning strike.

From this blackened husk of feathers and ash emerged a young woman not much older than Serena. She sat up and locked eyes with Serena, who gaped at her in wonder. It was Alice, as she was in the picture, with bright sapphire eyes, ebony hair and fair skin. She was beautiful, with sharply defined features that Serena recognized from the sketch.

The woman watched Serena as she reached out to wrap an arm around one of the branches of the sinking Devil Tree. Her slender arms gripped the branch, her white dress singed at the edges and her hair scorched from the fire. The tree blazed, and the flames licked at Alice, burning her skin as she clung to the branch, causing her fair hands to turn pink from the flames. Her blue eyes locked with Serena's brown ones. They stared at each other as Alice sank along with the tree into the belly of the earth, to the depths of hell itself.

Serena ran to the edge of the circle and extended her arm to the woman. She could have been her—a heartbroken mother who would have done anything to see her baby just one more time. Alice ignored Serena's outstretched hand, but kept her eyes locked on Serena as she disappeared into the ground. The churning soil closed over the tree and Alice. Then all was still.

The earth closed up. Alice's black hair was the last thing Serena saw before the ground sealed. Serena wiped a tear from her eye. She couldn't help but feel sorrow for Alice Lake—sorrow and pity. She was sentenced to hell for all eternity, never to be reunited with her baby.

Yolanda crawled over to Serena, her back bleeding as she moved. Jack came running out of the house with towels, and he fell to his knees to wrap one around his aunt and gave the other to Ashton. Tinker followed along behind him, barking and trying to lick his face.

"Are you okay, Sissy?" he asked over Tinker's barking.

Serena's arms found Jack, and she pulled him close as she rubbed her hand through his hair. "It's all right. The wounds aren't fatal. A bit of mugwort and a good compress will heal us in no time."

"And a bit of magic," he replied. He looked over at the smoldering ground. "What about the others? All those souls inside the tree? Are they trapped in hell now as well?" Jack's voice was small and fragile, like a piece of shattered glass. The earth was shifting inside the circle, reforming back to solid ground.

As Serena stepped inside the circle, a tiny sapling emerged from the ruins of the Devil Tree. Its green leaves sparkled like emeralds. The earth had healed from its blackened wound of hate, and replaced the evil with something pure and good.

"Out of the fire comes rebirth, and so a baby apple tree is beginning its new life," intoned Aunt Yolanda as they watched the emerald leaves unfurl. Little silver orbs hovered over the sapling, sparkling like stars in a night sky. The orbs circled around Serena before taking flight up to the heavens, disappearing into the moon.

Ashton stood beside Serena, her arms wrapped around her body. Serena sagged into her. "You saved them," Ashton said. "The souls are free now, and maybe in some other parallel universe Alice is with her baby."

Ashton's breath was warm and her words smelled sweet, like honey. She tasted the moment, a sweet taste of peace and calm. Jack would be safe and Serena no longer would worry about the raven. It was nothing more than a nightmare.

Epilogue

Autumn had come to Conjure Lake. The air was crisp and held the scent of ripe apples, cinnamon, and nutmeg. Serena inhaled the surrounding aroma. Round orange pumpkins with twisty vines and tall stems lined her garden. Serena smiled, thinking of the delicious pies and homemade bread she was going to bake from the new crop.

Jack ran down the path, his backpack bouncing and heavy with books. Just like every day, Serena had been waiting for Jack to arrive home on the school bus, with Tinker at her side. Jack quickened his pace, leaves crunching under his steps as Serena held her arms open and Jack flew in for a giant hug. Tinker barked happily, jumping up on Jack's legs.

Jack hurried Serena and Tinker home. Serena and Ashton had promised to decorate the cottage for Halloween. They had worked all week on making black bats from cardboard, ghosts from cheesecloths and scarecrows from old clothes and hay.

Jack always looked forward to his after-school visitors. Ashton had taught him how to throw a baseball clear across the yard, and to hit a home run with one tremendous swing. Ashton was the coach for his Little League team and all his teammates looked up to her. She always brought him the most interesting books on the history of the sport. Yolanda came every Tuesday and Friday night for supper. Jack worshiped his great-aunt's recipes. Each one was more scrumptious than the next, and she regularly joked that was because of the magic she'd baked inside. This week she'd promised pumpkin stuffed shells with almond pumpkin bread. Yolanda told Jack that pumpkin bread would bring him dreams of victory and success in his next baseball game. Her food always brought pleasant dreams to Jack, and he no longer slept with a night light. Maybe someday he'd even get over his fear of spiders. Or maybe not.

The apple tree in their yard had grown big and strong, with solid branches, perfect for climbing. Now the tree bore the sweetest fruit in town. Serena promised the local farmers she would donate a bushel to the cider house. Everyone was eager to taste the delicious fruit that had seemed to appear overnight. Farmers had come to the property to admire the tree and congratulate Serena on her gardening skills, for the caretaker had disappeared, and Serena worked the garden and cared for the house herself. Serena opened a booth at the local farmer's market in town, selling cabbage, carrots, turnips and kale.

Everyone agreed that her produce was by far the most delicious crop in two counties. Everyone asked what her secret was, but Serena would only smile and reply, "It's the love that goes into the garden which makes the vegetables so tasty and pure." No one knew she was a witch, but people would come to the cottage seeking advice on love or how to make blueberry preserves so sweet you lost your heart in one taste. Women would visit with Serena around her kitchen table, sharing a loaf of banana bread and leaving with a pocket full of magic.

People were drawn to Serena. They sensed wisdom in her—others her age paled in comparison. Maybe they assumed it was because of the love she held for Jack, or the way she could be found at night in her garden singing to her plants. Possibly it was the love she and Ashton shared. Women would stop on street corners to admire how Ashton would tenderly tuck a strand of Serena's hair behind her ear. Women longed for love as strong as theirs. The townsfolk of Conjure Lake would say that Serena must be magical to be blessed with true love.

Serena walked through life with a dreamy look on her face, a look that represented victory over sorrow. She had been reborn since coming to Korwin Cottage. She no longer feared life. Her magic had opened a new world for her, one where she could be free to love and to accept love in return.

*

Want to see more from this author? Here's a taster for you to enjoy!

Ambrosia Hill: Amethyst
Rebecca Hill

Excerpt

"It's just for the summer." That's what my parents told me as I boarded the train to spend three months in the countryside with my great-aunts. The city skyline faded into the distance, replaced by rolling hills that climbed high into the horizon. The gentle rocking of the train lulled me into a trance. Three months in an old house, on top of a tall hill overlooking a silent lake in a sleepy village with nothing to do, was enough to make me lose my mind.

"Great," I said out loud to myself, my thoughts turning to the city that I was leaving behind. There was always something to do in Manhattan, whether it was going out to eat, going to a skateboard park, catching a movie or going to the mall. By the time the conductor announced Ambrosia Hill, I was the only passenger left. Me, myself, and I, all alone, a ticket for one to the last stop on the line.

I peeked out of the window and saw the glistening ripples of Lake Cauldron. The black turrets of a tall Victorian-style house touched the clouds like a church steeple in an empty town. I could almost see both my aunts sitting on the porch overlooking their enormous garden, drinking freshly squeezed lemonade with their long black dresses, wide-brimmed hats and crimson boots. As the train rolled to a stop, I grabbed my suitcase then left the car. The station was quiet and empty, much like my plans for the summer. I swung my bag over my shoulder and rolled my suitcase to the parking lot.

I took a moment to remind myself that this was just for the summer. My old life would still be waiting for me in September with the same boring school, the same bullying kids and the same depressing apartment with my parents still on the verge of a divorce…but it was my life, and I resented being sent away from it. I brushed my long hair out of my face, wishing I could grow up by September, skip high school and be off to college, or go backward in life to when things were happier and be a little kid again. Anything would be better than being thirteen in the twenty-first century.

Charlie was waiting by his old pickup truck. The rusted hubcaps were a deeper shade of orange than the last time he had met me at the station, and I thought a headlight might be out, but overall, the car seemed functional enough. Charlie flashed me a big, fatherly smile. The wrinkles around his eyes traveled down the sides of his face, and for a moment I couldn't believe how time had caught up to him since my last visit. "Well, look at you, Zinnia! You've shot up like a string bean."

Charlie reached straight for my suitcase and threw it into the truck. His hearty laugh filled the cabin as we both buckled in. "I almost didn't recognize you there with how you've grown." I looked down at my cramped legs, desperate to stretch out as my knees touched the glove compartment. Charlie patted my back and turned the key inside the ignition, bringing life to the beat-up truck as the engine groaned like an old dog too tired to wake from its nap. "Here we go, String Bean! Off like a herd of turtles at the races."

I cracked a smile at this, almost by accident, before wiping it away and looking out of the window. I could admit that I liked Ole Charlie. He'd been neighbors with my aunts for over forty years, and I'd known him all my life, so I thought it was safe to say that he was basically family. "Wait till your aunts get a look at you, string bean."

I rolled my eyes as I tried, and once again failed, to conceal my smile. Every time I visited my aunts, Ole Charlie gave me a new nickname. *I suppose my nickname for this summer is going to be string bean.* I whispered it to myself for a test drive and annoyingly, it wasn't so annoying.

"It's been a few years since you and your mom visited us on Ambrosia Hill." Charlie looked over at me with his old brown eyes full of affection. "Not ashamed to say we've missed you, string bean."

Mom loved coming to Ambrosia Hill. The aunts had raised her after my grandma became sick and couldn't take care of my mom anymore. Mom said visiting with Grandma during that time was the hardest thing she'd ever had to do, and it was a sad relief for everyone when Grandma passed away. That was the day Mom packed up a suitcase and moved to the city, where she eventually met my dad and had me. But she never forgot where she came from, and every summer she and I would come up by train to Ambrosia Hill and visit our aunts. At least until my parents started fighting.

I was nine years old when they had their first big fight and I remembered hiding under the kitchen table hugging the wooden leg, hoping that if I stayed hidden, it wouldn't be real, and everything would go back to the way it was. But that didn't happen, and the fighting only got worse. Mom was too ashamed to visit the aunts after that. With her marriage on the brink of divorce, she felt like a failure. She'd left home to chase her big-city dreams on Broadway, and instead of achieving that dream, she had gotten a reputable job, one where she could achieve success. But even if she didn't live her exact dream, at least she was in the city, married and a mother. She'd had a good life before all the fighting began.

I rolled my window down and stuck my head out as we began the long slope up Ambrosia Hill. The village was named after the hill and apparently my aunts' house was one of the first settlements on Lake Cauldron. Most people with lake houses invested in updating their homes into fancy summer getaways from the city. But not my aunts. They'd lived in their house for the majority of their lives, and they refused to change even a single detail, including their old purple porch.

My great-aunts loved purple and black, from the violet-painted siding to the ebony trimming along every window and doorframe. Even their garden was filled with purple and black flowers mixed amongst the green foliage. The house was the same on the inside, with rich black wood furnishing and purple wallpaper. My room was in the attic when I came to visit and it was a fairytale room hidden from the rest of the massive house. When I was a little girl, we'd painted the ceiling a deep indigo with pale crescent moons and diamond-shaped stars. The walls were papered in pale pink with blue roses. Pink and champagne ceiling lights hung across the attic and warm fairy lights covered every square inch of the room. An old-fashioned canopy bed with four black posts sat in the center.

Growing up, I used to pretend that I was a princess locked in a tower waiting for my one true love to rescue me. But what I didn't admit to anyone, at least not then, was that I never wanted to be rescued by a prince. I wanted someone else, something different from what the other girls my age wanted in life, and the typical happy ending didn't feel right to me. Fairy tales screw kids up. It wasn't who I wanted to rescue me that was the issue — it was the fact I thought I needed to be rescued by anyone. My parents were desperate to understand what I wanted, and when they couldn't, they started insisting that it was simply a phase, and that I'd grow out of it once I met the right boy. Truthfully, I don't think they even had the time to worry about me. They were far too busy arguing with each other.

Still, my dad was persistent that time away with my aunts would clear my head and eventually I'd forget all about the girl from my class. The girl with the red hair and freckles who had stabbed me in the back. The girl who had been yanked out of St. Hope and enrolled into another school the second her parents discovered the letter I had written to her. A letter that had gone around my entire middle school and had labeled me forever. It had hurt at first, knowing that kids in school slapped me with a label like I was different from them. I wasn't *different* — I was just me and I deserved to be myself like everybody else in the world. I wouldn't allow some meddling bullies to affect me. I would not let them win by showing them how they'd hurt me.

As the truck stopped outside the garden gate, Aunt Stella and Aunt Luna jumped up from their rickety porch chairs and ran down the driveway to greet me.

Aunt Luna was carrying a black kitten in her arms, and Aunt Stella was holding on to the top of her wide-brimmed hat, which shielded her eyes from the glaring sun. Almost unconsciously, I ran to meet them, flying into their arms. The tears that I had been holding back rushed out of me like a waterfall. They burned my flushed face as I clung to my aunts. They comforted and cuddled me like momma birds.

"It's all right now, my darling girl. You're with us. No one will hurt you." I looked into Aunt Stella's loving eyes. There with them on Ambrosia Hill, I could be me. I didn't have to wear a mask or pretend to be strong—I could allow my tears to flow freely.

"You are our little love and always will be." Aunt Luna cupped my face in her chubby hand, and I reached for her like a child hugging a teddy bear.

"Come now. I know exactly what you need," piped up Aunt Stella.

"Yes, yes, yes!" clucked Aunt Luna as she handed me the black kitten. "A glass of chocolate almond milk with a chocolate chip cookie is just the thing for this occasion." Both aunts turned on their heels and shuffled back to the house.

"Come along, dear!" called Aunt Stella. I turned and waved goodbye to Ole Charlie, who tipped his cap at me with a wink before getting back in his truck and driving away.

The purple and black walls swelled when I walked inside the dark house, then surrounded me like a giant hug and for a moment, it felt like the house was alive and greeting me with love. Nothing had changed in the three years since I had last visited. Black candles sat inside tall iron holders. Old dusty books decorated the built-in bookshelves along the far wall. Dried herbs hung from every rafter and exposed beam. Inside the large wood-burning fireplace were towers of quartz crystals. Branches of eucalyptus draped around the mantel, trailing to the floor. Wicker baskets littered the house, filled with yarn, empty glass jars and pouches of dried herbs.

I inhaled, breathing in the scent of my summer home, my other life...a part of me I had almost forgotten existed. Suddenly, I was overcome with the realization I had forgotten my true self. Standing amongst my aunts' collection of tarot cards, pentagrams and spell books, I remembered the inner strength I had inside me. There is another identity to the Fern women, an identity my mother tried to hide from the world. Only in Ambrosia Hill were we free to be who we truly were — a lineage of magical women.

My aunts scurried back from the kitchen with Aunt Luna carrying a tray of homemade cookies and three glasses of chocolate almond milk. Aunt Stella caught me eyeballing the clutter surrounding me and placed a hand upon her hip.

"Darling girl, a clean house is a sign of a misspent life." She raised her eyebrows to support her statement.

"Come along, dear. We have something important to do," Aunt Luna said as she skipped past me, stopping to kiss the kitten, which was, by then, curled up like a baby in the crook of my arm.

"You won't want to miss it, dear!" added in Aunt Stella as she raced up behind me, shoving me back out the front door and onto the porch. A tote bag was draped over her shoulder.

The aunts placed the tote bag and tray of treats onto the porch table as they chirped back and forth to one another in playful banter. "She forgot what day it is! Why, this used to be her favorite day of the summer. Apart from her birthday, that is." Aunt Luna laughed.

Aunt Stella nodded, positioning a stack of card paper neatly on the table. "She's been inhaling too much smog in that city. The fresh air will do her lungs some good, she'll remember any moment now," she replied. Her heeled boot tapped against the weathered wood floor. I sat down between them, setting the kitten on the table next to a vase of purple orchids and some black candles.

"What am I supposed to be remembering?" I could feel the creases in my forehead grow deeper as I desperately tried to recall what special day it was. My aunts both looked at me with their eyebrows raised gesturing at the random items scattered on the table in front of them. I shrugged in apology, still not grasping the significance of the day.

"It's the summer solstice!" they sang in union.

I turned my wrist up and caught the date on my smartwatch. "Oh, my gosh, it's June twenty-first."

Coming from a historical line of green witches, the summer solstice had always been a significant day with an important purpose for the Fern women. Every June twenty-first, my aunts wrote about the things they wanted to let go of in their lives, things that no longer served a purpose. After they wrote their messages in gold ink, they folded the paper into a tiny boat and placed a tealight inside it. When the crescent moon appeared in the night sky, they lit the candle and released the boats into Lake Cauldron. It was a symbol of new beginnings and a chance for positive self-growth. I shook my head, amazed that I had forgotten about the summer solstice.

Both my great aunts had lived their entire lives as green witches, just as their mother and her mother before her had done, going back three hundred years. My aunts had educated me at an early age on how to be a green witch. The very essence of a green witch was to be a naturalist, someone who connected with nature on a personal and powerful level. Green witches were wise women, herbalists and healers who helped those around them by using the properties of nature. We may never use magic to harm others or for personal gain. I was a green witch by birth rite, and fourteen was a significant year for a teenage witch. I hadn't identified as a practicing witch before. I'd never cast spells on my own. Any spells I had done were guided by my aunts. However, at fourteen, Fern witches developed individual traits and branched out into our own magic. I could feel a change coming. One that would redirect my path forever.

"Ha! She remembers! I told you she would. You worry too much, that's your problem, Luna."

Aunt Luna placed her hands on her round hips with her head cocked defiantly to the side. "I do not. You're the one who worries."

Aunt Stella waved her hand in the air. "Pish-posh. I am as calm as a cucumber, but you could worry the horns off a billy goat."

I giggled, breaking up their banter. I reached for the gold pen and a piece of black cardstock. I stared at the paper, unable to find the words I needed to write. I could feel them stirring inside me and I could see them take form in the shape of *her* face.

Aunt Luna reached for my hand, understanding my internal struggle. Aunt Luna was the maternal one of the two sisters. She lived to nurture those around her, and her maternal instincts were fierce when it came to me. Although Aunt Stella was stern, she had an intense love that ran deeper than any river marked on a map, and I could feel that love surrounding me as I stared at the pen in my hand. It baffled me why neither she nor

Aunt Luna ever had children of their own. I made a mental note to ask them someday.

"Draw, dear," whispered Aunt Luna. "A picture can be just as powerful as words. If your artistic expression helps you, then draw whatever you need to let go of."

Before I could respond, my hand moved involuntarily, sketching the outline of her face. Of all their faces, everyone who had hurt me.

About the Author

Rebecca Henry is an American author living abroad in England. She is a devoted vegan who gardens, practices yoga, crafts, travels the world, and bakes. Rebecca's favorite holiday is Halloween, and she is obsessed with anything and everything witchy! Besides writing fiction, Rebecca is also the author of her vegan holiday cookbook collection. Her love for animals, baking with her family, having a plant-based diet and cruelty-free food all came together in her holiday cookbook collection.

Rebecca loves to hear from readers. You can find her contact information, website details and author profile page at https://www.finch-books.com

FINCH
BOOKS

Sign up for our newsletter and find out about all our romance book releases, eBook sales and promotions, sneak peeks and FREE romance books!